SINISTER UTOPIA

H. F. Heard's DOPPELGANGERS is a book like no other you've ever read, a book that will fascinate you, challenge you, thrill you . . . and perhaps frighten you.

For the world of the DOPPELGANGERS is an apocalyptic nightmare built on the soundest principles of science and sociology. Its vision of the world at the end of this century, and of the titanic powers that struggle for dominance there, is so intense that you may find yourself looking around you, and wondering . . . is this tomorrow . . . or today?

Here is a book comparable only to such classic works as Bernard Wolfe's LIMBO and George Orwell's 1984.

DOPPELGANGERS

by

H. F. HEARD

ACE BOOKS, INC.
1120 Avenue of the Americas
New York, N.Y. 10036

"He who meets his Going Double must go himself."

—OLD GERMAN PROVERB

I

THE DIVE

"You would do anything?"

"Anything." It was the drill answer, but he gave it with conviction.

"Then read this." In the silence could just be heard the faint fluttering sound of paper being handled. There followed a click and a fine pencil of rays formed a small spotlight that tracked to and fro for some dozen passes and then, with another click, vanished.

There was a pause. Then the first voice continued, "You said, 'Anything,' and you have taken the active-service oath. Now you have seen your instructions, and I gather from the impression that they have made on you that you will not forget them. I will now, therefore, burn this small memo."

There was a short silence but no flame appeared.

The first voice again was audible: "I am also taking for granted your consent, for you know that anyone who sees an instruction is not open to change his mind." Another pause. "That's obvious," the first voice went on; "there can't be people going about who have seen a specific direction with which they have declined to co-operate."

"But living clay, living clay."

"Well, it's an apt term. There's nothing to be gained by being imprecise in brief instructions. You're being more highly trusted than any of the front line. You are to be given the one undetectable weapon."

"What do you mean?"

"You won't have to wait long. We've succeeded. And now it's straightaway for you."

A match spurted, but its light was under a table. The concealed flame wavered a moment or two and then sank. A chair was pushed back. After a moment another rasped on the stone floor. In the dark a narrow oblong of light began to glimmer.

Now sunk to a whisper, the first voice said, "At corner 45.67.23 at 21:15."

Two blurs of darkness appeared on the oblong. The footsteps died away up a flight of stairs.

In the street the man under orders stopped. He was by himself and would be for long enough to be able to think. There were a couple of hours until the time given for the assignation. He was to have had a meal, but that was out of the question now. There was no way out, of course. But why should he be pitched on in this way? When he'd first joined—the cubs, they were called—they used to see if they could raise gooseflesh on each other by running through the different kinds of executions and beatings-up an agent might expect. He'd been good at the test; perhaps that was why they'd picked him now. But being killed can't last too long, and beatings-up and the whole sadistic box of tricks was different from this. They'd been taught the way "to hold yourself in."—Oh yes, the underground had its defenses, and they were pretty good. They'd been scientific, without a doubt. They'd all been drilled in the air-locks, the special twists of internal muscles, even with the tongue swallow, so they could go out when they felt they were near breaking. And, as far as was known, none of the boys had broken, though about half must have been killed already.

Yes, the central Mole, as they called him, no doubt had a brain and was always one step in front of the silly brutes that swaggered and stamped on the surface. They had a cliché joke, "Talpa can always cap Alpha:" But one never thought that basic brain would think up this. Well, that was the curse of a big one; it always had a surprise up its sleeve. And no one had ever accused the Mole of mercy or of endangering the cause by showing any consideration for any agent. One couldn't help wondering whether that big brain had thought up this as a real ruse for undermining the enemy overhead, or simply as a new way of testing-training, just to see what the boys who could stand any of the standard stuff, and were proud of it, would do if met by something that just picked the stuffing out of them. It wouldn't be unlike him, after all. He was always getting a finer edge on his most edged tools. He was always looking for that last little hold of self-respect to cut it out as a dentist cuts nearer and nearer the nerve to be certain the last piece of soft decay had gone—and then builds up a defense, a front that won't break, harder than the original tooth. But the simile wouldn't do—too close to what the truth, the nauseating truth, seemed to be—though, again, you never could be sure. That was, at the start, the excitement of the assignment. But in the end one began to wear. One could be sure of one thing, that if you failed you were got. The trampling Bull above might be clumsy with his goring. The Mole below never missed his bite. But if you obeyed you weren't treated with any more leniency than if you revolted.

That proposition ran in his mind. What were they living for? Of course, for the future when the shadow would be gone and they'd all come out into the light, and, more, those who had gone deepest would be most on top and those who had been most in the mud and horror would be names in everyone's mouth and seen everywhere. But it had gone on a long while. True, they had become more and more skilled, but somehow their strokes, brilliant as they were, had never gone right home. True, they were so

7

well planned that always it was possible to try again. Nothing was ever given away, and certainly Alpha and his tribe were kept in a state of quite unhealthy misgiving as to the ground under their every step. But as long as he and his mouthpiece kept the public ear he had an immense advantage.

You couldn't be a realist—and any sentimental hopefulness was a major disqualification for the Agency—and say it was just a clever coup d'état of a few scoundrels. The people may not have been behind it at the start, but they were now. Alpha could count on popular support if any government could. And that was his main defense, that great open country or belt of land, the good will and so-called patriotism of the people. That had to be crossed before you actually came up against the more scientific and specific defenses. What fools the people were!

But, again—if you were to have that cold mind that you had to have—were they such fools? Alpha gave them a good time, and, damn it, they were healthier and cheerier than they used to be. He'd not only put on monster shows and given them good food—*panem et circenses*—but he'd given them the vivid clothes and ranks and badges they'd always wanted to wear but which respectable democracy had said was in bad taste. Democracy's a gentleman's delusion, a preanthropological pretense.

And this newest of the dictators had learnt everything the others could teach and added a lot more. The elite could be virile but the people could just have a good time. The nonsense of inhibition for which the old totalitarians had fallen, this shrewd mind had seen through. A sour smile twisted the agent's face as he thought of that day long ago in Cuba when they were going to get the temporary tyrant out but he side-stepped them when the mob was ready to rush his guards by giving the cinemas a mass of pornographic films. The stalls filled, the streets emptied, and peace reigned in the capital. Of course, Alpha had improved on such crude inspirations of the moment. He didn't offend the churches by being too frank with the maximum lure. Indeed he was said to be increasingly interested in synthesizing or at least syncretizing Religion. And he'd had

8

the biggest film men to help him. They knew the knife-edge on which to work.

The agent' had been walking aimlessly and, like moth to candle, found his feet had taken him to one of the big, brilliantly lit parks in which one of the free cabaret shows was being put on. Troops of people were streaming across the grass to the seats, people as gaily and brightly dressed as if they were performers, too. And weren't they marionettes? He looked at his watch; yes, there was plenty of time before he need be at the corner, and the show might divert him. The shows were always first rate. Authority knew they had to be, and paid top prices for this, the first line of defense, the line of distraction. There was nothing about patriotism in them. That was stale—it was all fun and fooling.

As they all converged, a brightly costumed girl turned and smiled at him. You couldn't say she looked oppressed, unhappy, inhibited, nervous of tyranny or interference—the reverse, quite the reverse. Will we be able to make people as happy? he thought. Will good sense and freedom and responsibility make them as gay and carefree? He remembered the phrase common among his branch of the Agency: castrated animals grow fat. Yes, but these people weren't castrated—they were full of life but not of querulous questions. Surely something had been cut out from them! They were a pollarded people.

The phrase of the old standard psychologist Sheldon came into his mind, Anemectomized—the soul cut out. But what was a soul? Could you cut it out? Has the Mole a soul? The jingle had been quite frankly repeated among his fellow agents. Certainly no one felt it was disloyal to doubt if the central brain had a conscience—how could it, considering what it was always having to do, in lying, killing, yes, and torturing? For their counterattack had two edges: there were the agents like himself, more or less above ground, real men taking the fighting, and there were—others. You couldn't be long in and not know that, though that was never talked about. Perhaps every now and then one of the toughest of the tough, in a moment of hard exultation, when perhaps he'd just picked off one of the fairly high-

9

ups on the other side, would, with a sort of sham modesty, allow that he had his uses but that he was a clumsy fool beside the real workers, the men really near the Mole, the men who, when you did succeed in bringing back your game alive, really praised you for not killing. Because with a live one in their hands they could always make him speak.

"We never split or bend, we just die in their hands as dumb as a log. But when we catch one of them and bring him home alive, in the end he always squeaks and speaks, whole volumes. Oh, yes, the Mole may have no soul, but, by the powers of the ultimate underground, he has a brain, twice that of anyone above. That's why we'll win."

Yes, that was the favorite argument why they must win and why, no doubt, the Mole, who certainly didn't seem to be one who cared a rap for flattery but cared a whole hecatomb for obedience, let this kind of jest run about among the agents. Suddenly a thought ran through his mind. Maybe it was because of something that a captured official of the other side had let slip that he himself, Agent numbering this week 6.x51.L. (your number was changed every month or so, so you had no identity), had been given those instructions which, though now ash, still gave him, when he recalled them, that shock of disgrace, the goose-flesh that pimpled his skin as he'd read that phrase, "living clay." He shuddered, and the girl, who had now, because of what she took to be his assumed indifference, taken his arm, laughed.

"That's a good opening and quite refreshing. I can't remember when the last man I picked up shuddered when I touched him. This is going to be better than the usual run. You're what we used to call an innocent."

She was perfectly natural and frank. There was no coquetry, still less harlotry. She was not an animal, but she was a woman with a child's mind. The people were that now, adults who were let go back to childhood, not expected to have good taste, high views, noble ideals, grit and heroism, but fun and foolishness and enjoyment. That's what they wanted, you couldn't doubt. Carniave, not Carnivale.

10

Carnivale meant farewell to the flesh, a last wild wave of the hand before repentance engulfed you. Now the flesh was being welcomed back. *"Io saturnalia!"* but no frenzy, for there was no hurry. There was plenty of time; and sugar and skilled gluttony were just as much fun as sex and skilled pornography. While—so he'd heard—as you got on, you needn't get sour. The arts eased you out until they, too, modulated into religion and you found yourself ushered soothingly and in the best taste into Nirvana. She had drawn him down to a seat and laced her fingers through his; but as soon as they were settled and she had cuddled up to him she was engrossed by the show. Like all these cabaret acts, it only lasted for about twenty minutes and then the people—all the younger ones—got up to dance, and the others to eat or play at one of the games provided.

"Shall we meet again?" she said. "I don't usually, because new people are so exciting, but somehow perhaps one could take two bites at you. You're slower than most are. Nobody has any mysteries now, and usually I don't care for that kind of stuff. It's all making oneself out to be important, I believe. But I suppose there is some difference between one handsome face and another, or one wouldn't keep on changing, would one? So if you're different I'd like to know why."

She spoke as frankly about herself as about him. That was, of course, common enough. But what he found catching in his mind was the thought—the thought he didn't want to hold—that she was under no fear, she didn't seem aware that the whole of this thing that suited her and these thousands and millions so well, was all based on force and fraud and fear and violence, cruelty and treachery—fought by cruelty and treachery; that this was a flower garden of rather garish flowers, where underneath, in the rich beds, centipede, ferret, rat, and mole, dug and bit, writhed and struggled. She was kindly, too, in an unsentimental way.

"Why not let yourself unbend? I'm not much, but quite a good sort. I don't hold onto men—and that's always an advantage, I think. You know where you are with me, and I shan't fool you. When we're not enjoying ourselves, well,

11

we'll quit quickly, and not spoil the first fun. But there's no point in not getting that, for fear it won't last, is there?"

Was there? He said something noncommittal—that if he were free he'd be there the same time next day. She didn't press; she smiled and waved her hand and was lost in the crowd. He felt curiously lonely then, and what was ahead looked even darker. Why had he gone to the park? He should have stayed somewhere quietly. Why shouldn't he come tomorrow night? Tomorrow night where would he be, what would he be? Somehow, having been with that bright, careless human being made his life look insane. Weren't they right? Hadn't life always to be happy and careless or full of confusion and struggle, always leading to greater complexities and horrors? Could all the men who were above ground and who managed this life for the careless, carefree masses, be calculating brutes? Did they know any more of what the system was based in, than the youngest, rawest activity-agent, who joined last week with adventure and heroism filling his callow mind, knew of the Mole and those round the Mole. Lord, what thoughts! Of course he wouldn't be killed for them—oh, no; but if in the dormitory they even came out in the random runnings of dream speech and were recorded in the microphone which was said to be in every one of the bunk-burrows, he'd be in for treatment, and treatment, whether it was the pentathol or electric shock, always meant that you were never the same. For one thing, in a little time they found you needed it again and then at more frequent intervals until you became—an old term from the old prisons—a trusty, a creature who always said yes and would do anything. It was said that such trusties were used by the other side especially when attempting "extractions" from the Mole's losses. It was said that such trusties were used when extractions were being made from a captured officer from the other side.

His mind had slipped again. He made an effort and suddenly something broke, skidded in the opposite direction from which he'd meant to pull it out. Suddenly he knew, he couldn't go on. Once or twice he'd felt such twinges, but, thank his stars, always when with others. They were never allowed to drink alcohol, but they had their synthetic-seltzer, as they called it, one of those chemists' brews that fizzed; after you'd taken it you could be sure your black mood was out, though your "trigger-finger" was as steady as ever. But of course no drugstore here on the surface had his medicine. He'd have to ride the storm alone.

But why? Why not stay on the surface? Living was easy. One could always get a job or relief. The old suspicious official attitude had gone, had been carefully smoothed over—on the surface. Everything, everything hard, the government and the opposition, was now underground; on the surface everything was bright, easy, generous, and apparently open. He felt cool. He'd think it out. What was the reason for going on? He'd gone in from high motives, courage, and the wish to revenge certain horrid wrongs of which he knew. He'd gone on asking questions till he'd dug up some horrible-smelling stuff, and he'd resolved, romantic young sprig, that he'd dig right to the roots and make the whole of the earth, right down to the subsoil and the deepest graves, smell as sweetly as the hay and the flowers on the surface in June. They'd soon knocked that out of him, and it was, of course, indefensible rot. There was always decay and muck underneath, and flowers and grass grew from that and went back to that. Then what had he been fighting for, ever more foully? For fear they'd get him if he turned back? Well, he'd been no coward when he started. When had he become one? Was it mere habit? They'd always said an agent's no use that can't think for himself. But he'd never really been alone; now he was—really alone.

The pull of the world to which he had come to belong, the world of the Mole, was now exactly, at this moment, matched by the pull of the surface world of the Bull, Alpha. He'd dismissed that surface pull by calling it debauched, mean, sham, cruel. And his world, of dark shadow, as brave, true, real, clean. But surely that was simply the most snatchy judgment that sentimentality could make. There was none of that boasted detachment and objectivity they were taught to prize, in such a notion. But if not, why go on? There was no answer.

Had he been underground at that moment there would have been the routine, the seltzer, etc., to drag him over

13

the dead center. Here there was nothing. The present was the lit, pleasant streets, the gay crowds, the easy, relaxed, deliberately entertained, amused, and distracted life. Below was a life going ever lower. And for him? In an hour or so a fate which he had to own was worse than death. He would be sacrificed for the Mole's ever more obscure sense of purpose and goal and right. The moment had done it.

He wouldn't go on. He wasn't breaking. He'd broken, broken with it all. He'd meet Alie; that, she'd told him, was her name. Tonight he wouldn't be at 45.67.23. That spectral spider's-web map of cryptic, sinister reference that lay and had lain all these months in his mind over the bright city would vanish away. He'd see things again as sane, aboveboard people saw them. He'd leave these nets and toils to those who cared to play with imaginary futures and nightmare presents. He wouldn't judge them. There had always been, perhaps always had to be, people who played at that—the government and the opposition, whether they debated or, as now, actually dueled. But politics wasn't life, and, more, it never got anywhere. He'd learned enough now to know that and, thank the bright sky, he'd learned enough to know how to get out of the cellars and tunnels back under that bright sky again and see that he wasn't snarled. That was worth the learning. He knew enough to know how to keep clear.

It was a lovely summer night, the moon full and sailing free with a few stars and some scales of mother-of-pearl clouds in attendance. His spirits rose to a level he hadn't known for—he couldn't remember how long. Often in those past months he had felt keyed—proud, keenly, grimly alive. But this was different; he felt careless, easy, a new sense of health began flowing in him. What fun to be meeting Alie tomorrow! He felt hungry, too. That was a good sign. He went into a restaurant and ordered a good meal. As he finished it, he saw, with an amused relief, as he looked at the clock, that he was already handsomely late. He dawdled out into the crowded, dense streets—wandering with only one will and direction—away from the rendezvous.

14

No one would miss him. A man who went on an assignment disappeared, as far as his few bunkhouse companions went. To inquire was absolutely forbidden. You never mentioned him again, if he didn't turn up. If he did, you went on, and so did he, as though the days he'd been out had disappeared. He'd be starting a fresh life anyway—anyone on assignment did. His Number, which was all that he was known by, would be shifted, someone else would be in his bunk. Oh, yes, they had brought anonymity to the frontier of total disappearance of the personality—so why not disappear? Besides, as his assignment had shown, no one had ever yet been planned to disappear so completely. He was being annihilated as a person. All right, he would go, go for good, for his good at last.

His mind grew clearer and clearer. He wondered why he hadn't done this before. He began to feel a kind of gratitude to them for pressing him out, extruding, exuding him. Who knows, perhaps the Mole, who seemed to know most things, *had* known he was through, and so used this method of shooting him back to the surface—as in old submarines when they'd sunk, you could escape by getting into the conning tower and shooting yourself back to the surface by opening the top hatch and going up in the uprush of the escaping air. The Mole would know he wouldn't ever want to go down or make trouble again for either side. Melodrama and the Mole, you couldn't think of them together. He cared for any personnel so little that the idea of revenge would have seemed to him as nonsensical as love at first sight.

He was thinking this out, so true and so reassuring, that, as he was waiting for a traffic light to change, he saw the middle color flash. He hurried to cross and was nearly over before the GO sign took over. It would still have been all right had not one of the cars, drawn up and ready to go ahead, been impatient. It swung out a little ahead of the others. The driver was evidently a little tipsy, too. He made straight for the tardy crosser, but then, when nearly on him, fortunately swerved. The mudguard just missed his thigh. He would be missed by less than an inch. But as the door swung past it fell open. Queer—his mind thought

15

even in that split second—a door opening the wrong way round. But, queer or no, he was caught in its jaw. He'd be knocked down and go under the hind wheel. He *was* knocked off his feet, but, by some kind of apron or web hanging between the swung-open door and the cab's floor, he was caught, as mail used to be caught from a hanging bag by a grapple net held out from a passing train.

He crashed, but fairly lightly, onto the cab's floor, heard the door snap behind him, and felt hands take hold on him. It was dead dark in the cab but the hold told him all he needed. He knew those holds as well as a fingerprint expert knows the whorls on a glass or the butt of a gun. No one held like that unless he had had one of the basic trainings.

Evidently Alpha wasn't such a fool. He'd been wandering about in the upper world all those hours. Someone had been on the watch; this little dredge had been sent out, and here he was in the landing net, being hurried to the fish market to be filleted. Well, if they knew their moves, he knew his. He'd wait, and then when the pain became too skilled he'd step out from under.

He didn't then feel frightened, hardly angry, only a bit disappointed and a trifle annoyed with himself for thinking so much about getting free of the Mole that he'd stepped right under the hoof of the Bull. Certainly his holders didn't feel they were to do anything. As long as he didn't make them break his thumbs or push out his thyroid they weren't going to forestall their successors' duties. They'd deliver him intact as they had picked him up.

He could hear nothing but the whir of the engine. They were going a good pace. And they went for a good while. The swish of other vehicles passing, also, had become rarer and rarer. They must be out in the country. And, after about half an hour of that, the swing and heave of the car showed that they must be on a byroad. That went on for a considerable time, too.

When it changed for a hollow sound, he was pretty sure the journey must be practically over. They were now in some sort of tunnel. Yes, this would be one of the undergrounds.

Alpha, who was the people's friend, the friend of the good times, of children, of fun and frolic, the one who had banished tragedy from life, was up to date: he didn't advertise the force necessary to keep the surface smooth. There weren't any prisons, of course. There were mental homes, out to which most people who contracted hysteria or economic illusions went for a short treatment and generally were discharged cured, so that their friends and relations vowed that they were far nicer to be with than they had been. Of course, behind the mental homes were the country hospitals. No one ever saw these. But the patients often wrote from them saying they were quite comfortable and were making progress but that visits from relatives would upset them and delay cure.

Alpha confessed he was no wizard. He couldn't keep everyone happy or prevent a few people proving incurable.

"But I am trying," he would conclude one of his hygienic talks. "You go ahead and keep happy and healthy and I'll go ahead and see how far down I can work your casualty rate." And in the television sets you would see his flashing brave smile, that row of large white teeth that gave a humorous curve to the powerful mouth, those deep, capable eyes with the lines of a care that laughs at its own seriousness.

Yes, the clichés about the Bull were true enough, and now he would be seeing, in a few moments, the truth under these easy phrases that the people loved to hear—what it cost to keep men carefree.

The car had stopped. Without shifting their holds, the guards put him on his feet. Yes, he owned, they knew their stuff. Outside it was as dark as in the cab, and, after he was out and evidently headed where they wished, a hood slipped down over his head. In complete silence they walked perhaps a hundred yards. At one stage he was sure they went up a fairly long gradient. Then there were several turns and twists. He tried to count but was not sure, and he couldn't hear a door open or shut. At last, though, he felt something touch both his shins and, as that limit was reached, the holds were raised. He was loose.

17

He stood for a moment, rather expecting a quick blow or perhaps the sudden thrust of the well-known hypodermic in the arm. But no. He listened. He must be alone. Cautiously he bent forward. Surely it couldn't be anything so old-fashioned as the oubliette. He almost smiled when, putting out his hand gingerly to feel the brink from which he was just curbed below the kneecaps, he felt a bed. As he explored he made its shape, pillow to the right, an extra blanket thoughtfully and neatly folded across the foot. He could not help chuckling when, right in front, he found that not only was the sheet turned back but silk pajamas were laid out—what a neat laying-out our great artist in living does design, nothing neglected.

He felt his way about. The room was undoubtedly on the small side, and smooth as the inside of an egg, so smooth that you couldn't feel the door. Well, there was nothing in his store suit with which he had been provided that would give him away. The Mole knew enough about such things for him not to have to think of that. He threw off the coarse cheap worsted, smartly colored and cut as all suitings today were, but tawdry. It was a slight relief to put on the silk.

Knowing how to wait was part of knowing how to keep cool. You had to live in the actual moment. In fact, he'd been one of the best pupils in the Chen method of standing torture—and the Chinese certainly were good testers—by dividing up the moment of consciousness into finer and finer moments and presents, until the pain impulse couldn't get through or be sustained. He threw himself on the bed. He found that his mind wished to think of Alie. He let it; that again was part of the drill of detachment. He yawned and threw his arms behind his head. He was quite relaxed. He saw her as vividly as he had those hours ago in the park. They were wandering about together. She had just said that at last she'd found someone who seemed to grow more interesting every time since that first time they met months ago. He was on his back on the grass. It was summer. . . .

But why have a rug over one's feet? The air, too, had a tang. He roused himself. Asleep? He'd never known the exercises to end in unconsciousness until you intended them to! What a fool he was! Of course this was a gas chamber. The air was getting right, however, now. And light was coming. Very little and in a small beam. But it lit one spot and there was a tray. Of course, the stuff might be drugged, but then, what was the need? He'd been knocked out as delicately as a frog is pithed. He felt hungry and, anyhow, if he felt they were using any of the old-fashioned poisons he could always make himself vomit. He ate the meal and it was good. From his appetite he judged he must have been asleep some while.

The light began to die. It shone, a faint circle, through part of the wall—one of those steel-hard plastics, he thought. Before it went he noticed that his clothes and watch had gone. He lay wide awake and his mind didn't wander. He was then all the more surprised to hear a slight cough close to him—that kind of gentle clearing-of-the-throat someone will use who wishes deferentially to attract attention.

"Who's there?" he said, but he didn't put out his hand. Somehow he shrank from that.

The replying voice would have been a whisper but there was no sibilance in it: "We want co-operation." Well, anyone might say that. "We'd much rather have a friend than have to use a tool—have someone who shares our point of view."

Yes, that could come from either side. Sometimes messages from the Mole had that sort of beginning. It worked with some people, with most, as long as you were new and had about you a good deal of the old superficial and surface vagueness.

"You were picked for special reasons."

What was that? Did the counter-counters know?

"It will be no end of trouble and perhaps a number of months, years almost, before quite such a fit can be found. Oh, yes, as you know, we can get brains as we like and make them take shape, but bodies are, we now know, harder. It wasn't to be unexpected that you'd start under the shock. Your mind-body chart showed that. Your soft spot is physical vanity—the ordinary tough's quick under his talon. So we were prepared—not surprised, not offended—quite natural, quite natural; and quite remediable. It would be serious only if that weren't so. And we just can't afford to lose you, so it won't happen."

The voice was very low and quiet but into its neutrality there had been fed the slightest note of reassurance.

"You slipped out and of course we slipped after you. We knew you would make that reaction, so we fetched you."

So he was back with the moles after all! That meant that in spite of all this rather puzzling preliminary he would be in the discard some time in the next few hours. Well, he must face it. They wouldn't torture. Perhaps they'd let him stop his heart himself.

There was a pause, and then the voice said, "You don't yet quite seem to understand; we mustn't have a second. You still really don't want to go to the discard, and we want it even less. You can't go back to the surface. We can always pull you down from there with more ease than a shark pulls down a poor swimmer. We have now a sure plan. You are the pin in it. Many boys would cut half their fingers off for it. And it really means that at last we'll hit the bull's eye."

He waited, but evidently the speaker had ended with a question. They had perhaps half a dozen exchanges.

At the end he said, "I'll think it over." Then he thought of some more objections and began to put them. But nothing answered.

He got up and groped round the room. It was undoubtedly empty. He went back and lay on the bed. It was clear that he was back, right in the middle of the net and they weren't going to kill, yet; indeed, would go to almost any lengths not to kill: but would, if they couldn't get their way. He must gain time.

He spoke to the silence, "What if I consent?"

There was no answer for a time, and then very faintly he heard, "Very well, very well."

"But why do you want my consent?" was answered more quickly.

"We *must* have co-operation. You know that as well as we. Why, even in these first steps, you can ruin all. Certain

20

grafts won't take unless you'll help. Still more, certain modulations, the person himself alone can make. They just can't be made, unless the man at the center of the machine cooperates. We can hand you in the tools, but you alone can, inside, make the adjustments. They are far too delicate for any outsider to make. Who could make a singer sing by manipulating his chords for him? But men are taught how to use their own chords. And then, later on, more and more, it is you who will guide the bomber. You must be on your own.

"Of course, we'll kill you if you fail us. But if you don't, you have us behind you; yes, ready to do as you, at the top-point, tell us you want done. You see, that's the choice: fail us and we will kill. We must, though we certainly don't want to—it's an immense loss, more than you can judge. Come in with us and you can have all you ask and get the prize singlehanded. You can't get out of it now, except by death. There's no choice for you but this big thing, for which any of your colleagues would have given their lives, or your life."

He still hit back, "Why not choose one of them?"

"Don't be forgetful. If you forget what you have been told, of course we'll have to kill you at once. Forgetting—how often have you been told in your first training—is treason in an agent. He forgets because he wants to fail. We've told you that you have been chosen because you alone fit physically; you alone, of all the possible cadets, could act as a model. We knew your damned vanity, but that can't be helped and we have put up with your attempt at a breakaway because your vanity can be cured, while your physique, at least in the selection at our disposal, is unique."

There was a silence after this. It was the longest speech he ever remembered having been given during an "instruction period." He thought it over. It was clear that they were being lenient, uniquely lenient with him, and it was just as clear that, having made the circumstances as clear to him as they could, it was now up to him to die at once or to go on. After all, he could always die when it became too tough. And also it might lead to some new kind of liberty. A way out could possibly lie ahead. No way out now lay by going back. He went over the steps again. Yes, it was clear enough that was the only thing to do if he ever wanted to sleep again in a bed or have another meal.

"Very well," he said, and already into his voice, he recognized, there had crept a slight tone of equality. The old blind obedience, the service of the great hidden mind that directed them, the willing pawns, was over. He was now a man bargaining as an equal. He had something they would give anything to get and they could take his life if he wouldn't yield. But dead he was almost as great a loss to them as to himself.

And he thought he could just detect something almost like relief in the level super-whisper which answered, "That is right." Then after a moment it went on, "Now that you are once more in with us and have accepted your promotion, you must be told of the various steps. We shall want you to be in the very best of health for this training, naturally. You are tired, and the success of our work depends greatly on your health being superfine. You are not only going to act; you are actually going, first, to grow, to grow quite a lot. You understand, don't you?"

It was a grim question, but he managed to get out a gruff, "Of course."

"So, of course," went on the voice, "you will need to be free of all toxins. You will be given deep colonic lavage in an hour's time. It is very restful, besides being hygienic." Again he grunted a consent and passed the hour checking back over the conversation. He always reached the same conclusion. There had been nothing else to do. So, when the light glowed again, he was passive.

"It will be slow acting, so rest," said the voice of the figure which had been kneeling behind him.

It certainly was soothing. He stretched and his mind went back to the bright scene in the park—the last lit thing that he remembered. Again he was walking there. He would live over those moments again: they were lovely and light. He would lie on his back and recall everything in detail. He thought with vivid imagery for a while.

But why was the sheet over his face? It was drawn quite tightly, almost uncomfortably, over his cheeks. He put up his hand to push it aside. But his hand was somehow caught. He tried the other; caught, too. He twisted a bit. A voice, *the* voice, was speaking now, speaking to him.

"Better lie still. Everything's gone very well; don't trouble to speak. You'll find it easier in quite a little while. This is all that has happened. You know the newer Avertin. You've seen it used, of course. A good anesthetic, as you know; and interesting: a great improvement on the old Avertin. It gives a really long rest—but the going out, as you recall, is rather long, even longer than with the old, and if interrupted, if the patient gets roused, then he's apt to spoil everything. Why, it's hard to know. But, you see, everything has gone well with you. And with the new super-sulfa dressings, now that you've been under for the best part of three days, most of the healing is well under way."

That, then, became his nightmare life for weeks, perhaps months. The days of dawdling, wrapped in bandages that pulled and ached. Then another swamping injection, and out one went, to wander in a limbo of confused memories, vivid and bright but incoherent, and then back again to this world far more dark, insane, incomprehensible, but having one terrible stigma of reality, that it was always the same. There was one small serial change: first he could feed normally, but, as it went on, he fed through a tube, sucking his substance as his jaws were bandaged up. I'm sinking back to a suckling state, he thought.

If only he could have stayed asleep or been put under for good. But now he was in their hands and that was the last thing they wanted. He would mutter in his mind—he could hardly use any part of his face—"Living clay, living clay." Yes, it was apt.

One day, however, they told him he must see, for they wanted to watch him move at instruction—wanted to be sure they had left the controls in good condition. He was sat up. The light came clearer until one could see the whole room. It was not much to see. His touch that first night had told him really all there was. He was inside

23

that smooth plastic cell which had just room for the bed and space for a person to stand on each side of it. They were evidently doing so, for he could feel their arms holding him and then their hands manipulating his bandages.

The one thing that must have been added to the room was across the middle of the bed—a wide mirror with a lamp above it. He looked and saw his still-bandaged head. Then, like an exhumation, these grave-clothes began to be unswathed. He saw his hair and forehead appear as the unwrapping reached where the two small eyeholes had been left. But after that, recognition tried in vain. There wasn't a face there. Loops and curls and volutes of skin and flesh he could see.

"This is just preliminary," said a voice at his left. "Will you pull your mouth to the right?"

He did so, and through the stiff skin and stretched flesh he felt something moving.

"Very good, quite satisfactory! We just wanted to see if the muscle co-ordination was quite in place. No need for surprise. You've probably understood, these are merely grafts getting ready. When they have made their new attachments and the circulation has started through the new rooting, then we can cut them free from their original base. Everything is going well. Now wrinkle your nose. Now contract your left cheek. Good, good!"

Yes, he could make this tasseled and looped mask move a little. He wondered why he obeyed. He concluded that it was less trouble. The dressings were replaced and the bandages readjusted. Once or twice he nearly roused himself to pull the whole thing off. He thought, though, with a dull clarity, that it would only hurt and he was tired. They couldn't be meaning to leave him as he was.

He was in no pain, only ached and was tired and muddled. Into his mind there floated a story he'd read as a boy about a mad doctor on an island who tried by surgery to make animals into men. Of course it was nonsense, but this was the living nightmare. He simply sighed.

But it was only a beginning. The grafts took. Then they showed him the face they were shaping again. Again he could see only a clumsy sketch of a man. So many scars ran across it that every feature that made it human was camouflaged by a cut, furrow, boss, or line which made any clear recognition impossible.

"Of course, the secondary, scar-removal operations will remove all that," said the voice that supervised these inspections.

He only sighed. Perhaps now, like the man who in the terror tale went down the maelstrom, he had touched bottom, and, having expunged him, they would start drawing on the *tabula rasa* what they wanted to reconstruct in the place of what he'd been. But no, there was further to go. They took careful measurements for a long while one day—if day it was—it was a couple of hours, he judged, after his first taking suck after a sleep. Then he was hoisted up and wrapped and injected on the face and the big work began. But it, too, was slow and was done in two divisions. First there was the extraction program. Upper and lower teeth went. More than ever like a creature reduced to a foetal state, he sucked his food day by day over the sore, aching gums. But they healed, too. Nature never seemed to take resentment, to curse life and die; no, the life in him hung on. Provided it was given the chance to repair, given the dressings that permitted it not to be too discouraged in its resolve to live whether he liked it or no, whether he was still recognizably human, it would patch and fuse as though it were glass being bent and twisted in a flame and blown into any fantastic shape. The life in him didn't seem to care whether he suffered or not; not even his physical pain—for now that came in shoots and dull, stretched spans—seemed to affect it at all, still less his shame.

The second part, when the gums had healed, was preluded by fresh careful measurements. They were fitting him, gauging him against some most detailed set of readings. They checked and rechecked. At last they were ready for what he heard one call the big step.

"There, there's no ground for alarm, and that's why we're ready to tell you everything, we're going to explain," said the voice one day as they raised him up.

He could faintly see the masked surgeon-figures round him. Indeed, now he was allowed to get up, as his bed slid away and the operating table took its place—Oh, yes, he was now quite the big boy who could be trusted to co-operate and take a part in the common building up.

"This technique, you'll be amused to hear, was invented by the beauticians. People with receding jaws suffer so much from a sense of inferiority, that it's become quite standard practice to lengthen the jaw. Yours will need, for the full effect, to be brought forward a bit. It's quite a standard piece of surgery, though still a little slow if it is to be done comfortably. We just cut through both sides of the lower jaw and bring it forward."

He was glad, before they were finished with this part of him, that they had been slow. Certainly anything faster must have been agony. But the long days of close bandaging were a prodigious weariness. He often wondered whether one could die from sheer frustration. His body answered for him. He might be weary of life. It wasn't, and it held the reins. They had picked a good body, as they said, and it was theirs, and loyal to them now, no longer to him. When the jaw was finished he could eat smooth things, and that was a relief. He noticed bitterly how the will to live siezed on any little comfort as helping to make its case for just going on.

But *they* were still going on. They, now, having reached the foot of his face, began at the top. It was time now for his eyes; getting back the use of his mouth, he had to give up the use of vision. His whole forehead was bandaged. They were working round the eye sockets. But at last that too was over. Now he would have rest, surely; surely now they would get to work at removing the scar lines and puckers and he would know the end of all this ghastly carnival—true carnival at last, true farewell to the flesh, true and actual pruning down to the stock the tree of life.

But no, though the face was finished and through stiff eyelids he once again saw his cursed featureless cell, they were ready to start another campaign and another sense was to be taken for a term of imprisonment from him. They opened his throat. They kindly explained what they were up to when they had done a certain amount of work which had made even swallowing a problem and made all speech impossible. They needed his co-operation—"and shall increasingly," said that soothing voice. He heard a recording machine start up, and they asked him to speak. He heard a strange tone come from his throat. They played from somewhere a few notes and he was told to sing them. This rehearsal lasted about twenty minutes. His throat felt strangely odd and he could not clearly recognize his voice.

"Pretty good; pretty good."

Then the gramophone shouted out some words in a hoarse, powerful voice.

"Try and get that," the teaching controller of the performance suggested. He tried. "Fairly close, fairly close. We should get it next time."

Next time was after a number of further small operations and rests. At last it was over. They made a jagged chart appear on an illuminated strip that ran on a small screen in front of them. Then he was told to speak, certain words over and over. On the bright field alongside the jagged chart that kept on making its queer saw-edge pattern appeared another pattern almost identical.

"That's the best test. Far closer than the ear. For the magnification is so much greater so that the sound impulses show up. We'll measure these angle impulses. All the rest is really training. We've now given you an instrument that's undetachable and undetectable: you have armor that no one can pierce."

This kind of rhetoric was unlike them, he reflected in a dull reactive way.

"What do you mean?" he asked, wondering faintly whether they might possibly mean that his hell was about to alter, if not to end.

The answer, though not reassuring, was in the same tone of suppressed cheerfulness: "You wait and you won't have to wait long. Yes, we've succeeded. You were a good pick, for there wasn't really much basic work to be done, really only a few superficial redrawings; and the flesh was even more responsive than we'd hoped. Living clay!"

That horrible phrase, how long ago it was that he had first recoiled from it? There was hardly any spring left in his spirit now to recoil, but he felt with a huge weariness

27

of recollection how much more horrible the whole set of ordeals had been than his worst fear had imagined. There was all the suffering, of course; but that, one might hope to put behind one; the mind heals as does the flesh. But this more than mutilation, this obliteration, this just smoothing out the person, and then, on the blank, modeling another—that was a smearing blow that left life a blank. And yet the damned body that had co-operated with these carvers was now as ready to live as ever, it was longing for life at any price.

"It's the straightaway for you now. There's no one in the whole underground that won't envy you."

He thought of saying there was no need to sneer, but it just wasn't worth while. He lay in a sunken silence. A meal came and he swallowed the usual mush.

"Can't I even have a dotard's comfort and be fitted with false teeth?" he called out into the silence as the strength at least of protest came with the intake of the food. But his voice wasn't his own. It was half a dotard's mumble and half a bellow.

A voice answered out of the wall, "Certainly, but all in good time. The jaw has to settle down a bit; it will make all the more for your comfort."

He knew that must be a lie and gave up.

Some days passed. Then a voice remarked, "We shan't trouble you with any more drills beyond this one. We just want one more movement check-up, to be sure you're completely mobile and at home with your new instrument." The lit mirror flashed on in front of him and he was aware of two figures standing at each side of him. "Turn head right: left: up: down: smile: yawn: purse lips: wink one eye: wink both."

Like a loosely made rubber ventriloquist's doll, he writhed these roughly modeled features, grimaced, went through the command performance. It seemed to him simply a tangle of grotesque leers.

But at the end they said, "Fine! And now pull it into a repose. Yes"—and it was clear they were speaking to each other, not to him—"yes, that will do. When it's got proper backing that will be a very convincing piece of assembly. No visible tremors, strains, or tension, though of course one can see that there are a few stiffnesses and resistance reflexes hanging on under the surface." Then to him, "But we'll deal with all that quite soon."

The horrible mirror flashed off and he heard it sliding away. He lay quiet in the dark. He wasn't quite sure—hadn't been able in the first flash of the light to see with any exactness. They didn't care whether he saw as long as they could see him doing what they said. But it must be pretty bad. He could stand that voice now embedded in his throat and which made coarse guttural growls, the sound of an old rasped organ. The blow was in what he thought he'd glimpsed of the face.

He'd tried to start at the top—the rest was writhing under the orders too much for him to be sure he made out anything clearly. He was sure the forehead and eyes had aged fifteen years fully from that time perhaps not fifteen weeks ago when he had stood unconsciously fully satisfied with the appearance through which he looked out at the world. Something wonderful, diabolically wonderful, had been done—a black magician's marvel of grafting and blends. From that upper piece, on which he had fixed his attention as soon as he could focus, it was clear that not only had they forged new features, new profile, new oval—they had made a new, or rather an old, texture, an old skin out of a new, fresh, healthy one. Large pores, coarsened texture, the first faint blotchy discolorations of oncoming old age—yes, he'd seen enough to see they must all be there to give that effect of tiredness and general loss of tone. It was just as when out of fresh, innocent wood a faker of antiques turns a good, simple piece of furniture of the right build and size into a weather-beaten, time-eroded period-piece, a museum curiosity.

He threw himself back on his bed. Coldly, comfortlessly through his mind as he lay in the silence ran the thought, "So we do care so much for ourselves, for what we feel we look like!"

The first time he again paid any attention or tried to understand was when some time after a voice said, "You will now have something enjoyable." But his shudder of

29

anticipation was cut short by, "Your muscle tone can be put back quickly by massage and you will have a good spell every day. You'll feel wonderfully better."

True enough, two masked masseurs came a few minutes later and with the first manipulations he discovered to his surprised relief that he was in the hands of men who wished to give him comfort and knew how. It was the first real rest and relaxation that he'd had. It was hard to keep up those submuscle tensions, that qui vive of the deep sinews, when these strong reassurances, so much more massive and deep than any words, came to him from the deepest sense, touch. He could not doubt the friendliness of the hands that dealt with him, if he still knew nothing of the eyes that were looking him over from behind their masks.

Then one day one of them spoke. "I'd like to show you how to do something of this for yourself. Especially round the head and neck you should keep this up. It will keep you free of tensions and set the circulation flowing well through all this new skin."

He was willing to learn. He was shown how to soothe a nerve with a few fingerings of its power-line.

"The back of the neck, though, is the central switchboard for all the head," was the next instruction.

After he had been trying with his teacher's help to get himself by the scruff of the neck, he was told to work first with his hands in front of him: "Get the movement there and then translate it back." But he still didn't, evidently, do it right.

To his surprise, and somehow quite considerable pleasure, the masseur—there was only one now—suddenly turned his back to the bed, knelt down, and said, "Look here, put your hands on my neck and that will show you. I'll be able to tell you how to do it; best that way."

They had several lessons in that method and he learned to feel his way along the nerves and muscles and see where the tensions lay and smooth them out. Then he could put his own hands and fingers on his own neck almost as aptly. The work interested him, too, quite apart from the relief. He had been so long without anything to do that his hands, just as had his flesh, seemed to be craving to get to work, to live again in action. But as soon as he had learned that, he saw his friend—as already he had begun to think of this strange, masked—masseur—no more. The life kept on its nightmare quality of irrelevance. For, a day after the massage lessons stopped, he was told by the invisible voice to come along. He was sitting on the edge of his bed after putting on the two-piece suit in which he spent his time when not in bed. He rose uncertainly, and as he did so a small section in the wall, just enough to let a man through, opened. He stepped out into a passage faintly lit through its plastic wall. It went straight for perhaps a hundred yards, then turned right and seemed to end after hardly more than fifty feet. But when he was within arm's length of the terminating wall, it slid aside. He stepped through and he could just hear the panel slip back into place behind him.

He was in a bare room, but it had one reassuring feature— an ordinary, obvious door was at one side of it and, even more reassuring, the door was ajar, while from the other side of it a loud, unguarded voice, full of careless inflection, called out, "Come in, come along." He stepped across and looked in. That room was larger and full of reassuring things— it was a big kitchen and at the farther end its cooking ranges glowed cheerfully. The man who had called to him again shouted, "Come in" over the noise of an egg beater which he was using.

He was told he could help. He found this, his second teacher, gay, amusing; and learning with him became interesting. He was taught all sorts of cookery by one who was evidently an enthusiast. The hours were not long and the drudgery was off their hands: for all the soiled things simply were put into a transit-duct and the clean utensils were returned by another. In between as they ate their meals—or rested (they seemed to be cooking for not more than half a dozen persons or a few more, besides themselves) —the cheery chef would talk vivaciously and amusingly. But all his life and anecdotes circled round his profession; where he had led it and why he had come here, there was never a hint of such things.

31

Wearily the captive reflected, this is probably one of the top men, who just chooses to act the part of a chef the better to observe me when relaxed. He himself was too old a hand at secret-service work not to know that vivacious type which is bubbling over with a talk which, like a thick foam, hides the deep, watching mind far better than any smooth stillness. But all that he learned was cookery, and that he learned thoroughly. If this, his new jailer, was an actor, he was the most thorough he had ever met in a profession which puts the highest premium on three-dimensional, all-the-time acting.

After what he was pretty sure was six weeks or two months—for he was told he was an apt pupil—he was told he knew enough, unless he wanted to become a chef, and no doubt, said the chef with a laugh, he only wanted to be an amateur.

"Besides, if I told you any more, I should have to initiate you into the real culinary mysteries and then we should be confreres, and that wouldn't do, would it?"

For a moment in that rhetorical question he thought he caught the far-down echo of a real one. Anyhow, that was the last time he saw the chef, and indeed the last time that he saw anything of that sunken life into which he had gone a young man of promise and full of his own sense of who he was and who he might become—and from which he would emerge, what? For the next day he found an ordinary suit lying on a chair by his bed.

The voice that he had become so used to, that came from nowhere, said, "Straight down the passage and then straight on."

He went down, carrying the suit over his arm. At the right-angle turn the wall opened in front of him and he was in a fine bathroom. A masked attendant, after massaging him, shaved him. With a motiveless detachment he thought to himself, how well they must have done their work to leave quite a steady flow of stubble to be reaped. Well, they had left him a man, if he had lost the particular manhood, the male personality, he had had.

"I'm shaving you," said the voice above him, "because you'll need for a little to learn to handle this skin of yours."

The shrouded barber took up a big fold of the skin with his fingers. The man being shaved remembered that he used to enjoy that—coming up from some particularly deep and dirty underground dive all soiled and prickly and under that stimulating rasp becoming smooth again and svelte. It was contrast that counted, really. There had been for a short time a short-wave invention that did away with the need to shave. Three radiation treatments left you with a waxlike face-complexion that lasted three months and more. But after a little it was thought a bit effeminate. Men preferred to go back to the stronger complexion texture given by the latent beard.

Looking up, he found there was a large polished-metal boss that held the diffusion glass under-shade of the light hung above the barber's chair. In this he could just see a miniature of his head, and, as the barber's hands flicked to and fro, he could catch glimpses with each razor-sweep-off of the foam, of a face emerging. It was hard to be quite sure because the flesh seemed so loose. And as the barber took it up in his thumb and finger there seemed so much cheek and chin that any clear outline never seemed to be detectable.

He felt, however, increasingly sure of two impressions: the upper part of his face, grown on him closer than glue, was someone else's. Whose you couldn't tell, for as far as he could glance there didn't seem enough of it. For the lower part of it, the greater part of it, was no one's. From the cheekbones almost to the Adam's apple it seemed there must be hanging a series of doublings and folds which, if they had had in them any thrust, might have been called chins. The whole mask, that he felt was so lax that, from drooping eyes downward, the miniature creature up at whom he glanced (and through whom he presumably was looking) appeared a cartoon for a deflated, dismal debauchee. No, it was worse than that, it looked like one of those rubber toys, just a crumpled swath of folds that may, when you inflate them, turn into a pig or a bathing belle.

As a fresh coat of lather was slapped on over this clever wrecking he sighed. Perhaps it would come straight when he could get upright. But did it matter into what shape they had cut and stitched him? The former man seemed already to have been stripped away with the face they had skinned and scalped from him. When he had been put through that last drill, to see that he could move all this curtainage and shrouding, he hadn't, while he pulled it to and fro at command and, as they said, "assembled it," he hadn't realized what it was, how far it fell short of being a face, when it really fell into repose. But even now he wasn't sure. All he could actually see was a manikin emerging out of foam, and he noticed that the barber's hands, which were shapely enough, looked in their reflection up on the polished boss quite a bit distorted. He thought grimly but with little grit of resentment, They might have turned me into anything, into an ephebe, a hermaphrodite, a monkey-man, a seal creature, or some sort of grotesque modernization of a centaur—one must be thankful for being let remain one of the featherless bipeds. After he was left he showered himself and once or twice caught his reflection in the small puddles of water. What was the use? And muttering with some bitterness, "Narcissus," he put on the clothes.

II

THE MISSION

THE VOICE directed him back to his room where his breakfast was ready. His gums were now quite hard but still they gave him pap and no teeth to bite anything else. He took it down: his stomach caring little for his appearance, or that of the food, as long as it got its mushy pabulum. What a surface creature this I is, he thought, and before he had turned his mind from this useless and inevitable reflection the voice said, "You will find the office to your left, down the passage." Again, when he reached the end of the first straight, the wall opened, but this time on the right, and he was in a small but quite normal room in which there was sunlight falling, books, and flowers.

He sat down in a chair looking at these with a relief that was so strong that he felt a surprise at its intensity. He was sufficiently master of himself, however, to realize this was his surface self, that had tried in vain to make his animal self give up the wish to live, now going over to those who had remade him. He had capitulated to the brutal terms of "life at any price" and "only let me live." He looked out of the window at a small lawn and garden, the close view ending in some graceful trees about a square sheet of water. The view rested him, and he was so determined to take it and disregard all else that he refused to look round when he heard another door open. He would not even turn away from the quiet scene when he heard someone take a chair close to him.

He waited until quite a cheerful voice began, "We don't deal in apologies, you know, but we do allow praise, and we cannot say how highly we think of the organic reaction that has been made to this brilliant and brilliantly successful experiment. We are sure now that all the main difficulties are surmounted. The rest presents no real problem. As in chess, there are some more movements to be made but the checkmate is now the definite six moves away. Only a fool could throw away the game now. Not a master, on the other side, can save the situation."

He turned round slowly. He did not remember ever seeing the man who was talking to him before. But then, you wouldn't. The face was remarkable for one thing: there was absolutely nothing whereby you might remember it— it had features, of course, but in the memorable sense, it was utterly featureless—smooth, unaccented, like the voice. You could not even tell the age—a male adult, that was all you could say, and no scrutiny would help you to remember more.

"It may interest you to know that you are being spoken to," went on the voice, "by one of the preliminary trials —a successful one, in its way—of course some, both before and after this particular case, broke down, nervously or just in the way of crude physical healing power. Sometimes the repair power seemed to give out. At others it wasn't possible to get results that wouldn't show—there was distortion, or that slight lack of subcutaneous muscle-tone which makes the face look suspiciously wooden—what you used to see on the old scar-removal surgery cases. But in the case which you are now viewing the aim was simple, just to see, as a trial, not whether something could be built up but whether it was possible to remove all likeness and reduce the face to complete nondescriptivity, nonentity. Well, I am told that the effect is quite successful, and I should like to add I have found that it is not merely physiological.

"I find, myself, that if clothes make the man and the uniform makes us uniform, having one's face made neutral does a great deal to make one's character lose those queer and inconvenient quirks which we are always building up as part of our character-pose. After all, what's personality, when you analyze the word, but a mask, an instrument through which one gives tone and flavor and accent to what is otherwise the common cliché-collection and vocabulary of everyone!"

The speaker paused. He had spoken in his partless part

perfectly, without accent or emphasis, as though to himself or to some large unknown audience and as though it were all so obvious as hardly to need the saying.

"You'll be surprised and pleased," the faintest glow of mild complacency came into the flat tone of the voice, "to notice how much a real change in physiognomy does for the psyche. In some of the earlier cases they did try pretty thorough glandular alterations, hoping then, by thyroidectomy, interstitial graftings, and such neat surgeries so to change the endocrine balance that the basic alteration of physique and appearance desired would come about. But it was more ingenious than successful. Of course, it had to be a hit-or-miss procedure.

"They produced naturally (or should I say unnaturally?) some quite interesting, and indeed unexpected, results. Indeed, very interesting for pure research into the problem. What is personality? But then, of course, as you know as well as I, this laboratory is not for pure research. It's for a very special, very particularly applied, research. In my own case, they were still hoping something might come from glandular surgery combined with radical change in appearance. So I was given a fairly extensive thyroidectomy," the man touched a fine vertical line by his Adam's apple, "but I don't think it really helped. The utter change in appearance is what counts and really affects and alters character—slower, of course, but in the end much surer—a sort of natural seasoning, maturing, weathering, from the surface in. Put a man into waiter's clothes, keep him in them, never let him be in anything else, and gradually he learns to wait; he becomes a waiter and wants to be. There was a successful actress whose final hit was the playing so well of the part of an ancient arthritic lady that the run ended by bringing her to a standstill. Off the stage she woke up to find she had actually become arthritic!"

He almost smiled. For a moment his listener forgot himself as he tried hard through that waxen mask to tell whether buried under that smooth smudge there might not be the face of a man whom he had once known as a comrade. It was no use. It was certainly lost. And his own attention was switched back to himself by what the creature was now saying:

"Your case, of course, is as much beyond mine as mine was beyond anything they had done till then. I am really only a trial piece, a halfway house, though I can be and am used as a useful kind of super, and no doubt a number of such featureless models will be made, for of course we can serve a number of general purposes. But yours is an attempt at uniqueness while ours is the reverse. We are, if I may so say, that kind of generalized skeleton key with which a number of ordinary locks can be picked. You are a key forged for one master lock."

"I would like you either to be more explicit, or to stop," he suddenly found himself saying with an emphasis that made him master of his mumbling mouth and dedental jaws.

"Quite a right remark, and I will," was followed without a pause by definite instructions.

"Then I go out today?"

"At once."

"Without teeth?" he gobbled.

"But you know, with all the beauty operations, the gums and jaw must settle."

He got up. The model rose with him, and they went past the window to the door by which it had entered. His mind switched from self-pity to an outer disgust. He found he could not think of this neat automaton as really a man. As they went past the window the slanting sunlight fell on that face. It was as smooth as a child's. All that long diary which man writes so unconsciously but so minutely all over his face, the caution round the eyes, the anger reactions in the pulls under the lower lids, the scorn stifled by still curling round the nostrils, the humor round the mouth-corners, the pulls of repeated resolution on the chin muscles and tendons, all gone, leaving not a wrack behind. But as he looked again, in that strong crosslight, he could see, as fine as the shadows of a gossamer spider's web, the faintest, neatest lines, crossing and running right across the face's smooth contours and the rise and fall of the main members. They were the only traces of this prodigious surgical battle that, on this field, had succeeded in annihilating a man's written and engraved life.

He was taken to the door by which the model had entered. It opened on a flight of stairs going down. He followed until it was clear that they were in a deep basement, when, passing through another door at the foot of the flight, he found himself on a small platform where, on the other side, a car was drawn up. This must have been the underground terminus at which he had arrived—how long ago and how different a man. And that looked as though it were the vehicle which had delivered him to his ordeal. The model opened the car door. Yes, it must be the same tumbril. It had no windows and was as smooth inside as had been his cell.

The model handed him two envelopes. "This," he said, "holds sufficient currency notes for your expenses, and this, your instructions."

The man waved him into the car. He obeyed, and as he sat down the door was closed, the car started. It was completely dark inside. He felt about. The door had no handle. There was nothing to do but wait and listen. He heard the hollow echo become more open—they must have left the tunnel. Then there were the quick turns and swayings which he remembered he'd diagnosed as the side road. After that came the longer sweeps of the highroad and the ever more frequent rushing sounds of other cars passing them. Finally the full sounds of city traffic began to rise round them. The story had been rewound. He was back again—but was it he who was back? A dim light came on in the back of the cab. It showed the interior as smooth as his cell.

He counted the currency notes, quite enough to live for a week or more as well as one might wish, longer if one was careful. He then tore open the other envelope. Queer to give instructions—he thought while doing it—and leave no means to destroy them. But when he had read them he smiled with his still stiff and rumpled face. He remembered the old rule: never destroy, but always leave the apparently obvious. The instruction was a piece of printed pasteboard. It contained only one piece of writing and that

39

was a date and hour. It said that one of the big semi-official employment agencies had an appointment for him at 11:30 A.M. on a date. Everything in the new state was semi-official: "free enterprise with nothing but general welfare supervision"—that was one of the first successful slogans. He guessed the date given must be the day that he was now living in. That showed that more time had gone in his country visit than he'd thought.

As he was trying to think back he was suddenly physically swung back. The car had stopped. He waited, sitting forward. But nothing happened. Then just as he thought they were about to start again, the door swung open. This time it opened the normal way.

"Get out," said what must have been the voice of the unseen chauffeur.

He didn't need urging, and there wasn't a moment for delay. He saw they were with a number of other cars drawn up at a traffic signal which at that moment was changing lights. The cars behind were already getting under way, and he was a track away from the curb. He leaped for it and ran, getting to the sidewalk just as the car on the track nearest the sidewalk swished behind him. Turning, he looked at the wave of cars sweeping down the receding boulevard. Of course it was useless in that number of standard hulls to try to pick out the one that might have been his prison ship. As neatly dropped as picked up, he thought. Then he glanced up at one of the big street clocks. It was ten past eleven. He looked at the street name and number. He was not more than ten minutes' walk from the place where he was to go. Good timing, they used to be told, is the essence of planning. Well, the central office evidently lived up to its advice.

He strolled along. It never occurred to him not to go on. The momentum they had given him made going back not only absurdly rash—they could and would kill, he knew, if he went off the tracks again after all the trouble they had taken. The Mole was always said to be able to cut his losses grandly. That was one of his strongest points. He would cut the whole thing out and start on a clean new idea—and with a new instrument. He scrapped his

40

old tools with an utter disregard of any kind of attachment to anything but the end. Yes, that was strength, and it was too strong for any of its agents—especially when it had put its obliterating stamp on one, as it had on him. He wasn't going on, then, simply because he calculated it would shorten his life if he didn't—he was past such an independent calculation of choices and the choosing of a path. There seemed nothing else to do—the whole thing was now increasingly inevitable. He didn't even feel much interest as to what lay ahead. It would just happen and he would act as events dictated. He'd once or twice, when he'd been young and in the game at the start, heard one or two of the novice-instructors saying that was the right state of mind. It had seemed just silly to him. A man who serves a great cause should have fire and dash and a clear sense of what he is doing and of the greatness of his goal. But no, they had been right. This, he now knew, is the climate in which the really definitive and decisive things are done.

He began then to take a casual interest in the crowds. The last time he had seen them he had still been taken up with himself and his prejudices and indeed his personal hopes. Let me see, he thought, and it was evening, too, wasn't it, and I met a girl. Certainly the crowds looked, if anything, gayer today. It was a day of lovely lighting.

Alpha and his crew had always said they believed in making the people happy. They were out to give service, to let the ordinary sane man have a good time and get what he wanted. They'd done with all the nationalistic nonsense—they were just the enemies of all rigid ideologies. They wanted the average man and woman to sit back and have a good time and live to find life worth living and enjoyable. Of course, that meant that someone would have to work for them, to relieve them of the task of just tidying up. Hadn't we given over our children, whom we used to try to teach, to the skilled teacher and the school, from the infant-school crèche right up to the university? Even the "traditional state," in the last phase of nationalism, had done that—it had unraveled that tangle

41

of the animal and the sentimntal called the human family.

The next thing, after the closing up and liquidation of the home, was the closing up and liquidation of the nation. Alpha had claimed that was his generous aim. And in a way he'd done it, and, without a doubt, most of the population were grateful. The great base of the pyramid of life, the ordinary self-centered person, settled back with relief, relief from no longer having to be on your toes reaching for a better life for everyone, or some great silly, out-of-the-range-of-the-senses aim. Only the peaks whined and protested and then went underground. Trying to do what? To overset the pyramid?

The thoughts went through his mind, but not as a personal challenge, as they had that last time he had strolled these streets. He wasn't thinking what he might do about it—that was settled and closed, as closed as the scars on his face, as hidden as that old appearance and character which these skilled cuts had swallowed up forever. Yes, the people were happy, gay, merry, as they had never been before. They wanted to be bright and careless, and Alpha had told them that was their duty and his aim for them.

"We must wait on life," was one of his easy perorations. "We don't know what it wants, but the old liberals were right: we must have freedom so as to be able to wait and let it develop as it will. We will tolerate everything save intolerance. That is where the New Liberalism has learned the lesson taught by the failure of the old. We have no quarrel with anyone save those who want to dragoon the people into causes and sacrifices which the people don't want and life doesn't want them to want.

"But we know that the people, because they are kindly and simple and ought to be off guard if they are to be easy and carelessly creative, can be exploited and seized upon. Their liberty is our concern, and we will watch that they may daydream if they wish. Theirs is the creative role. We are merely their trustees and guardians. We have no quarrel save with those puritans and self-appointed fanatics who want the people to sacrifice themselves for any aim save clear, immediate happiness. The common man

42

doesn't need to be told what that is. He knows, as a child knows what food will agree with it, till its taste is spoiled. We intend to give back to all of you your inspired and natural skill in knowing by your taste what agrees with you and what life wants of you."

Yes, it was simple, so simple and so successful that you couldn't think why someone who wanted power hadn't thought of it before! Of course, he beat all the grim puritans, the old nationalists, the old ideologists, the hard fanatics, the men who thought the masses wanted to be drilled, when all they wanted was the fun of going about in some uniform and some kind of performance a little less dreary than the utilitarianism mixed with the inhibitions of the gentleman, which had been the only alternative formula of the old liberalism.

Here was the proof. The crowd was as bright as a May day festival, a pageant. The last vestiges of that hangover of nineteenth-century good taste that had lasted right on to the final failure of the economic revolutionary phase, the hideous male semi-uniform, as dreary as the worst unifrom, the so-called lounge suit, then named the store suit, had gone forever. Men wore what they liked, but most were in that athletic kit which the thirteenth century had stylized —the jersey or belted tunic reaching to the mid-thigh, the long hose, and the boots of the soft plastic that had taken the place of leather. The textiles were of hues which made silk look dingy. And these iridescent crowds were made kaleidoscopic by their reflections in endless mirrors. All blank spaces were large looking glasses.

"If people look at themselves—and it is that they'd rather look at than anything else—they'll never trouble to look further." He remembered that when he was a young fellow and he was talking to his professor in political science, the man had said that to him. He now suspected that then they were feeling out, making a first test of him, as if he might be one of those few young on whom the bait of pleasure and ease wouldn't take. If so, he would have to be taken into the machine, go under the smooth surface with its finely painted decorations, and see the actual structure underneath that supported all this and the engines that ran it.

Instead, he had been caught by a fellow scholar who had made a contact with the unofficial underground, and for Bull they had exchanged Mole. Well, it was done and irrevocable. Between him and this gay crowd there was a gap as wide and unbridgeable as between the living and the dead. It was too wide for blame or praise to come into the question. For that would mean that choice could be made. No comparison was possible. The living don't blame the dead for having gone. It just can't be helped and had best not be thought about.

Of course, there were officials about in this irresponsible crowd. It didn't take his trained eye to pick them out, either. Alpha was not such an old stick-in-the-mud as to try to hide everything. The actual machine was hidden well underground, but there had to be contact points, holds, and controls which emerged onto the surface. Such things didn't disturb the masses. On the contrary, it gave them a sense of security. They were told half of the truth quite frankly, so frankly that, as they wished to believe it was the whole, they never inquired further. The world, it was said in all lessons on sociology, was divided into two classes as a genetic fact. There were people who could be content to take their pleasure and their ease, those who had by nature, in their blood, the art of living. That was the great mass of people, and no doubt they were the aim of life. And to keep the world fit for such sane people to live in, for men and women who were so natural and healthy that they didn't need any other reason for living than the physical fun that healthy living gave them, nature had provided another type, of too high nervous tension ever to be able to relax, a type which needs to live for something else and never could live just for the life's sake in them, just for friendly fun, who had the itch to work in their blood. It was clear that this was life's aim.

All this was now taught in every high school as the moral and peroration to all lectures on biology and evolution. Life had tried to produce this kind of society, it was pointed out, often before—in all the social animals, supremely in all the social insects. But just as man had done with his first three revolutions—the religious, the political, and the economic—the fault was that the worker type could not see that it was obviously menial, clearly a means to the full, open, wanton life of the non-worker. So the worker bees kill off the drones; and every puritan who—till the last, the fourth, the final and glorious, revolution—had dominated and then exploited a new age, all these hardworking kill-joys had tried to make themselves, who were mere means, the end. Then, of course, they had to have religious wars and political national wars and economic wars, just because, poor one-track creatures, they could not find any interest in the marvelous manifoldness of actual immediate living. They could live only in some conception of service, and that was right enough. But when they had served, then their real pride came out. They were determined that just to have set men free to be happy in the careless way that life has planned happiness actually to be—that was not enough, was wrong, base, ignoble. So they set up the fancy aims of crusades and causes and pointless heroism, until it ended in the insane nonsense of war for war's sake and sacrifice for sacrifice's sake and life for death's sake.

Of course, when the psychological revolution—the final revolution—broke out, men saw through all this nonsensical pseudo-rationalizing, saw it for what it was. And so the great Alpha had said the first word of the really new age. He frequently remarked laughingly—through those fifty million television sets, his great, wide, generous mouth bellowing out the humor the crowd loved—that he was simply a dolt, but that he had tried to be sensible and really enjoy fun for fun's sake. Finally he decided that Life meant him to take it at second hand, to get his fun out of seeing other people happy. Well, it was probably a pretty poor and faint thing. But then he didn't ask anyone to share it with him. All he asked for was tolerance. For though he was sure that the ordinary man was right and was the real aim and crown of life, and from him would come the really creative ideas, the real progress that can spring only from real freedom to do as you liked and do noth-

45

ing if that pleased you better—yet there were odd people like himself that kept on turning up. And he asked for a place for himself and his kind. He was ready, too, to show that he and his sort could in their humble way have their uses. They could keep the tracks clear. They could guard the rich liberty of those who wanted to enjoy and create rather than have to watch and prevent the fine free impulses from being thwarted.

"We," he used to say, referring to as much of the Party as the people were let see, "we are in our way quite a natural growth, though, I grant you, hardly ornamental, and well kept out of the way. We are the roots to you, the flowers. We serve a purpose and get our satisfaction out of working. Life will produce muscles, and they are necessary for holding out the five senses to the sun. And if you produce muscles you have to give them exercises—that is their low form of enjoyment; they get their fun just out of work!"

And the people cheered to the echo his cheery compliments of their gay sloth, the people who had been told this in every key through every stage of their schoolwork, till it was commonsense, obvious fact, till it was the conclusion of every history lesson and why the old nations had made anarchy, why the old religions had made hell and persecution, why the old economics had made death and destruction, till it was the conclusion of every lesson on sociology, biology, physiology, till all science was shown to have pointed to this conclusion and all art to spring from it.

So Alpha recruited those who wanted to rule and who were ready to prove the purity of their passion for power by preparing to forswear all the alloys which till then had been mixed with and had weakened power: the wish for display, for pomp, for wealth and any indulgence. If you were of what he called the service type, a few good-natured jokes were made about you, and you became a worker; you were gradually initiated into and inured to the machine. There, too, he and his advisers had shown their psychological skill and they could indeed claim that theirs was the capping revolution, the only one that had understood man in his variety. And therefore this was the final one, the lasting change. As for you, you the private person, Life's picked pet, you could go just as far as you liked.

They had, of course, taken over Sheldon's classification, and that at once gave them a realistic power no dictatorship had ever had before. They had at last something approaching a real map of humanity, instead of those queer selective shadows and profiles of themselves which till then reformers had often honestly taken to be the picture and likeness of mankind. So the good easygoing type—the viscerotonic—were claimed to be life's end: and they had least to do with power, for power (that was one of their camouflage slogans) was just a menial thing like drainage and, like drainage, best kept out of sight. Half of mankind were in that first type. Then there were the somatotonics, the athletic type. It got tired of sitting about in the sun, but that did not mean it was fit for real power, psychological power. It was simply its muscular tension that made it want to act. You gave it games and competitions and explorations, and got rid of quite a lot by shooting them off the earth on planetary flights from which they never came back—expensive, but really quite cheap considering the riddance—and you put up small monuments to them in the quieter corners of the great public parks—or you kept on sending them down in bathyspheres to be crushed in trying to touch bottom of the ocean abyss. Those who survived that kind of testing were then given the high-power planes of the mental hygiene inspection corps and dashed round and round the world. You could generally wear them out in ten or twenty years of use and never give them a moment to make trouble. Indeed, naturally they gave no more than the pleasure seekers as long as you kept them on the run. Pen them up and they *were* troublesome. But the cure was simple—just simple, straightaway speed. The ones who were a little more than that and who had fairly mixed in them the cerebrotonic element, well, they were quite useful in their limited way. One needs strength in asylum attendants, and quite large numbers were required to staff the arrest squads who were always ready for preventive work and for the actual dealing with those picked up and needing treatment.

As the remodeled man looked around him he could pick out these, the top layer of the machine. There was no attempt to disguise them. Indeed, they were quite noticeable. For while the crowd of Lifers—that was the popular name for those who could loaf for life—was dressed in all ranges of color and hardly a single person wore less than several tints, these public servants wore, though in bright color, suits which were of only one tone. You could see here a couple in plain yellow and there another in Lincoln green. He had been out of the world so long that he had forgotten what the various tints meant, what service corps you belonged to, and, besides, Alpha was always thinking up some new stunt. The attitude of the people, though, had obviously not changed toward these their servant-masters. They regarded them as though they were a mixture of a mailman and a garbage collector—necessary, no doubt, and worth a bonus, of course, but still always rather a mystery as to why a man who could really enjoy himself should care to go on working just for work's sake. Of course, the psychological textbooks at school had explained it all rationally. But still, emotionally, how could careless, carefree men understand such cranks? Thank heaven, though, there *was* someone who liked hard dull work, considering how hateful it is to all well-constituted bodies.

Yes, that was the formula that had won, and—by the deepest of all undergrounds!—it was more true anthropologically than any of the old formulae in the name of which —"The right of private religious judgment! Man is born free and equal!! All profit belongs to labor!!!"—the other revolutions had been made, formulae that always narrowed down man: down from one obsessed by religion, to the lesser man of politics and to the final *reductio ad absurdum* to economic man, interested only in money! No doubt it wasn't right; it was too simple, this shot at the psychological-anthropological solution. That was shown by the things that Alpha the Bull had to do in his underground.

The remodeled man had joined the Mole against the Bull because of what he knew about the Bull's subterfuges. He asked himself now, would he have left the surface for the underground had the Bull been really able to make his case, had he had the whole secret and his explanation needed no helping out from underground violence? Now that he knew the Mole's way, too, how closely the two underground burrows ran, how parallel. Was the Mole anything else but the Bull in opposition? Wasn't he simply the Omega of Alpha?

His mind grew weary trying to find the fine straight edge of right, that once had seemed so clear and strong and noble, amid all the twists and bends that actual practise seemed to force on it, and the strange lights that actual living threw on it. He looked at the crowds flowing past him—weren't they real enough, so strong in their rooted carelessness that you might as well think of turning them from their set gay thoughtlessness as a tumbling, sunlit torrent from its course? He was the shadow, they the thing of abiding strength. Yes, so far the Bull had been right, they were life.

He began then to think whether the crowd noticed this ghost among them. Of course, he was in the kind of clothes they wore and they had left him his good figure, and with the brightness of the costume the looks of facial features counted for far less. He remembered that when he had been reading all about Machiavelli he came across that strange Baldassare Castiglione's *The Courtier*, a book these people ought to republish, for it was the real answer to all that rationalistic, pre-psychological, pre-anthropological stuff of Machiavelli's *Prince*. The author there had noticed this very point. He remarks that Spaniards, the type of the thrusting, domineering, totalitarian, imperialistic nationalism of that day, had brought in the ostentatious fashion of wearing black, for this drew everyone's attention to one's face, while a young man who was modest should be able to preserve his anonymity by speaking little and wearing rose-colored velvet. Yes, that was right. And it accounted, no doubt, for the fact that in these crowds hardly a person looked more than twice at his face. Surely it must draw attention to him. He turned to one of the large mirrors. For a moment he had difficulty in picking out himself.

Then he saw a creature of good form and carriage, but the face, if you once paid attention to it, was unpleasantly arresting. In all these crowds the faces were as generally vaguely uniform as their gay dresses: a certain standard of good looks was everywhere. The free medical services, the psychophysical hygiene looked after that.

The problem of hair had been solved by glandular study endowed by the state. You could have practically any head of hair you chose for a few treatments—injections and diet —and most people chose bronzes and golds. Well, the people who had remodeled him had taken care of that: his hair had been quite good and now it was one of the standard dark tints, somewhat cleared off the temples and a wave which he'd had was taken out.

It was, of course, the main features of the face and especially the mouth that were wrong. There was that top part, far too rugged, too emphatic, in a crowd where all excess was evidently ridiculous, and then there was that treble collapse of chins, like a cascade of half-melted wax, one of those face-modeling accidents that now with the new techniques had became old vaudeville jokes.

He went close up to the huge looking glass. There were plenty of other people frankly admiring themselves; that inhibition had been gotten over. But he still felt shy and made the acted excuse that dust had gotten in one of his eyes. When he was close he scanned in the full daylight and at full length and framed with fellow men, this new mask. So that was what he was to be for the rest of his life. That was absolutely certain. Because flesh at his time of life had its limit of tolerances and would never take such a tormenting again—like the three wishes, if you had used them all up, then you hadn't that last one to get you back safely to where you were before you dared to wish. But in spite of being hideous, it looked natural. It was simply one of those few misbirths with which beautician surgeons didn't like to meddle because you'd have to tease the flesh so much it might refuse to heal and go malignant. So you gave "Suggest We Don't Mind" mental treatment instead and asked people not to stare and they didn't. Yes, he was simply a misshape. To his most careful scrutiny all that was revealed of the strange secret was the fine gossamer straight lines he had noticed in the sunlight on the model's face as he left that hospital, the faint print of metamorphosis. But, now what he could give careful scrutiny to this fused-on mask, he saw how different it was from the mask worn by the model who had given him his last interview as he left the underground hospital. In that creature's face there was nothing left but an anonymous smoothness; he wasn't bad looking or good looking but blanker than a Chinese coolie's face looks to a Westerner.

But this further experiment which was now fixed on him for life—a far more awful confinement than ever the man with the iron mask suffered—he was now able to study in detail. There had been that growing exposure while he watched in the little mirror his face being shaved. He had seen from casual glances in mirrors as he passed its general disproportion but only now did he gauge how slipshod and unfinished it appeared. There were a number of apparently strong lines on the upper part of the face, deep furrows and convergent folds, and then they seemed to peter out and come to nothing. They should have swept down round the cheekbones and the setting of the nose and bound themselves round, finding purchase in a firm, strong chin. But the whole mask just lapsed. There were big puckers round the mouth and lapses on each side of the nose, and the lower part of the cheeks sank and hollowed. He tried to hope that his teeth would somehow remedy the effect and give back a little strength to that large, drooped, suffering mouth.

He wondered what the effect would be, every time he caught sight of himself, to see this rather beaten, weary object looking at him. Surely, to his divided thought, it would act as a steady suggestion to further discouragement. He feebly thrust his tongue across the toothless gum of his upper front jaw trying to make the cheek take a less dismal fold. In vain; the cheek was far too loose and empty to be filled; it simply made a grotesque grimace. They had removed all the bicuspids as well as canines and incisors. Only the molars were left—like some degenerate ru-

51

minant, he thought dismally. They had not been content just to let his face fall in. With their hateful mutilations, they had added skin and flesh, making his mouth and cheeks and lips too big for even the support of the teeth which he had had. He would be a scarecrow even when they should give him back his teeth. For some reason they had wished to break his vanity, evidently, perhaps to make him a better, more selfless, agent, and so kill two birds with one stone, make him disappear, the handsome young agent whom one of the Bull's agents might now know by sight, and also to ruin in him the last vestige of self-love so that he might become their slave for life. They had just mutilated him, as lecherous tyrants turned men into eunuchs to guard their harems. He must give up looking at himself.

Well, it was time to be keeping his appointment, and he was tired of waiting, for he no longer had any will to strike out for himself; there was no longer any sense in such a thought. He had been making his way all the time easily to the destination, and, sure enough, there was the great façade of the office just across the boulevard. As the lights flashed a clear-way for pedestrians, he walked over.

At the door the man scarcely looked at him as he took his card. He was shown straight up to a small booth in a vast office room and he was scarcely seated before a clerk came in with a small file and began at once, "A situation has been found for you at 46832 Avenue 23 west. You will be there for interview at 2 p.m., please. Refer to us if anything should need correction. That is all for today. Your registration fee, as you know, is deducted from your first six months' pay by monthly installments. Good morning." And the door was being held open for him to pass through. "This is a memo of the address and notification that you are sent by us. That is your serial number on our books."

As he went out, he realized that his name had never been asked and the whole arrangement must show some clear understanding between this huge agency and the Mole. But again curiosity was dead in him. He no longer found that secret agent's secret pleasure of watching the other agent when neither must betray to the other that they both know. He did not look at the youth who repeated the formulae, but passed out, only nodding to show his assent and taking the card held out while the card he had carried was taken from him.

He went and lunched comfortably. There, too, Alpha had shown his power to understand the new anthropology. He had made his people into gourmets. They were taught to appreciate food and to think about it as a large part of their living. The most stable civilizations, said one of the new history books, have always made a great art out of each sense—and no sense is so sane as taste, the appetite for food; every fanatic has been forced to confess that without a taste for food you cannot be healthy. One of the wisest of the old statesmen, Talleyrand, said eating is the one pleasure that can be enjoyed three times a day and with skill can be made each time to last an hour. The most stable civilization of the past, that of China, evolved the most elaborate cuisine and menus. So men were taught how to eat well, discriminately, healthily, appreciatively, slowly and at their ease. Yes, he had forgotten how good food could be and how well the Alpha crew ran their world and knew it. They had taken his looks but not his palate, and the dishes he chose could all be dealt with by his remaining teeth. To do justice to one of the middle menus took all the time he had till his appointment would be due after he had walked off the comfortable weight of food.

He went out into the early afternoon light and headed for the address. As he came up with the numbers on his card and was scanning the buildings, one of the sidewalkers, as they were called—the smartly uniformed public informationists, as was their official name—came up to him and asked if he could be of service, took his card, and showed him the entrance he needed. He felt sure that was a check-up but he had evidently passed the test. Under the guise of incessant courtesy and helpfulness, these public servants, most people knew who troubled to understand, were the first line of Alpha's informants. It used to be said when people, in the first novelty, used still to joke about

Alpha's innovations, that information please worked two ways and that though you mightn't know it you always gave away more than you took in.

III

THE AMBUSH

HE ENTERED the outer office and found to his surprise that
he was quickly led through into a large kitchen and beyond that into another small interview room. He waited
there for a moment, and then a large, red-faced man entered, actually wearing the chef's traditional costume. He
flung himself in the chair at the desk and held out his hand
for the card, looked from it to the face, and then remarked,
"Well, I hope they told you I have a temper like my fires.
I believe in hot fires for cooking and an equally hot temper for scullions." It was a breezy opening, so breezy that
the natural reaction of the old-time agent in him made him
think the part well acted on the whole though perhaps a
little on the obvious side.

"What's wrong with your mouth?" was also just the same
formula of forthrightness.

He replied, "I was getting a new set and found the changes were more expensive than I had thought. You see, I
was changing my job and so my pay had run down. I have
to wait till I can earn enough for them."

There was no further question as to why he was out
of work and where he had last been at work. Of course
these big employment agencies took that task of inquiry
and references off the hands of the employers now. Still
he might have asked, and, though it was a relief that he
had not, still a mind trained to suspect clues in everything
asked itself, Was this an oversight? Was the man really as
roughly bland as he seemed? Or was it a deliberate avoid-
ance, because this new ,employer of his was himself still
rather new to the niceties of dissimulation? A practiced
hand would never first play the part of the bluff, open-
hearted downrighter and then avoid an obvious question

which, playing his part, he ought to ask. The "Well, be here sharp at four; I like to get my dinners under way by six," was well enough done to seem possibly the real thing.

"Your name is Anwerp, but that's too fancy for this level. All my underlings have a series of names—the last in the job you're taking over was José so you'll be José. You're good at pastry and you'll have plenty of that work—the tables I serve like that—but you'll have to turn your hand to anything. I'm often rushed, and my orders may come at any time for very varying amounts; be sure I'll work you hard and take nothing from you but hard and willing work."

He turned in again that evening. He had brought his cook's clothes when he went out. He was kept till after midnight. The dinners that were being served evidently weren't for many people. The cook apparently worked for a clientele who lived in houses not far away but not in this stack of buildings. The meals were put in insulated containers, sealed up, and fetched away by housemen who came for them. He made, of course, no inquiries as to who the cook's employers were. The cook was in fair spirits and had plenty of assistance. Besides himself there were three others. They paid absolutely no attention to him. For all they cared, evidently, he might be the José who had been there before. He was simply a name for a pair of hands.

But over one dinner the old chef became anxious, then irritable, and finally explosive. He thought it must be because perhaps they were behind schedule with it. Certainly there must have been some hitch. The actual supplies were delivered late, a delivery man rushing down and depositing a series of sealed cartons while on his heels marched in the two men who were to fetch it. They looked over the still unpacked food but didn't make any remark about unpunctuality or, indeed, say anything. They were dressed in plain uniforms which might have been those of chauffeurs, their only concession to the public rule of color in everything being that the tint was lemon yellow. They stood about with their hands behind them watching with a patient interest the cook's efforts to get on with his job. One propped himself by the stoves and looked on at every action the cook was taking, evidently making the master nervous. The other stood by the big table where the food was being prepared. They seemed to be the type of well-trained servant who is so bored with his own job—and does it so perfectly on schedule—that he has time to watch with a detached interest the incompetent way other men carry on their tasks. Their eyes flitted over every activity of the five men with a faint impression of superiority. Nothing seemed to escape them and yet nothing seemed worth more than a moment's cursory glance. At last the things were ready, for this meal wasn't an elaborate one. The two lemon-colored onlookers took possession, saw everything bestowed in its special container, and carried the whole off.

When they were gone, after a little while another house-man came in for another dinner, but this one was practically ready, with the usual good timing which a good chef understands as well as his own breathing. The cook's temper, which had been edged by this incident, however, was not mollified, and till the day ended, on the verge of the small hours of the next, he remained thunderous, with lightning-like explosions of irritability over the least thing.

José, as he had come to think of himself, thought a little about the cook. Why this failure to have that meal ready in time? Did it link up with that little hiatus when this seemingly unguarded man didn't ask where he, José, had been before he became José? It was too soon to say, and one of the things that secret agents know is never to forget clues and yet never to try to make sense of them, to force them into sense before they fit in of themselves.

He still kept himself from coming or trying to come to any conclusions, still less from thinking of framing any questions, when two nights later the same thing occurred—the same failure of the supplies to arrive in time for a particular dinner, the arrival of the two men in yellow, their quiet, silent patience, their idling onlooking at the cook and his staff's nervous hurry to get the food ready against time and under that cold and evidently contemptuously careless inspection. He had been there for a couple of weeks and these particular men had come perhaps four or five times and always with the same apparent unexpectedness. They would walk in and the cook seemed always taken

57

aback and had to rush to prepare. Yet he seemed to know what dishes were wanted. He must, then, have been told earlier in the day, but evidently the hour was not specified. Of course, that would tease a good chef—but still, was the matter as simple as that?

While he was still thinking this over, in the way that a chess player will play out problems to himself that are no part of any actual game but just because he has the chess mind, another small incident occurred in the kitchen that certainly gave him one more fact, but one that made the puzzle-problem more complicated, not simpler. The three other assistants were out one afternoon. He and the chef were alone and the old man had seated himself, after some fuming, on a stool near his stoves and was watching him as he took some lobsters from their containers and laid them on the table. They were, of course, still fully alive as they were drawn out from the damp seaweed in which they were wrapped. The pot was ready with boiling water and he was just picking them up by that one place whereby a live lobster can be held and not bite you, just at the end of the head-carapace, when the cook came forward, fussing.

"What are you going to do with the creatures—put them into the boiling water? Don't you know that that spoils the flavor? That they must be put in cold water with the same salt content as seawater, and then the water must rise to boiling point?"

His, "Cruel, that?" was answered by a queer look, half of interest, half of assurance and a kind of "I told you so" expression. But the words gave the lie to such a notion: "Don't be a fool, and don't answer back! Learn your job; thought they said you knew it!"

While this fuming went on, the portly figure had twirled round, snatched a set of fine skewers from where they hung on the wall, and, selecting the smallest of these, a fine rustless-steel stiletto, the chef siezed with dexterity one of the lobsters and immediately drove the needle-pointed bodkin up behind the head-carapace. The claws which had been waving about flopped onto the table.

"Put it into the pot, and here, do the same with the

others, and if you're too mealy-mouthed and delicate to stand cooking as it's taught, here's something that may help your conscience. You might have a job where you'd have to kill your own poultry and other meat. Well, what I've shown you will help your fine feelings. All you've got to do is to touch the animal on that spot with a very fine sharp skewer and it flops. You can kill a sheep or indeed an ox that way and the flesh is as good as if you'd cut its throat. For I suppose you are merciful and not just a mollycoddle about blood. When it's dead you open its throat, hang it up, and death has been so quick and central that the blood drains away almost as clean and quickly as though it had died from the cutting of its arteries.

"All you have to do is to get the animal to lower its head to some fodder if it is a big one, so that it opens the cervical vertebrae, push your skewer between the two top ones, and that drives the point in close to the medulla oblongata and so its breathing stops. Yes, a cook should know the outlines of anatomy. We were taught it at our cuisine school, and quite rightly. That spot saves a lot of trouble. Have been told it would work just as well with a man—all animals have it as their Achilles heel—a bit high up, but as long as one knows what one is looking for the name doesn't matter, does it?"

And, evidently pleased with his own address, the chef actually chuckled.

The incident was so small that he would have forgotten it, no doubt, but that a few days later he found on returning to his room a notice from the post office that a package was waiting him. He went down there before work. Naturally, it would be his teeth. His disappointment was keen when he saw that the package handed him was far too small. He opened it as he went along to work, and his annoyance was shot with surprise when out of it he took an Alpha badge pin. Of course no one had to wear these badges. The administration often said they wanted people to be happy and they believed that happiness was the cement of agreement. The didn't want people to be loyal but to be satisfied, and they didn't believe that loyalty or manufactured satisfaction was durable. Still, most people at the big festival of freedom did wear some such badge and nearly everyone who was in one of the public services wore them rather more often. Well, if that was his instruction, he had better live up to it—it didn't seem a very subtle piece of window dressing for the Mole to think up after a number of days—but the obvious can, with the very subtle, have an edge which is concealed by apparent bluntness.

As he was approaching the place where he worked he put the badge in the breast of his tunic. It was a small rod with an Alpha on the top like the Constantine Labarum. He was fitting it into his buttonhole when the top twisted loose. Poorly made, he thought, as he drew out the top and left the stem in the button-hole. But as he tried to fit it together again he saw that the joint which had come loose, just under the capital A, had, depending from it, a dowel that pegged into the stem-hollow. And it was a very long dowel, almost the length of the stem. He had now arrived at the side street in which his work-place was. He examined the object which he was holding by its capital letter head, which made a fine grip, and saw that he had hold of a very fine and sharp skewer about two inches long, double-bladed. He tried it on the hair of the back of his hand. It was as sharp as a razor. Of course the two incidents could be coincidence. But were they? And if not, to what did they point? He put the badge together, put it right in his buttonhole, and went in.

One evening, though, his mind tired of this solitaire. Why try to solve problems of other people's behavior when that of your own and your own position is completely enigmatic to yourself? He must have company. But who'd want an object like him to spend an evening with? Suddenly, with the conviction that need will give, he thought of Alie—Alie would understand. She'd said she liked him because he was different, that she was tired of handsome health. Well, women were sometimes like that; they had pity—"And pity from thee more dear than that from another." The line running into his mind set it. He got up from his meal and went down to that park. A show was on—nothing might have happened since then. He walked about. No one noticed him. He went to the place where they had sat. Broad bands of flush lighting were flooding the lawns and concentrating on the outdoor stage. But just where they had sat there had been a heliotrope shadow made by the light being broken by a screen of bushes. He came into that mauve dusk. Sure enough, that must be she, and she was alone. This must be meant; luck like that could only mean that she did come here—waiting. He came up from behind and sat down in one of the rows of seats immediately behind hers. He could see her profile when he bent forward. She did look grave, sad even. He rested his hand softly on the back of her chair. He could control his voice now, if he spoke softly so that it could sound as it had formerly sounded.

"Alie"—she did not start, but he was a good enough observer to see the neck muscles tauten—"Alie, I had to be away—away on a hard bit of work." She didn't turn. But he thought he saw her head almost involuntarily bow. "Alie, at that, that work, I've been—well a bit knocked about—I'm injured?" There was a question in his voice. No, she wasn't going to cut him short either by going away or turning around. "Alie, you said you might like me, if only for a little, just because I was different. Might we, please just try an evening together?"

His voice was pleading. He did not know till he let it find words how deep and cruel his need was. Certainly his tone told. She was silent. But suddenly he saw that without turning round she had put her hand backward. She touched his knee.

"Thank you," he said. "I don't know how to thank you."

The fingers gave a small pat, as a person pats a strange dog they are sorry for but are not sure about. He put his fingers gently on hers. She did not draw hers away. They sat like that a little, and he thought he had never rested before in his life.

Then she said, "Yes, I couldn't get you out of my mind; and, do you know, I was full of some kind of fear. I thought something must have happened to you. I somehow knew you'd have come otherwise.

There was again a silence. The play had stopped and the

crowd had thinned. They were alone in that series of seats. He waited a few moments. Then, taking her hand, he got up gently and moved to the seat beside her. Suddenly her hand was snatched away. She had risen.

"That's a common trick and a mean one!" Her voice was shrill. "You've simply got my name and description from, I suppose, the man who gave it you when he was drunk—so that you'd get off with me in the dusk!"

"But I'm that boy himself. Please, please believe me. I told you I'd been injured, facially injured."

"Dirty liar, and dirty-minded old lecher! You, injured —you, a fresh young kid only a few weeks ago! Why, you've not been thirty for a dozen years! No, my old scrounger, you didn't get a face like that and a skin like that in any accident. You're just an old piece of debauched skin. Get out!"

He turned round and was back in his room in twenty minutes. Yes, they had seen to it that he was shut out from life. He had a couple of bad days as the shock of hope died down and he settled again to his sunken living.

It was, then, with no relief that a couple of days later he found another notice from the post office waiting for him on his return from work. He had to be early at the kitchen the next morning, and it took twenty minutes to get to that post office. He arrived to find a queue at that window. When he at last received the small package it was nearly time for him to be on duty. He had no time to go back to his room to open it. He guessed what it was—his teeth. He went down into a public lavatory and, locking himself in, tore the package open. He pulled the wadding away and smiled unpleasantly as he saw grinning up at him, like the remains of a skeleton, the artificial pieces of tooth-shaped enamel with the hard sham gums in which they were rooted. Well, there was no time for Hamletesque soliloquies. There was no mirror to watch for effects, and why should he? Wasn't that, at least, dead in him? He slipped them in and was pleased to find what a good fit they were. Those surgeons had understood their horrible art. He felt the firm grip again and could set his jaw once more; it was curiously reassuring and he felt the powerful mounts push out and stretch and hold his lapsed cheeks and chin.

He ran his hand over his face. It was firm and taut; the very feel of it was encouraging. He felt his jaw thrust out by the new support. "I suppose," he amused himself by thinking, "it's the feeling a poor ruptured body has when they build up its abdominal wall for it again." But there was no time; he ran out and up the stairs, and as a taxi passed he sprang into it, calling out the address. He leaped out as it drew up, threw the fare to the man, and ran in, just on time.

His long experience of complete loneliness had now driven him into a level of interior feeling. He felt as though he were always fingering his way about like a blind man in a complicated prison. He paid much more attention, therefore, to such explorations of his own states of mind than to the impression he might be making on those around him. He was slow, then, to notice that in the kitchen his appearance had begun to awaken interest that in the freshness of his first arrival had not been stirred. And he was even slower to think out why he should now be given some attention. It was, too, the kind of attention of which formerly he would have been most aware. When he turned suddenly he could not, after some time, fail to notice that one or the other of the rest of the crew, sometimes the chef himself, sometimes a couple of them, had actually been looking at him while his back was turned and made the usual clumsy attempt to pretend that they had not been doing so.

Finally the half-dead interest in himself stirred sufficiently under those small prods to make him wonder vaguely about the change. Of course it must be the teeth, but then, surely they had got used to his appearance, and if they asked the chef he could have told them that as soon as he could get his pay he would have his new set. In this world where personal, physical happiness had been deliberately made the goal of every sane person, people would often have their teeth-profile, as it was called, changed because their beautician had convinced them that the type of beauty he was building up for them would be given more point if their smile were re-accented. It was natural, then, that a person should be changing his teeth; and, as it was expensive, it was just as natural that he might have to work in a quiet place for a few days till his new set could be given him.

Yet all the day that furtive interest seemed to simmer round him. That evening, too, the couple of yellow liveries came to fetch a dinner: There was the same little fuss, the same obvious nervousness in the chef and, to a certain amount, in the other assistants. But with it, he could not help noticing that there was something else, an overtone, and in that he was somehow involved. Usually the two yellow figures stood, one leaning against the stove, the other gazing blankly at the big serving table. But today he twice found that, though they were in their usual positions, their eyes had turned to him.

It was a long day, though, and by the time that he was let go, toward midnight, he was too tired to wish to work his mind on any little problems. He changed out of his white overalls to his street clothes, went out through the kitchen, through the little office, and into the short passage that led to the main door of that entrance of the building; it was on the side into a small street that was not a thoroughfare. The chef had told him to turn out the lights as he left and had gone five minutes ahead. The others had all gone earlier, the chef holding him on with rather annoying insistence about some utensils being put away in better order.

When he had put out the light in the small outer office and let the door lock itself behind him, he noticed that the light in the passage must have burnt itself out. But he could see well enough in a dusk which was lit by reflections of the street lighting coming through a small fanlight over the street door. He walked toward that and had his hand on the inside doorknob when he felt himself held. Again his old knowledge told him that this was no common holdup, just trying to get a payroll of a late worker. That hold was seldom known save to men long trained at picking up wanted people so that the pickup could sometimes be made in broad daylight in the crowded street and the man be held so securely and with such a grip that he would go quietly, for at the slightest struggle he could be dropped dead on the sidewalk while the men who had killed him could quietly call the attention of the police to a case of sudden heart failure.

He therefore stood still. The door opened ahead, he was pushed through and into a car that was waiting at the curb. The door shut behind him and his two companions; the engine started up. My second abduction, he thought. I suppose the Mole must somehow be displeased with my conduct. Perhaps the dismal park incident, or perhaps the attention I awoke today? I wonder which of those, my late colleagues, is really my underground colleague? What a world of shadow and shade. Or has the Mole got planted in that kitchen one of his small recording tubes and can I have said anything within its range that might seem to him to need a personal checkup? Or should I have done more, have I forgotten, was I meant to report regularly and have I failed? The questions ran through his mind; but though, out of habit, he used the old phrase of reference "I," it had little color with which to hold his attention.

The drive was much the same as the one before, in the way he was treated: silence and darkness. But it didn't last so long, and as far as he could tell they never left the city. True, the traffic did become a little less as they came toward the end of the journey. So he judged they must be in some quiet part of the town when the car stopped. But as the door opened he could see nothing. It was night, and he was pushed rapidly across a piece of empty paving into a tall house that spread above them. They seemed to be in some kind of large porte-cochere. But inside it was even darker. He could just tell that they were in a passage, stone-flagged, he thought, and then they entered a room which was completely black. There he felt himself put into a chair and handcuffed onto it. The chair was fastened to the floor, he soon could judge. He waited for, he thought, about five minutes and felt pretty certain that the two who had brought him in had gone.

Then a voice—not one, he was sure, of those he had got to know in his last ordeal: "You have been condemned to death."

Well, that was a fairly straightforward opening, he felt with a certain relief.

"Whether by absurd vanity or for some other reason"—then they didn't know his background?—"you have done something which even if it isn't your fault—as may be—makes no difference. The safety of the state makes your removal imperative."

Again he felt the relief, and with a certain humor reflected that many Asiatics would rather die than "lose face," and as he certainly had lost his, why shouldn't he also die?

"Your life, then, is over. About that have no doubt. But there is one way that you can escape physical death. You can cease to be, completely, as a person. Alive in that sense, your absurd escapade or your ill luck—it makes no difference—can serve our purposes."

It all sounded very unlike the Mole's way of working, but, then, what was the use of saying that? Didn't he know that the Mole's power was just that: he never had one way of working. What you might be sure of was that whatever you heard was not meant to give you light but to make you think you saw, the better to hoodwink you. That commonplace reflection ran through his mind once or twice; there seemed no other reflection to make. But when he had gone over it again, no fresh material for reflection was provided. He sat still in the dark, waiting. After about five minutes, however, he heard a small sound in the complete silence; it was the kind of sound that switching on a microphone circuit sometimes gives. He judged that he was being listened to by someone not in this room. He saw no reason for giving them anything, however, and after perhaps another five minutes, he heard (as though voices were at some distance) one say, "It is extraordinary; clearly, there is only one thing to do."

Then the voice became clearer. The speaker must have drawn up to the microphone. The voice was clear but spoke in a whisper or such an undertone that all character was taken from it. Yet, as it went on, he kept on wondering whether in it there were not tones which somehow he associated with a voice that was in some way familiar. But what it was saying was enough to keep such speculations out of any mind that retained even the slightest interest in its self and its future.

"I have now viewed you for myself and I find the report perfectly accurate. You will now be brought over and if you co-operate you have nothing to fear; if not, your life will be ended tonight."

Co-operate, yes, that was the old phrase, but what in the name of the uttermost underworld could the Mole now be up to? He had almost become vividly interested, by the time that he felt himself taken hold of again, loosed from the chair, led down the passage, and ensconced in the dark cab. They drove for perhaps as long as the first drive had lasted; the city sounds muted and then dropped, though he could still hear a distant hum.

The door opened onto a small dark court. He was bundled into the building that rose round it, hurried into a small elevator, and silently they went up, some ten floors he judged by the clicks which must be landings being passed. The door switched back; a small carpeted passage, his feet told him; then a door opened within a yard of his face and he was given a push by his attendants who were now behind him. Light came on. He was alone in a small, well-furnished apartment.

"Sit down." He obeyed the voice which came, he thought, from the left-hand wall. There was silence for eleven minutes. He knew this accurately because there was a fine timepiece on the bookcase on his right. He noticed that it was five minutes to one when he arrived; it was six minutes past when a door, opposite the one through which he had been pushed, opened.

His first thought was, "Can the Mole have got disguises on the brain?" Here was he himself obliterated and here facing him was another triumph of "living clay" make-up, for the man who faced him wore a face, the face best known in a conventional way to everyone. It was Alpha's. Of course, he could see it wasn't quite the Alpha known by a billion reproductions to five hundred million people. But it was of a most creditable closeness. And the absurdity? Seriousness belonged to the living who had to go on living, not to those already made free of the complete non-relevance of death. The other man evidently, though, knew his part better than to co-operate at that grave-level.

He remarked, "I have viewed you already. This work now I must and can only do myself." Then he stopped and seemed to wish to impress his listener with his weariness. It was quite a good piece of acting, thought his audience of one.

"I presume you understand your situation," the one with the speaking part went on. "You can go on living at one cost, and it's a reasonable price: that you cease to be a person and become a double, a shadow. I am told that such accidents do happen. Those who handle such supervisions reported to me that there had suddenly appeared a man who was my double. They were, of course, for killing him outright. But this was, as it happens so often with me, providential for me, and maybe for him. The inquiry shows that he obtained a post in the place where my food is prepared and that of my staff; that he had either had some injury or was undergoing some kind of facial treatment and that on obtaining new teeth, the set of the face was completely altered and he appeared as my double."

The listener kept his balance as his view of his problem went through this capsize.

"May I see a mirror?" he asked.

The man who was now standing in front of him put his hand in the breast of his tunic and held a small mirror in front of him. He could see his own face—or what he supposed was what his face had now become—and the face of the other just above it. Quietly he checked over the two images. What a piece of work and what a piece of planning!

The man in front of him put back the glass into his tunic, sat down in front of him, and went on in the same commonplace voice, "It does not matter whether you realize what has befallen you or not, and I don't care how it happened, for though none of my staff sees the appositeness of this, I do. This was meant to happen and is one more proof, if I needed one, that I am the one person who really knows and understands the age and epoch in which we are, and through which I am leading all of mankind that counts.

"Only a few weeks ago I was wondering how I could

carry on without endangering unity of command. For the others are only hands, at best. I alone am the head because I alone understand the Revolution. I had to have a substitute head without a brain, a mask so as to be able to duplicate that work which I plan, but, as I cannot carry it all out without fatigue, I cannot actually perform. And, naturally, the people are right—they will have no substitute. That is all you need to know about your general situation. All great central figures get a dummy, if they can, for appearances, when only an appearance and no action is required. But, as usual, I have thought out the matter further. Now speak."

"If that is our position and I am your ventriloquist's dummy, then you must tell me what to say."

Evidently his answer did not displease, for without a pause his interlocutor's voice suddenly swelled, "On this occasion of the anniversary of one more of our new freedoms. . . ." He repeated the words, and he noticed how closely his voice seemed now to have the coarse, vibrant tone he had just heard, and with which half the world was so familiar.

"Yes, I have provided for that. Many of my records are ghost-voiced for me by phonetic experts who train speakers to get the tone. There will be no difficulty in getting your voice in proper pitch and intonation. Now I will take you through your area. You will live in this apartment. Your sleeping cell is here." He threw open a panel, and a small slip of a room, containing just a bed and chair, with built-in wardrobe, appeared.

"I shall call you whenever I have need of you. Your food will be sent up by this hatch and is present when that bulb glows. You put what you want cleaned in that other hatch. All supplies will reach you that way. Anything more you may require will be sent you by the same method. Remember, you are under observation all the time and will never see anyone but me and the couple who'll train you save on those occasions when you will be taking my part for me.

"By the way, you need not wear that loyal piece of filigree. I'm not a vain man. I have no need to be. And I shall not be impressed by your loyalty if you wear it. I know men, and they are of two types: those who like to lounge and those who like to work; one has to provide for both types. I have. If you give the actives enough work they will serve you and if you never give the slack anything but leisure they will never support anyone who might upset you and then put them to work. That is my simple secret—or all you need to know about it." And the creature, that now more nearly ruled the whole world than had any man ever before, turned on his heel and went through the door.

When he had gone, the remodeled man sat fingering the little emblem. But he did not take it out of his buttonhole. His mind was busy arranging the volume of information—not much, it was true, but bringing together all the weary weeks he had been through into a single point. So the Mole, after all, was a really big man. He had begun to doubt. But now that he saw the width of the planning, what he thought was dead in him—admiration, cold and detached, but all the more sincere for that—rose like a star in his mind. The Mole must have watched his opposite number, the Bull, and realized that his psychological crisis was coming on; he must, he supposed, have gathered it from studying the countless photographs and getting them enlarged and so detected and diagnosed the small tensions and perceived the little tics that showed in the film pictures. He knew that Alpha must be wanting a double and did not know where to get one that would actually stand up to the constant photographic scrutiny which the present master of the earth could not avoid—the real white light that beats upon a throne. And when the Mole was sure of that, then he picked from his servants the man whose general form measurements were quite close, took that victim and carved him into shape so that the key would fit the lock precisely, and next planted the key where it would be picked up, must be picked up. It was daring, but really of a simple directness that, if you could find anyone to undergo it, it would have a high chance of success, and you would get your prospective victim actually to take on board the instrument which was aimed at him. It was like those old tales of witchcraft where the final skill of the sorcerer—without which all his magic cannot avail—consists in making or persuading his victim voluntarily to receive the object or the familiar which is to destroy him once he has willingly but unwittingly taken it into his possession. Yes, if this was Alpha, then the Mole was Omega—the last word, the one who laughs longest and loudest because he laughs last. Such a mind was worth serving.

All the old element of adventure woke in him. Certainly this was a supreme exploration into the unknown. And he was being treated as an equal. He was left with no instructions. He could do as he pleased. The life here might not be impossible. It was obvious that he might very well be indispensable to the central figure of the age and might become increasingly valuable. He, the remodeled man, needn't do anything unless he wished, unless he felt a co-partner with the Mole in the cause. He could lie up here snug as a ferret, sent down to turn out rabbits, can lie up in the rabbit burrow and refuse to come up, serving its own ends on its own. He was quite safe. That was as clear, too, for after years of effort it was undeniable that the Mole had found that he could not strike directly at Alpha; all the attempts had failed, and with each failure went the increasing risk that one day the Mole himself would be rooted out.

It was clear that this amazing plan, of which the remodeled man was the tool, had been attempted only because there was no other way through; and, if it were attempted, the only possible thing was to leave the tool free to do as he liked when you had put him in reach of the prize. After a period of great passivity—in the exact sense of that word, the sense of suffering and patient enduring—he had then come out for a small spell into a busy routine life in the kitchen. And now a third phase had opened: he was to call the tune and he need not call it until he decided it was time for the music to begin again. He suddenly felt a great tiredness. He went into the little bunkroom, undressed, and fell asleep at once.

When he woke, his trained eye saw that nothing had been touched—he had not been able to resist the routine of his

71

old training, as fixed a habit now as a child's repetition of its nightly prayer, to check up on everything. The way he had thrown his robe over the chair, the place his socks were in, the fold of his garments—he memorized them all automatically, and now, looking over these and a number of other small place-clues, he judged that no one had been in the room since he had fallen asleep. He got up and went into the sitting room. There, too, the disposition of everything, he would have given his word, was unaltered. Yes, he might be observed but he was evidently not to be intruded upon.

That he was observed was pretty clear, for, by the time he came back from his shower, the bulb over the service lift was shining, and, opening the hatch, he found his breakfast ready for him. He ate it with relish. Alpha certainly had practiced at home—at least for his guests—what he preached abroad. When he had finished, he put the tray into the other hatch as he had been told. As he closed the panel he could just hear a gentle whir; yes, he was certainly being waited upon with instant vigilance. He leaned back in the chair a moment. Then he sat down to wait. He had been taught how to do that and he had plenty to run over in his mind. There were excellent cigarettes, too, in a small glass box on the table beside him. They were of that new synthetic smoking mixture which was so much more fragrant than tobacco, was a true stimulant instead of a narcotic, and which did not hurt even a singer's throat. He had much to think over and recheck.

He was just trying to put out all the pieces, to understand the particular place and problem of his late employer, the chef, when a voice which was the very antithesis of that tempestuous bass that had been called "the ground-swell of Mankind's Tide" said, "Good morning," just behind his chair. Of course, his watch and his meal and everything but the daylight which never came into this place told him it was morning. He swung round and faced a figure which was certainly as unformidable as the voice. A little fellow in silver gray stood bowing slightly. He was certainly a typical cell of the brain-trust section—one who, because of his excessive cerebrotonia (the standard classification of the day was now used by everyone) must have been picked and conditioned almost from the kindergarten. He was the type which would have worn spectacles had not eye-surgery and exercises made such clumsy hangovers and hangouts an anachronism.

"Good morning," said the remodeled man.

"Ah, what a pleasure to an expert," was the odd but immediate reply. "That tone, quite wonderful. Not, of course, quite the thing. Privately—though in saying so I am actually speaking against my own science—I can't help feeling that we shall never get quite the unique thing. After all, a scientist need not cease to be an artist. And though—please don't misunderstand me—we shall, of course, get an effect which the ordinary man, which every ordinary man, will mistake for the sublime original, we experts, trained to know the finest qualities and having by nature an artist's ear, we shall know. But," and his little modulating voice took a brighter, almost vigorous, tone and fluttered up from its sentimental coo, "we shall do what we are told to do, never fear. We shall deliver the goods, we shall achieve a reproduction which will serve; and, after all, if we serve, that is all we wish to do—not for us to create—if we copy so that the casual eye sees all that it is fit to see, and needs to see, then let the exquisite appreciation of an irreplaceable original belong, as a private and rich reward, for those who can, and have to, see more than ever their highest skill and most advanced science can convey."

The small creature beamed after this little flow of eloquence, which was delivered in a series of varied tones which made it even more odd to hear. What he was driving at became, however, quite clear in his next sentence.

"I was told when I received my instructions that I should find a task which would both delight and tax me. As usual, I have been told the exact truth, though, as usual, in this wonderful age, I still said, like the child I am of an earlier discouragement, 'Ah, *that* must be too good to be true.' And, as usual in these happy days, it is true. Indeed, he was right!

"Of course, I said to our club, it is just one more proof

73

of what we scientists are only just beginning to learn, in this the final phase of man, that what a really creative mind demands *must* be supplied. It just comes out of the unknown to his call. You have seen him in this room, I know, so I can be frank with you. He is so frank and open. He gave me this assignment himself. He hates any indirectness. As long as he has time he will always get straight into touch with the man—however humble— with whom he wishes to work. He told me the story frankly, so I know all—of how he knew he must have this instrument given him and he only thought about it and willed it to happen and, within the time that it took him to think out all the specifications he should need, what he required had emerged—that, I believe, is the right word— emerged."

The remodeled man did not feel any call to alter the term chosen by his visitor, who ran on, "And then—it is so like him and his modesty, which is innate—he said to me with a twinkle, 'But the gifts which are sent us in this way always are left with some little piece of work to be finished by us ourselves, and that is why I have sent for you.' You may be sure I felt my position, linked with him in service, unique service. He told me that all that was needed could be done by me and that I should find the work well within my science. He is always right, and now that I have heard I know.

" 'O Alpha,' I said on leaving him (and I couldn't resist saying under my breath 'and Omega,' for, of course, he wouldn't let me say it aloud—he's far too modest and, as you know, is always saying he's only the usher of the new age), 'you really mustn't mind if in one way we, at last being left alone and told that he can enjoy himself, and should not and need not care for things that he really doesn't, and can't, care for, and that all the rest like myself only want a chance to work and serve. But there are some of us in the little clubs, the A.A.A.'s, who feel that the finest thing you've given, of all the benefits now poured out on man, is just the power to admire a perfect achievement. You have given us at last a perfect case for loyalty.' And do you know, he clapped me on the back and told me to run along and keep my metaphysics for those who had the brains for them, for he was just a person who tried to do the next thing that came along a little better than he'd done the last."

To stem this queer eulogy the remodeled man asked, "What's A.A.A.?"

"It's the name of our club or clubs! It stands for 'Alpha, Avatar of the Absolute.'"

The creature beamed, evidently in a kind of quiet orgy of worship. The man watching him wondered whether the Mole had been able to rouse as intense a loyalty among men as capable in their jobs as this little fellow probably was in his. Probably the Mole thought that you could do without such gushes to drive your resolution. Perhaps the success of outward achievement always rouses a backing, which, wishing to be on the safe side and ashamed of its cowardice, tries to rationalize its timidity by calling it devotion. Of course this kind of emotional attitude had nothing to do with intelligence. Whether you chose to serve Mole or Bull, Alpha or Omega, didn't depend on your mental skill. There was something involved far deeper than that.

That this small emotionalist knew his techniques thoroughly, a moment more showed. He cut off abruptly the mood he had been in, picked up a case which was on the floor beside him, and, opening it, showed a voice-recording instrument.

"Now, please," he said with brisk efficiency, "we will try some tones."

For the next twenty minutes he kept the remodeled man busy, as, with terminals on his throat, with mouthpiece to his lips, the voice was gauged. He read off the records on dials, checked them, and then went through the whole process again. Finally, with equal briskness, he packed up his instruments, bowed, and said, "Tomorrow we can start our tone-balance lessons. I will work on all my data here and be ready for you then to give you your lessons, so—if I may so put it, and I am sure you will agree—what is a voice full of promise may become a marvelous echo of that voice which has called the world out of chaos, to order and happiness."

With that, the little fellow slipped quietly out of the door to which he had been withdrawing during the speech. The prisoner went to it after the latch had clicked. Yes, it was locked.

Thus began this odd companionship. He was being trained until his voice would take on the exact tones of his captor—a kind of human parrot in its cage. As he was certainly as interested in learning as is a good speaking bird and had a first-rate teacher, he made progress which charmed his trainer. He found his time with the little fellow also instructive in another way. He must try to understand what made the technicians—and this man was certainly a fine one: an inventor and not only an applier—so passionately loyal to the tyranny. There was no doubt that here—in what he still called their emotional immaturity—lay the real massive strength of the dictatorship. After all, under the strongest walls the final foundation is the natural earth. It carries the fortifications above, which otherwise must collapse. It was nonsense to say that the Bull had not behind him the vast majority-assent of all classes—at least so far. Of course, that assent must mainly be passive—even with this emotionalist. Of course, he did not see a real man in his Avatar Alpha; he saw just an opportunity of getting a worship symbol round which his sugary devotion, reaching precipitation, might crystallize. The remodeled man smiled as he recalled being told in a biology lesson—which of course ended with the benefits of living under the sign of Alpha— that the oyster will make a pearl round anything which intrudes on its soft comfort and the favorite nucleus for its shining and persistent devotion is the egg of a tapeworm.

After about six weeks—in which he saw no one else; "The other tones might disturb you," said the little voice-specialist, who himself now spoke hardly at all after those first gushers—at last he was told, "Now I would give my word for it, no one but myself could tell the difference. Listen."

A short record of a speech was played twice over. Turning round triumphantly, the little silver-gray figure challenged him, "Tell which was which? Of course I know, and

76

of course there is a wonderful quality which we shall never get, but can you tell?"

No, he couldn't.

"My work is, then, done and I am glad to say how co-operative you have been and how I have appreciated this assignment."

He felt that the little fellow, as he declaimed this, was speaking to others who were not in the room but were listening to all that went on in it. He hardly troubled to say good-by, though he guessed it was the last time he would see his small companion of the last few weeks. There wasn't really a whole man there: just a pair of wonderfully capable hands and ears and the parts of the brain that deal with those organs, and, behind that, just a little fog of emotion that, like a small, drifting, damp, vague cloud, was at present clinging to the side of this vast, forbidding crag that had reared itself over the flat plains of ordinary mankind.

But after his companion had gone he was not left alone; in fact, his life took on a varied tempo. There was now quite a lot of outward drilling and dressing to be done. It was not more than two days after his last lesson in voice-production that he went into his room to find quite a different sort of man waiting for him. He seemed to show by his every gesture that he was the super-valet.

Without introduction he began, "As soon as your breakfast is finished I am to come for you to show you some presentation detail."

He was turning back from putting his tray in the service hatch when the door opened and he was bowed out, led down a small passage to a door only a dozen strides away and so into a room larger than the one in which he had been confined. The man who had led him went to a wardrobe and drew back the sliding door. Inside were a number of suits, all of identically the same cut.

"These, as you know," he remarked, without turning round, "are the official uniform."

Of course, he knew them all too well by sight: the tunic of silver white, the white cone hat, the boots of soft white

77

plastic that came up to the edge of the tunic just below the knees.

"You will wear these. Put them on now so that I may judge."

"But if I am the exact double of Alpha, why do you wish me to try on?"

He didn't see why he shouldn't try to draw out this other odd "servant of Alpha and the public."

"I am an expert in carriage as well as in costume. The psychology of clothes has never been understood till now, and the enormous subconscious part they play in men's lives—all the more when they don't recognize that and think they don't care what they wear. Now, please put on one of these sets."

When he was uniformed, the other asked him to walk slowly up the room and back again, sit down, stand and raise his arm, make a small speech.

As he finished this drill his instructor remarked, "Any carriage expert in the crowd would guess something was wrong. Of course you will get used to the hang of it and the part, but if you learn wrong, as you will if you go your own way, then we shan't be able to get your acquired reactions out of you. This is the time."

And certainly they had a time of it. It was far harder work than that with the voice trainer. He was made conscious of every step and movement and every attitude into which the body fell when not moving. As the days went by his admiration grew for the machine which he had so long fought and so little understood. He had seen its underground steel tentacles. He didn't suspect (perhaps no one but the Mole knew—and did he?) the psychological care, study, and research and experiment, that had been put into this new method of holding people, this psychological tackle which was always finding new ways of impressing people's emotions.

The man who trained him was even less communicative than the voice teacher, and he felt it would be useless to ask him for any more information than he would give just to make the remodeled man become a perfect model. At last he, too, evidently thought he had done his job. He made his pupil rehearse in front of mirrors alongside of which were screens on which were thrown life-size cinema shots in full color of Alpha making all his conventional appearances, at fetes and rallies and great services, vast displays and social rituals.

It became a curious interest to the remodeled man to see how far he could go in becoming like his model. First he rationalized it as a necessary part of camouflage, of stalking one's prey, so that the hunter appeared, to the ignorant hunted, as innocent as a tuft of waving grass. Then he found himself thinking of himself as playing a part in theatricals. He had always been fond of them as a boy, and no doubt the melodramatic ideas of adventure with which the stage always has to deal had influenced him in choosing his profession—so disappointingly different when you got inside it from what you felt it must feel when you thought of it from outside! Well, now he could let his bent and gift have its way. At last he could combine the extreme of realism—the skilled assassin within one step of his strike—with the extreme of melodrama—the actor who actually plays a real part right on the stage of life and so that an audience, far vaster than any that any actor had ever played to before or could play, should be carried away with complete conviction of the reality of the performance, again in a way that no audience before had ever been able to be convinced. He realized that he was that type of actor who to do well must sink himself in his part, be his character. And surely once again he was unique in the whole annals of the stage, for no actor before had had so perfect a make-up, such an undetectable living likeness of the part he wished to play.

As he stood in the uniform reciting in the very voice he had for a decade heard giving out these very words; as he saw in the great mirrors the body, inside which he was making every gesture and sound and even detailed facial play which he knew so well as that of the master of the world, he felt a curious vague but convincing sense of identity come over him. There were moments, when he gave with full conviction one of the perorations or stood for a culminating moment with his arms raised to bless the vast crowds, when the tiny dowel of selfhood at the center of this vast column of build-up seemed to shrink—he used the simile again to himself with a wan inner smile—to the position of the tapeworm egg, the egg of the bold parasite that floated secretly into the hold of the oyster, thinking to consume the dull creature, having got past its defenses. But when it was in the life that enveloped it, that life threw round it, veil by veil, the iridescent coats which finally walled it up, making it the inert, imprisoned nucleus and base for a manifestation of its own triumphant power to react, defend itself, and recreate a new pattern of its energy out of what had been meant to be an assault on its life.

This feeling was redoubled when at his last lessons, lessons when he had learned his part and needed only to have it repeated till it was second nature, he was shown shots in which, ingeniously, from photos taken during his rehearsals, he saw his own figure—for so he was assured by his trainer, and he needed the assurance—actually dominating the adoring masses that stretched away to the horizon. The figure was—as Alpha's presentations to the people on the mass days now always were—magnified immensely, for magnavox had been added to and equaled by magnavision. He stood with these invisible electric "field-screens" round him which acted as lenses. He stood on the apex of the altar pyramid and his Brocken-like figure—but not a dark looming gigantic shadow, instead a great shining shape—thundered out, in tones like the roar of Niagara, the charter of liberation, of the right to happiness and enjoyment, of the individual to live his own life, to enjoy the light of the sun, the delight of love, the freedom of beauty, the creative spaces of leisure, the deliverance from sacrifice. And that voice that shook the crowds to exultation, that went roaring round the world, as the tides that brim round the earth's girdle of oceans go rushing after the moon, that tide of sound was his voice, that great moon of worship was his own figure, himself. True, for the moment it was only a build-up, but today he had seen what he was to become, today he had the promise, like a Moses who was let see the promised land with the promise that he should be let enter. Today perhaps he was no more than a moon that shone by reflected light—though like savages the people did not know that the moon was lit by a concealed sun. But tomorrow—which of them would be the real thing, what was the real thing?

He remembered when the revolution was making use of every means—of science and philosophy to win the educated, as it made use of pleasure and fine shows to win the masses—he remembered the use made of that queer old bishop's speculations as to reality. Bishop Berkeley's philosophy had been dug up just as in the last reaction from the dying Economic-Marxian Revolutionary phase, the German Nazis had dug up that other great master of philosophy, Eckhart. In the general classes given in philosophy to the boys who showed danger of preferring thinking to enjoying, it was a commonplace to quote the famous Berkeleian slogan, *"Percipi* est *esse."* Very well, if that were true, then, and if to be perceived is to be, when he was perceived he *was; he* was then the master of the world. Whoever played the part was the part, for there was nothing apart from the part. The people, of course, could never distinguish, but now at last neither could even the close-ups. Could he? Should he? Did he need to? Did he want to?

He felt a curious vertigo in his mind. Was this, he wondered, the feeling which the imago-insect feels as it realizes that not only has it long ceased to be its chrysaloid body, but that it is now quite another body, far more complete and powerful, that its old body is now only a withered and constricting husk and that it must break out, leave that behind forever and emerge a new and shining creature, with a completely different appearance and completely different make-up, organs, and powers? Perhaps, after all, the mind was the precipitation of the body, and, if so, a complete metamorphosis had taken place. Of course, if that were so, there would be no need to push things or to hurry.

On the other hand, if he were suffering from a kind of post-surgical shock, a sort of concussion through the habit patterns of a lifetime being recast, well, then, too, rest was wise; no need to hurry. He must get his bearings again, think out his position, and decide after sufficient deliberation what to do. Either the Mole was still the master mind and had foreseen all this—and in that case it was clear he had seen that he, the remodeled man, must be given time and allowed to choose his own time as to when best to take the final step or steps. Or the Mole had not foreseen, had not calculated for such massive displacement. One could become certain as to which of these interesting conclusions was true only by waiting and seeing. The Mole would have to wait. If he were still seeing a move ahead he would be willing to wait. If even he were at last in the dark and had done something, spoken a spell, which he could neither foresee nor unsay, well, then he must wait. Everything must wait, everyone must wait, the Alpha and the man who no doubt thought he was Omega, the Bull and the Mole, the powers above and those below, as he, small but wholly significant rider on the vast balance beam on which the three worlds hung, stood making up his mind, finding his balance, and deciding where to throw that minute but decisive weight.

How much bigger the whole scheme and plot, play and stage, was than he had ever imagined when he had the simple picture of "them" and "us," of right and wrong, of oppression and freedom, of courageous revolt and cruel tyranny, of self-sacrificing nobility and mean, selfish exploitation of mankind! Could it be that they were all not merely pawns of a far vaster Mole, but that they all made up, in some sanely insane way, a pattern, that hurt the mind to think of and yet delighted it in a vague agonizing way, a pattern that was always, when your vitality and imagination failed, becoming chaos and, as your vitality rose, becoming a stupendously satisfying design of inexhaustible richness? Could it be that Alpha and Omega, himself and mankind, the man who thought he was the inside realist and the mankind who didn't know that they were dupes, were all part of an immense being, as above so below, all aspects of an immense mind that was reflecting on itself, all valves and vessels of a fabulous heart that pulsed and beat, systole and diastole, in an unending cycle of experience and expression? These wild thoughts ran through his mind first when he was resting one night but unable to sleep after a peculiarly brilliant demonstration by the private

82

cinema in the robing room, showing him, as his trainer said, "only needing now to realize how convincing it looks to the outside, for the last of your own idiosyncracies, peculiarities, and personal traits to be lost for good!"

But though they first attacked him only at night, soon he could recognize them lying in wait for him at the back of his mind whenever he rested from the work. And of course the work fed this subsoil water-table with constantly fresh suggestion. For the first few days the theme was mainly in the mind's background and his reverie still went back to his old life, to the life in the hospital, to the life in the kitchen. But then he noted that not only was all that fading but that the theme, which had haunted him first as a drowse-reverie, was now present in a way in all his thought, flavoring it, but also that the theme, as it had first appeared, was now becoming clearer and more definite in all detail and in constant emphasis. He tried to explain it to himself. No doubt it was due to the fact that he had lived so long with no future, with his natural sense, the natural sense of what he would do and how he would live entirely subordinate to commands which could not be foreseen or understood. That absolute obedience had coiled up the spring of desire and wishful thinking, until now in the space given it it had uncoiled with a snap. He who had really had no future for years, living always in a kind of blankly potential present, now had in front of him a future which, just because he had lived such an unnatural life of abnormal, unconsidering readiness, showed up with its vast orderly formality stretching undeviatingly ahead, with a sudden, quite unexpected, relief. He tried to banish such thoughts, but he finally decided that it was better to let them have their way and run their course, just being content to prevent their going too far into the future, or from leading him to draw any conclusions, or making him to consider any actions in which he might have to take the initiative and change the stately course of this vast current by a violent intervention.

He had reached that state of agreement with himself, this provisional treaty or armistice with his old, central, if shrunken, self and this new accumulation of experience that already had built itself up as another encompassing body of conciousness, contemporary, self-consistent, holding the immediate future in its hands, and yet, quite inconsistent with what he had ever been or thought of being. He had reached an agreement not yet to force an agreement. That, he felt sure, was the right thing to do. Then, in a little while, when growth had gone on, he would be able to judge which of these two persons was the stronger, the more actual, and he would throw his weight on that side, for he realized that to try to defy the stronger must now mean madness. But there was no need yet—not the slightest—to say that his old self would not recover and assimilate this vast secondary personality which for the moment, because it was so great, showed a tendency to go on its own—the satellite to consume its own sun. He must give himself time, that was all. It was literally madness to go too fast at this point, and only he could judge the pace. The world must wait. The so-called masters of his fate, fighting for the mastery of the world with him as weapon, they must wait till the weapon decided, until the familiar made up his mind in what direction he was pointed and along what line, from what direction and to what goal, he would make the decisive thrust and stroke.

As he reached that conclusion, his spirits rose, and, as his second trainer took leave of him a couple of mornings after—when he told him that now the rehearsals of life could alone take him further—he felt positively buoyant.

He was, therefore, not in the slightest surprised or taken aback when, that very evening, as he was sitting back after supper smoking with the slow pageant of his presentations passing like huge hypnogogic imagery before his mind, while he rested as a quiet, contented spectator, the inner door, which had not opened since that first night, swung open and Alpha entered. The world-master stood looking at the remodeled man who did not rise from his chair. There was no need of caution, still less of courtesy. He was being inspected as a purchaser inspects a picture he had bought when it was needing cleaning and which has repaid his insight. For perhaps ten minutes the inspection lasted. It was quite impersonal on the part of both.

At last Alpha let a small sigh escape him—which showed the studied attention he had been giving—and, turning round, sat down in a chair some six feet off, took a cigarette, and, looking at the ceiling, remarked, "The insect is now hatched: it only remains to let it hop like the performing flea which is controlled by a hair unseen by the spectators and so seems to be a triumph of human affection in teaching a creature of instinct to respond to intelligent direction."

The remodeled man made no answer and none seemed expected. Each followed his own thought, if thought it was. In the remodeled man it went back to that vast lit procession, that shining stream of pageantal event in which, whenever he rested, his mind seemed to be drawn away, to be melted in its flow.

His day-and-night dream was broken by hearing his companion say, "Tomorrow you will dine with me. I dine early. This evening we shall have a little work to do, some small points to clear up. You are shaped for that now. When I have made a few points clear to you the matter will be settled. You will have nothing more to do than to hop when the invisible hair signals that your particular, if rather restricted, reflex is required of you. That is all for tonight. I expect you sleep well and soundly now, so you'll like to be sleeping now."

The remodeled man's double got up and went through the door.

"How does he know I sleep well now?" the synthetic twin reflected when left alone. "Like bodies, do they have like reactions? But we have only a surface resemblance. But how far do surface resemblances and habits finally eat like a Nessus shirt right into bone and brain, shaping them like the outer appearance?" But it was true, he was drowsy and he now did sleep well. "I'll ask him tomorrow what he meant. It's hard to be shy with one's own image, and anyhow I'm now far too valuable for him to risk hurting in any way such an expensive and irreplaceable work of art!"

Smiling he went to bed and woke again from those long, uneventful, vividly lit dreams of slow and beautiful processions, full of light and color and vast choruses, in which performances he always had the position from which the best view and the best hearing could be obtained. It was pleasant and soothing to be the central onlooker, and even when the central actor was, in a way, you, even then you were really only in the royal box, the more-than-royal-box, from which at last it was true that the onlooker, if he could be as central as this, saw at last most of the game. And, like an interior creator, he might well conclude, might he not, that it was very good, at least as a play, maya? Yes, he was more rested every day and he was quite content to lounge through the whole of that day. He owed it to himself. No doubt his nature had been more strained than he could realize, and now it was recuperating. Sufficient unto the day, sufficient unto this evening.

IV

ALPHA'S APOLOGY

THE DOOR opened punctually at six P.M. and Alpha beckoned him to come through it. He entered a dining room not much larger than the sitting room in which he had been confined so long.

As he looked round, his host remarked, "Yes, you're thinking these quarters are on the cramped side. But you'll find, when you have to be for much of your time in vast spaces, that one naturally best relaxes by contracting. The attitude of foetal humility, as it's called, I believe; my nerve doctor tells me it is the most economical of space but also the most restful muscularly.

"Time and again when I was thinking out this, the Last Revolution, the Psychological Revolution which ends the whole cycle of uprushes, I noticed one thing that the big settlers, the men who concluded each revolutionary phase, always did: they got themselves into small resting quarters after all the expansiveness and expansion. People thought it was simplicity or sham simplicity. No, the anthropological reason is that when you have to relax from too much expansion and imposition of your self, you must contract. Well, perhaps I'll like a bigger apartment when I get more used to having more time off and by myself—that's where you will come in. Now let us eat, and you can ask questions after."

The dinner was served. All the hot dishes kept their exact temperature of 120 degrees because they were made of a conductor which drew its heat through the table which was charged.

"A small invention which I had devised was this tableware." Alpha put his hand under the table, and the dishes which had been a rose pink began to flush a deep red.

A moment after and they had faded to a silver white. "No need to taste a thing to see if it is the right heat. That rose-pink tint I find the right heat. You may find it a trifle on the hot side. The resistance switch just under the table at your right hand controls your side of the table and sets your dishes at the glow that you find most palatable."

Through the meal of four light courses, each of which was exquisite and all blended like four singing parts, Alpha talked lightly, easily, entertainingly, of the gadget side of the new world. According to him, he had set on foot many of the inventions which made the new life so amusingly distracting—the cinema invention whereby the figures no longer appeared on a screen but, owing to electric fields making invisible projection screens, the actors appeared as though they were three-dimensional figures. Alpha didn't refer to the use to which his double knew this had been put, and, no doubt, for which it had been invented. He spoke also of textiles which had been developed together with lamps which sent out an invisible radiation, in which, however, the textiles fluoresced.

"The result," he remarked, "is remarkable. I have found it of great use. No, there is none of it here. Some small inventions have to be used with economy or their use is spoiled. I am no inventor and so I am not concerned to spill my results and cast pearls before peacocks.

"I want my children to be happy, and the world is my family, and as they are children and want to stay children and are wise in wanting that—that is the whole of my discovery in a nutshell—they don't want to grow up and there is no need that they should. I take care that not only should they not be troubled by questions they can't understand and problems which make them suffer for no purpose, but also that their pleasures should be rationed to them, always enough, always some little treat and change coming to them, but never a surfeit. Like a good father, I get ready a surprise for each birthday and Christmas. And sometimes—as with all good children—some small thing, done with the proper element of surprise, pleases them more than some big, gaudy show or something too clever and ingenious. I'm not here to dictate to the eternal child in man but just to find out what it needs and to see that it gets that. Then it is satisfied.

"I never make or set on foot an invention and let it come on the world directly it is found. Timing is everything. I put them into my reserve account. In the old-fashioned phrase, they are my capital. As long as I have a store of these—and I have a large sum now put by—I need fear no disturbance. A really new gadget has a lasting power of amusement, of distraction, of about six months. Then you must serve another, no sooner and no later—just like a well-served dinner, you must neither rush it nor dawdle.

"I hope you have enjoyed this meal; on the whole, I have learned as much psychophysiology from cookbooks as from any other textbook. Of course, the men who wrote them didn't know that they knew so much about the mind-body, but they were drawing on a huge experimental tradition of 'taste and see' and 'mix and try,' and it is fascinating to discover how the main classical sequence of hors d' oeuvre, soup, fish, game, sweet, entree, and dessert, reveals an intuitive knowledge of the whole rhythm of response of the nervous and chemical system of the body. It's that kind of knowledge—not theory, but practice that has worked and expanded step by step and had to prove its pudding by constant eating—that I have found most useful. I was always reading those textbooks of the great traditional arts of living—cooking, tailoring, acting, singing, to see what was latent knowledge in them: to see how it could and must be made explicit, though esoteric, knowledge.

"It had to be done, for the great tradition and intuitive way of life had almost completely given out. And *someone* had to keep people going. He'd have, himself, to do it deliberately and self-consciously in order that they might still carry on doing it unthinkingly and enjoyably, a synthetic extension of tradition, an *ersatz* instinct. Man can't live without a complete social pattern. From eating and sex, to clothes, games, manners, music, metaphysics, religion—it's all style, it's all fashion, and once the ancient regime, the grand manner, is gone, someone has to invent. But I mustn't

89

run on into theory myself." And he turned his guest's attention to the flowers on the table.

"Quite a naturally-unnatural extension of horticulture," he smiled. "I'd noticed that gardening makes men sedate and content, more than anything else. But not only is that difficult unless you live in the country—and many people don't want to do that—but you need a contemplative disposition that can wait for things—and the childlike nature is not patient. You also need, or needed in the old art of gardening, quite a liking for dirt, hard work, and the constant combating of garden pests—and most people hate fighting things. Then one day, when I was thinking about how valuable a strong taste for growing flowers would be in my people—how the contemplative orders, for example, found that gardening was the best corrective of the intense nervous strain their intense methods of concentration set up—I happened to be visiting one of my labs where we were working at one of the barbiturics—one of the sleep-and-disassociation drugs that have proved very useful tools if not overdone. But I, as the high-distance onlooker, saw something the chemists didn't: the chemical forms which were being precipitated were as a peculiarly beautiful and elaborate crystalline pattern.

"I set on foot another line of research at once. And from that simple cross-breeding of two ideas—owing to my imposing one line of thought on another—out of it came our modern floriculture. As you know—these are some of the new patterns—we can make, like a kaleidoscope, flower patterns of any color or salient design. People love making the chemical beds—neat and clean, and rapidly sprouting out of them, these crystal forms, as beautiful as any flower, of more variety of shapes and tints, of course free from all pests and, as the old hymn used to say, never-fading blooms. Of course, they have to be scented after they are grown, but that is just the little problem which you leave for the people to play with. Never give them a toy which they have to put all together for themselves, but, at the same time, never give them one that is perfectly finished and to which they can add nothing. I think we know our children and have found out the way to keep

90

them perpetually arrested in happiness by sending them round and round the maze of pleasure at such a pace and on such a span that when they arrive back at the same place it seems new—or, you may prefer an eating term, the appetite has recovered. Well, you have finished. Let us go into my study."

He led the way into another room. It was somewhat larger. At one end was a large curved desk with six microphones set round the left-hand sweep of its curve. There was a door on its left, immediately opposite the door by which they were entering. There were tall windows with blue curtains drawn. The floor was covered with a thick carpet, the pile of which was so thick that all sound of footsteps was completely lost in it. The pattern was a series of checks of amber and silver. There was an open fireplace set in the wall through which the door had just let them, and, in front of the fire, two chairs drawn up. Alpha waved his double to one of these and sat down himself, took a cigarette from the crystal box, but put it back and then handed the box to his guest.

"I think I'll inhale one of the salts instead," he remarked and took from the small table on which the cigarettes were, a tiny smelling-salts bottle.

"That was another line of research. I thought about priests—again men of great repressions and nervous tension—and their snuff, and how it had gone out. And then about the nineteenth century and that curious period of women having fainting fits and being recovered by sal-volatile. Then, as so often happens with me in my reading, I came across a Frenchman's researches of a century ago on the nerves on the inside upper part of the nose and their effect on the brain.

"After that it was plain sailing. I was bound to run across the other line of convergent research. We were using all we could get from tantra and hatha-yoga to train the men who had to fight the underground fortresses of democratic reaction and the atavisms left over by the spent revolutions. I soon found that the necessary breathing exercises had, naturally, a great deal to do with the lungs, but also quite a lot to do with an air massage of those nerve-ends right up near the brain at the top of the nose. Then, putting two and one together, I had made these different kinds of salts and got a threefold result. Perhaps you don't know that, besides the scents, which I have made into the basis of a supersensual art (so a man who has lost his digestion can still go on relishing all kinds of olfactory pleasures and people become nose epicures and despise as gross gluttons the old-fashioned palate addicts), there are stronger ones that act like a kind of drink.

"Of course, one had light along that path to popular conquest from, first, cocain, which was generally snuffed and generally ended by decaying the snuffer's nose, and the work in morphia in getting the toxic element out of that drug. We now—as always in our whole campaign—hit at dividing body from mind and keeping the body intact and letting the mind put on its own well-fitting handcuffs or, rather, surgical belts.

"But my third discovery was as useful. Besides detensionics and relaxants I found, of course—for discovery, if you have the mind, has about it an element of inevitability—you are in constant touch with your genius and daimon; I know I am, as I've already told you—I found the third use, the discovery of stimulants. I prefer to be like a refined lady of the nineteenth century and sniff my salts when I fear fatigue might bring on the vapors. And I do work hard, you may judge, and sometimes I have lately been near the edge where careful breezes are needed to be gathered to carry me off the rocks." And he snapped open the little crystal bottle, unloosed its glass stopper, and snuffed a couple of times the savor. Then, shutting it up, he added. "Now we are set: we have the evening before us for work, and our agenda opens, as the old British Parliament used to open, with question time. You ask me any questions you like."

There was a pause. All through this dinner the remodeled man had been trying to build up out of the mass of detail a clear picture of the creature who was talking to him and who, of course, held him like a tool in his hands. He must keep the old picture—whether it was right or wrong—of the ruthless, cunning tyrant, out of his mind, and use nothing but the copious information and observation that was being given away to him. But still it was too early for that. He must go from step to step and keep the interview going as long as possible. He pulled himself together; yes, that would do as a start:

"My first question is, Why do you let me question you, why should you?"

"That's easily answered—because I know what I don't want. I don't want a 'trusty.'"

"What's a trusty?"

He knew all too well, but it amused him that Alpha could think he might become a kind of unquestioning, doglike devotee. Alpha put his hand on the arm of his own chair, and the remodeled man thought he was going to rise. But he sat back after the hand movement and a moment later they heard the door away by the big desk open.

Alpha didn't turn round, only remarking, "Demonstration is always quicker than words," and then still without turning, "Number One, rearrange those flowers in the Kwan Yin pattern. They have lapsed."

A man came forward and, without saying a word or showing any sign of their presence, set to work to reorder in a variant of Japanese flower decoration the five strange crystalline blooms that rose from a small agate vase.

"Number Two." Another figure, which looked in carriage and appearance very like the first, now also came onto the hearthrug.

"Under the rug I have let fall my abraxid ring." Alpha put out his hand to point to the spot, and on that hand his signet ring, which all the world knew, was shining. "Get down and find it for me."

The man looked at his hand to see where it was pointing and then got down on his knees, rolled back the rug, and felt over the surface of the carpet until he had touched every inch. Then he rose and said in a completely even voice, "The ring is not there to my touch nor to my sight."

"Put the rug back."

It was put back. The man rose to his knees but did not get on his feet. The two servants paid no attention whatever

93

to each other. The first had finished his flower arrangements and stood aside. They could not be said to be waiting, it was obvious, for waiting means some degree of expectation. They were no more expectant than is a typewriter when not being employed.

Nor, though the guest—as he now felt it stealing over himself to regard himself—tried to detect any reaction, could he catch a trace of it when Alpha went on, "Those two are trusties. We took the word from the kind of convict which imprisonment took years to make—the creature which at last only wished to be left in the familiar safety of the jail and whose one reaction—it could even then be hardly called a wish—was to do as it was told and to obey the orders and carry out authority's wishes.

"Well, we worked up from that unforeseen natural product of unnatural conditions, life's reaction to a living death. We also thought about the whole problem of seasoning—one more example of that putting things together that seem poles apart and getting a new useful blend. It used to take years to season wood and stone and wine. But once we knew exactly in chemical terms what was going on, we could do it in a very low percentage of the natural time. So with making trusties. These men will do anything I tell them, but with no imagination. They are conditioned by the proper barbiturics combined with the right suggestion and periods of initial solitude, so that they, like dogs, respond only to certain stimuli and really listen only to me. And they listen to me only if I speak to them. They are now not listening to me and are unaware of each other. Whatever bizarre thing I set them to do, they will do with great persistence and remarkable skill. But, as I have said, they can never think for themselves.

"In the old palaces of the world—about four thousand years ago—they discovered castration; the word, you see, means a fortress, an inner defense. They made the inner guard eunuchs. It gave a defense against interior treasons, at least in the harem, though at a big cost in energy. Now we castrate the mind. It is more efficient and more merciful. As that initial thinker of our revolution, Sheldon, called it, this is animectomy—he charged much psychoanalysis with being that. Sheldon was, in spite of his genius, a man of his time and a bit of a conservative—as, of course, was unavoidable. But, as with all real genius, you can use its protests as much as its propositions. And with a single word he put an instrument in my hand." Without changing tone or looking up, Alpha remarked, "Go now," and then, without a pause, "You will find it a little hard to believe" —the men moved off round each side of the two seated figures—"that these men actually notice nothing. But you will get used to it."

What the guest *was* getting used to was a reviewing of the race between Alpha and Talpa. Had he been right? Was Talpa always in the lead? The underground could do quite a lot of conditioning, but generally with a good deal of violence and breakage.

As if to confirm his doubts, Alpha went on, "We have yet to find a type that is quite resistant, and all that go under are quite happy—appetite good, sexual energy fine, enjoy games, and show it in their quiet way. They don't make friends, but why should they? And altogether, friendship is far less common where kindliness and general openness are as common as they are today. Friendship, as Shakespeare and all the romantic poets knew, is a defense against the attacks of an unfriendly world and community." A stab like trigeminal neuralgia went through his hearer. "Why stay in a walled city when the country is quite safe?

"There are a few who resist, and in those cases I do think that relieving them of their bodies is kindest—for them the change into a perfectly conditioned body would, I think, be a real imprisonment and spiritual suffocation. That's just why your case is so interesting to both of us— unique, of course, because you are a double—one of the neat paradoxes in which life delights. It would, as I've told you, be no use just obliterating your memory, when it is your face we want. Neither would a trusty be any good. Think of a case in which you were substituting and some hitch occurred where you had to gag, as it were, and extemporize. Think of the million crowd watching what they firmly believe is me, me at a loss and having to be prompted and pushed through the part. They'd know I was failing.

It would be worse than my going on without help. The priest-king is absolutely sacrosanct, till his people see his failing. Then at once they kill him."

A question came into the guest's mind, and he felt he would like a rest from this intensive discussion of his future—no longer private, yet all the more concerning him as he felt his identity practically gone.

"What became of the men in the kitchen with me?"

Alpha answered quite amiably. "The arrest was made, you remember, at night. By the two men who went to fetch the food each evening I dined here. They are highups, and the chief of police—of whom I'll be telling you in a moment—keeps up that show of watching for possible poison. I think it's a hang-over of the romantic age in the chief's mind. Policemen are incurably romantic, but I let him have his way—food brought in sealed container by agent one and then watched by agents two and three—you know the old formula. But you have to let men do things in the way that amuses them, so long as when it is a real matter of life and death they obey. For some reason best known to his rather slow, if methodical, mind—something to do with his filing system, I expect—he didn't make the periphery arrests till the next morning. He got the three assistants, and they were treated amnesiacly. They are at large now with just that tract of time they spent in that kitchen wiped off their memory—as used to happen in post-concussion amnesia. But, strange to say, the chef, whom I was told—and I viewed him also through long-distance tele-visor focus at work in his kitchen when I was also making the first look-over on you—was really rather a slow mover as most fat men are, got away. My chief of police is vexed, but on the whole that amuses me. Such people can do us no harm, but a policeman is rather like an anxious housewife: she always wants the house cleaner than it need be."

The guest felt a certain small thrill of pleasure that the old man had got away; besides, it gave one something to think about, across this stream of unanswerable success and all-embracing power-planning. But he saw that he was expected to ask further questions.

"You said you wanted to inform me about the chief of police?"

"That certainly is your next lesson. Hardly anybody knows you are here. To be exact, of all that are capable of normal knowing and remembering, only the two who made the arrest—and they know only that you weren't killed or psychologically 'pithed' at once—and Algol. Yes," and he chuckled, "that is the rather romantic astronomic name that he chose! Let people choose their names and they'll tell you their characters—not what the name says, of course, but the kind of person who thinks up that kind of fancy mask. You may not know that after that last and dullest of the Revolutions, the Russian afterbirth of the Economic Revolution, there was that queer old reactionary, Lenin—quite rightly they mummified *him*—giving such theatrical names to his juvenile-minded leads! Kamenev, the Man of Stone; Stalin, the Man of Steel! So my chief of police, as soldiers in the old battle age used to get ready for the last war, is always getting ready for the last revolution. You can never get a man of action ever really to live in the present. But he has served his purpose, and I don't like to take away his fun of living over his past coups, though there is less and less to coup. So he recuperates by memory," he laughed.

"Besides, he could be a really awkward customer if you didn't give that spider-mind plenty of webbing to spin, even if there are fewer and fewer flies to catch. I sometimes say to myself that if this Mole he is always talking of really exists he's really a blessing, for he keeps Algol from spinning flytraps and webs round all of us. He would love to be making new rules all the time in order to be able to keep on arresting people and having to catch dangerous undergrounders. I believe that in his heart, as soldiers hated peace, though they said they fought to win it, he hates the success of the final Revolution. He hates the fact that we are really in the tradition of Lao-Tze and not of Machiavelli and that just making people comfortable has worked, while threatening them has failed; just getting them what they want has made them quiet, while continually threatening them and attacking them kept the revolutionary wheel spinning forever. It is so hard to make a man of means

97

not fall in love with his means and not fall in passionate love with repeating his old successes when they are no longer apposite. A good fellow in spite of a native stupidity, and a clever man, in spite of some considerable cruelty. He really ought to be treated, and I've often suggested it to him. But I have never really had time to make a point of it, and he always has some excuse for putting me off. Now, when I have more time, that is one of the things to which I must and will get down." He yawned easily.

"Oh, yes, there are a number of things I shall enjoy doing now that I have a little leisure from the routine work which will be taken off my hands. Meanwhile he is Pluto to my Jupiter and he knows his position, though at times I'm sure he thinks he'd make a far better king of the day than I do. But he is born for the night, he's moon to my sun, and now that the sun is at zenith he has less and less place in the sky, and the future."

The host paused. Then his mind took a wider sweep. "No one really understands what I've done. I've rolled all the past three revolutions into one and taken the odd little efforts each made to solve its particular problem and incorporated them all into one comprehensive art of living. That is why this is the last revolution: because it is the beginning of rightful progress, of a new cycle and eon of evolution. Revolution occurs because pressures are let accumulate, the crust chokes back the yeast, and then there's a burst. But evolution is the rule, and, after these adolescent efforts at alteration which have gone on like a recurrent fever for the last six hundred years, I have shown mankind how to grow without convulsions every time it cuts another tooth.

"But I have had to make a number of discoveries and inventions, not merely the ones I made simultaneously to bring off the beginning of this the last, the Psychological, Revolution. Then I had to solve the problem of how to stop the thesis of Liberty and the antithesis of Order strangling each other and exhausting all mankind. Freedom and Plan, like the Gladiator and the Retiarius, had dueled until the only end seemed that both would be destroyed. Then I saw and intervened with the synthesis.

"But just the idea would have been no good had I not

also seen that men are of two types, really three. The first wants to enjoy itself and be left alone. The next has to be found activity or it will pull everything to pieces and drive the poor stick-in-the-muds until they are mad or dead. The third thinks things out and sets these two lower types to do what they want without getting in each other's way. But once I had done that, and you must own it was much, then I had to see I had only begun. Having made a settlement, I mustn't settle down; having prevented another misbegotten revolution and put a live birth in its place, I must be prepared to carry through and on.

"I saw that all the other Revolutions had themselves been in three parts. First were the actual revolutionaries, thinkers who were completely abstractionists—as we used to call them, rationalists. Then came the man of actuality and action, instead of theory. The doctrinaires were demoded by the opportunist. He had to be a reactionary because he had to find something precedental and once-accepted to take the place of all the theorizing that hadn't worked. So you get the Napoleon type—what a blunderer!—not only a man of no nerve but of no vision. Do you realize, when he had time, seated out on St. Helena, to review the world, he never foresaw the industrial revolution in all his wordy prognostications? He was so blind that he not only couldn't see an inch into the looming future, but when he had to find a footing he had to go right back to the Roman base. That's really to play the Roman fool—not suicide, as Shakespeare thought, but Imperialism—the military dictatorship. But he was forced to make some discoveries involuntarily. He found he had to dress his part and that his figure was more effective for cohesion than his speeches. He found that the 'redingote gris' was a better rallying symbol, its plain mass amid the deliberately-made-gaudy marshals, than the imperial bee-spangled purple. Nap saw that some kind of slow movement had to come in. For he was to maunder about his son being a king of peace, but he couldn't see his way round.

"So, too, the poor old Russians, always behindhand, always holding the world back. First they 'afterbirthed' the Economic Industrial Revolution, when for a generation it had already miscarried in the Economic-industrialized countries, and then had to make their Lenin into a mummied Pharaoh and, finally, call back the Greek Orthodox Church. Slow movement and coda, you see, once more.

"It was that phrase, 'slow movement,' from the art of music, that gave me my next insight. Epochs, like individuals, have to grow up, but, like most individuals, they die from the excesses of their youth. The first movement can be vigorous but, after its initial splash and dive, then the swimmer must strike out slowly and steadily. I saw that.

"I had seen that militarism was as out of date as democracy. I saw that the future of the way up to power no longer lay over battlefields, because war weapons had become instruments of ludicrous imprecision—the atom bomb, like a huge periodmark, closed that, the soldiers' frank, bullying way, in which you club everyone impartially over the head. I saw that the next revolution would be made by secret police, by mining from within, by the discrediting or the capture and conditioning of all key men who made or could make trouble, and by propaganda, mainly amusing, debunking, ridiculous-making jokes and lampoons; and by getting 'noble' characters into 'discreditable' situations. I bought up scores of funny papers and put the men who liked debunking in to edit them with a free hand to attack and make ludicrous patriotism, militarism, all provincialism and all drill. I had comic songs made that guyed the whole bloodthirsty lot, and the songs and the cartoons stuck. It became silly to be patriotic or to care for arms—childish. Then the better people I won by argument and found places for them, so that the tough didn't know what was promised the tender-clever and the tender didn't know what the tough did.

"Though all my work was scientific, I had really no more use for a brute, still less for a sadist, than has a surgeon for that type as one of his dressers or nurses. No, my men had to be cold but never violent. Sometimes it was difficult to manage. Algol, I've told you, was at times a problem. But, of course, all that is over, and I mustn't run on into anecdotage.

"Besides, it was much more brilliant and interesting to

turn from this still rather gaudy fanfare to the next stage —the wholly original phase, the slow movement when one had to conduct the vast orchestra of more than half the world down into the quieter, more sustained passages after all the crashing chords. Now, after having been the irregular leader, the mysterious unknown that was the brain always thinking up new surprises and always suspected but never defined, I come out into the open and take on the part which can sustain the pressure of repetition, peace, and relaxation. I saw I must become that ancient enduring type, the priest-king, of whom Confucius, the architect of the most enduring society the world has known, says, 'As long as the Emperor—or rather, the Son of Heaven—sat still looking toward the south, all went well.'

"Well, you can't stay quite still in this new world—at least not yet; the pendulum must be let swing slowly to rest. And that is what I am doing. I am becoming the conductor of the great slow movement, the great choragus, or dance leader of the sacred dance that finally becomes a perfect posture. I have come out and I spend my time leading this vast pattern. It seems stupid and vain to those who don't understand. I am initiating half the world to a new service, a new ritual, a new communion. I'm not only blending them, fusing them into a larger unit, into a real mankind—a thing which no one has ever succeeded in doing before. I'm blending them, fusing them as part of humanity, of human history. That, and that alone, will insure the other brazings holding fast. I'm making them understand themselves, their place, their part, not only on the world's map as it is now, but in the world's story.

"The old reformers were always talking of teaching history to the people—and in a way they were right—though I noticed that historians weren't, as a matter of fact, better citizens of the world, less provincially prejudiced, than the man in the street. And all the old dictators before the end saw that something has to be made of mankind's past story if you are to educate the present generation to develop man's future and see their destiny in it. But, you see, there were two mistakes. The first was to leave people just to get it out of books. Life—the present—will always beat the book which mumbles about the past; the past must be made to live here and now in the lives of the living. The second was to make the story, which can't fail to be a big thing now we can see back so far, end in a provincialism which was just sheer anticlimax—the bathos of a Nordic Nuremberg as the culmination of mankind." He let out a gust of laughter. "The anticlimax of one of those monster Moscow Mechanist-Marxian Masques bellowing away all a-bout man being an economic instrument—why, history it-self laughed the whole charade out of court.

"But I'm making the masses—and don't they fall for it! —actually live through history, live it out in its fullness. I'm still only at the beginning of this experiment, and it's taking, I must own, more out of me than anything I've done before. Making a revolution is just child's play, or a boy's romp, beside taking on and explicating evolution. I expect you have thought about it when you were in one of the great rallies."

The remodeled man realized how much, in every sense, the Mole had kept them in the dark and misrepresented this strange effort, for clearly he feared it, and mightn't he have been right in doing so?

But Alpha was running on, and he must not get left behind.

"None of you can really have an idea of what I'm heading to. I'm going to show to mankind, and make him know it's true, because he'll actually experience it in himself and with his whole generation, that history is still living in him. I'll show them the real inevitability of what I've done. They'll not merely know—they'll feel—seeing is believing but feeling is knowing—that all history is still living in them—that all of them are needed, the whole of mankind in all its types united, in order to express history. They will see and feel that the whole of the past is pressing down into them so that they must know it that they may express it—no silly antiquarianism here, no revivalism, Gothic, Classic, Nordic, Roman, no: but the whole past brought to flower in a present which has more room to express this immense promise than ever before.

"In these great rallies I'm aiming more and more and

getting closer and closer to making the vast masses realize that they are now this, and can now be this, because the past had been thus. They are—if they will become and expand into One—they are the past's fulfillment. All its rivers flow into this, the estuary leading to the ocean. They are the latent word which all the letters of the past make. And as they come together and under my conductorship say it, affirm it, utter it, that is the creative word, the Logos without which the eonic message of complete meaning can never be completed and made able to continue its utterance down through the ages."

He had become excited, and the words had rolled off his tongue like a peroration. But a moment after he half sighed, and the sigh turned into a yawn.

"Others think that I do it out of exhibitionist fun. You wait—you, of all people, will be able to judge; I'm tired out and so I pick an understudy. Somehow those great hypnotized audiences draw something out of one—or it may be the actual position one has to take; again you will be able to judge. I think, myself, it is more the former than the latter." He seemed to muse. Suddenly he yawned again immensely. The listener heard the powerful jaw crack like a fraudulent medium's toe joint. "That's enough for you to know. Now you have your general bearings. Sleep over that. I must sleep. Off with you now. I'll give you your next lesson in a couple of days if I can manage it; for I must have you ready in the next week or two. I just must have a rest and time to think things out."

The host rose; the guest followed suit. As he turned round at the door the guest saw his host was already half through another that led evidently to his bedroom.

He certainly was glad for the next three days to be able to think over what he had heard. What a load of news for the Mole. But would the Mole be able to take it? Was it true? Partly, no doubt. Was the intention of making this change to peaceful methods of consent true? Perhaps. But, even so, would the Mole and his idealists—would he himself have consented to such a drugged, such a psychologically debauched, state for mankind? Wasn't this picture at its best—granting that Alpha at all meant what he said—

103

a confession of defeat—that humanity could not be raised from a certain low level, that equality was a myth, progress an illusion, and evolution had come to an end?

All our drive had come from the faith that the peoples were deluded and deceived and that once we showed them the nobility of sacrifice and the grandeur of fight against tyranny they needs must love the highest when they saw it; they would want ardors and endurances rather than comforts and amusements. But had we shown them a life of clean heroism? Was our fighting any less dirty than Alpha's? And, while *he* might now be turning to methods less brutal and cruel than those to which every underground has to resort before it can come to the surface, weren't we still down in the sewers of liquidations and eliminations— the long Latinized words for murder without trace and treason without repentance—where we were trying to sap and drain the towering structure above us?

Hadn't, then, every structure a base in the blind mud and only when it got through the crust could it build something that went on and tried to find the sky? That would mean that only if you let things grow past their violent stage would they ever become constructive. You couldn't force them past. And that again would mean that you must work with what is and only encourage it to grow better out of its less bad developments—that to attack it was to keep on making it return to violence and also to keep yourself down at the same root-and-drain level.

He must be frank with these questions. He was alone. Had anyone ever before—would anyone ever again—be so alone, so stripped! He was now the decisive figure for mankind, able to throw his unseen weight on either side and poised on the very center of the vast beam that stretched perhaps to the horizons of history. As it now trembled, he could swing up or down as he, the midget rider, inclined.

His thought turned from the two machines, and the two antagonistic minds, to the prize they fought for—mankind. There, too, was it simple? If the psychophysical revolution were really here, if Sheldonism were right, then your best service to threefold humanity was to give each layer the life it loved best and worked best in. We had outgrown the silly sentimental anthropomorphic notion of thinking of birds and animals as manikins and trying to make them happy and safe as we define happiness and safety. That was simply to try to give them our anxious sense of time when they were really in an animal immortality of an always almost wholly present moment, a vivid instantaneity of totally-focused living, direct, unreflected, unrefracted being.

Well, mustn't we face the same thing about mankind—three types in one species, a huge threefold symbiote? He remembered how much, when he was being taught biology, his simple, generous mind had revolted when the teacher began pointing out the conventional moral, even when they were only studying the lichens—how, though they were a single creature, yet they were two: they worked in with each other by combining quite different lives—that there was an alga that could live on air and a fungus that could eat the rock, and these two utterly different creatures made a fast-bonded, most successful, widely varied, and powerful form of living creature. They needed each other but only because they never became like each other. Of course, the lesson was: leave people to be what they feel they are happy in being, only point out what their mind-body indicates they would be most happy in doing. He had revolted from that—but wasn't his revolt mere emotionalism, that reaction back to the past, which psychology had now shown is the young person's natural reaction to anything new? It is the young who are the blind conservatives from the time when the child, with scrupulous ritual, insists that the "Story of the Three Bears" shall be told every night with precisely the same detail, so wearying to the fresher-minded adult. Anyhow, now his middle age—his suddenly imposed middle age—and this vast opportunity question had come on him together. He must think the matter out in the fresh light of maturity.

He went through his daily drill in ritual automatically, but that was what was expected of him. They taught him nothing new. He was simply keeping supple and imposed the patterns of carriage and attitude he'd been taught. He hardly needed conscious attention, these exercises were so like those limbering ones done by a pianist as a routine preliminary. He kept on watching the door of his deep mind to see if an answer was going to be delivered to all the questions he had sent down for judgment. But nothing came, save a great sense of waiting. Perhaps, he thought, some things can be determined only by doing. When I actually am in use, then perhaps I shall again see as clearly as I used, or at least feel. Not that the numbness was unpleasant. It felt like a waking dream in which you are aware just because of the bizarreness of the scenes that flit across the mind that the body is really at rest lying warmly covered up in bed.

He didn't even keep any tale of the number of days; their quality was so vague that he couldn't say when it was that the inner door late one afternoon again opened and Alpha called, as carelessly as an old friend who shares the same apartment, "Wash up, now; dinner will be ready in a quarter of an hour." When he had done as he was told he found the door ajar, went through it, and caught sight of a trusty just leaving the dishes on the table. A few minutes later, Alpha himself came in from his study, waved him to the same seat he had had before, and sat down opposite him. They spoke little through the main part of the meal, and it was worth giving attention to. Then Alpha broke the silence to offer him some wine.

"Alcohol has always been the problem of Western man as opium is of the East, though I think alcohol leads and has always led. So I set my chemists to work on the molecule of those ferments. It was, of course, only to do what had been done eighty years ago on opium—to get the toxic and habit-forming element out of the molecular ring. We have succeeded, but only quite lately, and it's not on the market yet. It could, of course, have been done a couple of generations ago, but those without the responsibility weren't interested and those with responsibility hadn't time. But I saw we must tackle drink as soon as we could.

"One day I'll get onto sex. Meanwhile, like a wise man, I let it have its head in those who haven't got a head; and, with those who have, I give them so much to do that they use up the gonadal energy and so avoid having that kind of bad conscience—which is really an evolutionary forecast.

It haunts them because they are using a basic energy just to give them the orgasm (right enough in the viscerotonics) when they ought to have ecstasy. Why, even the toughs know that sex isn't the thing for them—that a plunge in ice-cold water or battling a blizzard is more fun than any girl. Only the fat visceroes can touch sex and enjoy it without tearing it to pieces trying to find in the bag that enduring ecstasy which isn't there. The viscero is so close to life that he knows a lot; he knows how to forget, how to follow up and damp out the pleasant little glow of lust by sleep and food. Put out the fire before going to bed and always keep it in the grate!

"But now, all that can and must wait. Try this wine—I'm told they have a method of detection of the molecule atoms that give a bouquet so they can build up a flavor that is too fine for any human taste-bud to judge—as we can now make and record and visually gauge sounds too delicate for the ear to hear—as you know with your voice, which is now so like mine that anyone listening to us would think it was a monologue spoken by a two-headed monster!"

He laughed and filled his double's glass and then his own.

"Yes," he said judicially, "I shall be able to give a *cordon bleu* to that young chemist. He's done it. I used to be no mean judge of the old raw, natural stuff that we used to squeeze out of grapes. The best *has* been kept unto the last, in man's long banquet, after all. And it will give those who like it a lift as well. It is a true stimulant, this superalcohol, instead of being a depressant—that has been my aim all the while.

" 'Your objective,' I've said to these boys, 'is the seventh cortex of the brain. There lies your citadel. Try to win that over to me; don't batter it down. Get it to come over to our side.' They respond to that stuff. Always reward.

"I learned that from experimental rats, and the emotional life of most of us is very near theirs. Eight per cent learned best, were most inventive, when they were both punished and rewarded; that, of course, was the old liberal formula. Then came the old violent dictatorships—for as the state became more powerful it punished more and rewarded less

107

—and the results were praised and my rats confirmed the finding. Learning and invention went up to fifteen percent with the punishment-pressed rodents. But when, in the interests of pure science, we had to see what would happen if one gave sheer unrelieved reward—why, then the good results leaped up to one hundred per cent.

"Well, I don't pretend to understand nature but I do attend to her, so I told them to get along with counter-checking the results on chimps. And, sure enough, there one found that the more psychological the reward for these higher types, the better the results. It was approval they lived and pined for, and would leave food if only to be patted and praised. The suggestive power of fame will make a man continent, sober, poor as a miser! Well, I need not tell you, we have not been disobedient to these indications given us by the Life Force. But I see you have finished your meal. Not another glass of this vintage? Well, anyhow, take it with you into the next room. It will really do you good."

They strolled in together into the study like old friends and sat down in the same two chairs where they had had their first long fireside chat.

Alpha went on easily, "Last time I didn't explain to you that little gadget of the fire. The play of flames round logs, the gentle fluctuating heat, those small stuffy things I had re-searched into. I was sure these great stuffy clokes of heat were a mistake. I'd known about how in the hospitals for crippled children they got such wonderful results by exposing the surgical tuberculosis cases to sunlight in moving air —Rollier a century ago in Switzerland coined the phrase, *Le corset musculaire*—the muscles are gently massaged and the circulation kept going by the rise and fall of the stimuli. I saw at once that man's taste for an open fire must be right—his tastes always are unless you start arguing him out of them—for, of course, he can never tell you why; that's for you, the clever questioner, to find out. I found out.

"People rest best with the merry play of flames to watch. Gas fires made discontent; radiators, revolution! But I've no doubt they did balk something ancient in people. The hearth is the most ancient spot for relaxed contemplation and the hearth must have a fire. But we have reversed the motto and then disproved it. All fire but no smoke. This fuel was an accidental discovery from one of our huge retorts in which we were learning how, out of sewage, to recover the essential elements—such as organic phosphorus—which till then men either destroyed or threw into water and made a poisonous swamp. You know we deal with all garbage now in the electric furnaces every house has fitted, but the more valuable sewages we still extract in our central retort houses. I noticed that at a certain heat there were built up these crystalline forms which are very frondlike, just as corals grow in the sea, but this, of course, is pure chemical action, a very rich crystal form. We discovered that when the heat was raised, then these forms combusted, very cleanly. We next treated them with other salts and we had this fuel. Of great warmth, radiance—see how beautiful those peach-colored flames and those peacock-colored sparks are —and giving off no smoke, and you see that when at last it burns out there is left only that light-blue ash."

They sat looking at the fluttering glow with that ancient pleasure in the bright hearth. True, as the fuel burned it gave off no smoke and the ash formed as a pale-blue, feathery down.

"It makes a good top dressing for plants too. We still have to grow a great deal of food, but it's getting more and more efficient. One day we'll get synthetic food, I guess. But I'm in no hurry—not that the chemical problem seems far away from solving, now that we have synthesized chlorophyll, but because of the psychological problem. A large part of the people aren't ready yet to do without growing things. It keeps their tempo right. Of course, all the other revolutions lost their balance by thinking of the clever towns and not of the massive lands, of the critical types instead of the integral masses; those are the human chlorophyll. They do the great integration while the rest just break down and up, into pretty but transitory forms, the raw material. Now that we are relieved of that false fever, the belief in progress, in there being a wonderful day in the future for which the present is to live in perpetual discomfort, strain, anxiety, and violence, we can see things in balance."

The guest swallowed this fresh shock to his faith. He must listen. His mind must not close down or he would act wrongly when the time for acting came.

They were silent for a moment or two, and then Alpha went on, "As you won't need being told, I'm increasingly interested in the psychological side of everything and I refuse to move, even when results are quite laboratorily clear, till I've checked up and found what the psychological consequences will be, what will be the reaction of *homo sapiens*—yes, I see you are surprised that I use that old funny term—but, seriously, I am beginning to see he is far wiser than we thought or than he knew. Of course, I started out on this, knowing that it was the psychological revolution that would demode all the other three, the religious, the political, the economic. They are all pre-anthropological —they just know the nature of the creature they were going to shape for its own happiness. Now one can laugh their pretentious ignorance out of court."

He chuckled, and his guest stifled a small sigh and that ended in a smile.

"We should never have won unless we were on Life's side. Man had used up all his credit with Nature, and she was saying in tremendous tones, with the blast of the atom, 'Understand yourself or go! I don't ask you to understand the universe; I do demand you look at yourself and cease talking pretentious, murderous nonsense.'

"Well, I attended, that's all, and that's all that been needed to give mankind another lease on life. What lies ahead I can't see. I don't pretend to be a prophet. I do claim that I have been contemporary and all the others have been living fossils. I do claim that I have had respect for life, have known I was up against immense mystery, have tried not to dictate to Nature and to control her only in order the better to obey her.

"Indeed, it was that old-fashioned fuss over the first squirt of atomic energy which really began the complete discrediting of the old politicos—that, in fact, was its chief significance in the end. What a gain it was to get rid of that type of caucus man who, since the beginning of city government, was up to his little, smart games of rigging committees and gerrymandering majorities—a fool, incapable of understanding even his own experts, and whose one gift that gave him power with the gullible was his clever, cunning talk. You probably never heard about that part of mankind's protest which I used. It's very stale history now and of interest only to the very few who, like myself, have to know about the roots of what's now flowering.

"History used to interest quite a lot of people. Of course, it doesn't now. It was fairly popular as long as the present was nothing like good enough in itself. Then it was natural to take an interest in the past, because it looked either more romantic or better run than the present, prettier or more profitable. But if the present is really pleasant to look at and to taste, who is going to be as foolish as Aesop's dog and drop what's in one's mouth for a fading reflection?

"Of course, those first physicists who revolted failed. They tried to begin by taking things into their own hands when they saw that the politicos were too stupid to understand what was being told them. But the physicists themselves were really no better. Why expect it? Pure specialists, they knew even less of human beings and their ways than did the politicos, though they saw much more clearly what had been run into. Why, most of them, though working with pure force, were, would you believe it, still materialists, though their own physicists had shown that matter is only a mental concept that they and their like had thought up. That was stupider than if I should start worshiping myself. Of course they *had* to fail—knowing as little of mankind as of metaphysics; but when they had been batted down and the politicos went on messing and people wouldn't live in the towns, and the bombed places, when you did go back to them, simply gave you cancer or diseases of the central nervous system—well, once I started I didn't have much difficulty in bringing in all the researchers, specialists, technicians, on my side. They couldn't do it themselves, but, with them ready to serve me and seeing that I understood them, well, they went over en masse, and the politicos were left. All I had to do was to wave them out of the way."

He stopped and hummed to himself, his memories evidently soothing him. Then he went on reflectively, "The underground may be a different proposition. Anyhow, there's the possibility of a real psychological problem lying down there, a residual core of systematic revolt. But," and he shook off his thought with a guffaw, "those overgrown debating boys with their utter lack of understanding of the present, let along the future, their complete lack of intelligence, let alone any consistency, let even further alone the slightest suggestion of principle, why, they were simply moss on a diseased tree and as easy to get rid of. No healthy life suffers from parasites.

"Maybe I don't know what Life's for or what it's up to. I've always been called a cynical opportunist. Well, all I've done is to wait, take the step that was offered, and then see what would appear when you were there. There's something moving behind it all, I know, and you must somehow keep pace with it, neither standing still nor going too fast, neither thinking you see the goal nor protesting that you can't see an inch ahead. So I keep all mankind at all levels as my scouts—all out at every range enjoying themselves, doing what their age and temper tell them to do. I let the young have their fun and the old their philosophy, the active their adventures and the speculative their theories, the loose their liberties and the devout their devotions—and I wait.

"I have had to work hard and sometimes hastily to set men free from their self-imposed chains and to fight off those who wanted to rivet fresh ones on them. It's damned difficult to hit hard and yet have no animus. But the result is getting steadily better and we are learning all the while, and less and less force is needed—surely that is a sign of success, of Life backing one."

He stopped again and gazed at the fire. He was evidently now talking his mind out at the very limits of his speculation.

"The future," he began again, "the future, what a strange thing—it's there in a way, and in a way we are making it, and in a way it swallows us up in its own unsuspected denouement. What do I foresee? A double answer, I think, like a quadratic equation—and so both may come true. I see a humanity stabilized in a sufficiency of happiness to make a life, that means nothing but that happiness, worth while—and what is that but what used to be called, in the early Sanskrit, 'To go the way of the Fathers'?

"This is not a blind wheel of suffering to those whom it suits. They plunge into the bath of death after the day of life and come up fresh, ready for another day in the light and in the dust, in the field and the forest. There are species that have managed—all up the huge phylum or tree of life—to make their peace with nature by knowing their place and their pace. They have been on the beat, neither behind nor before, for millions of years; some, like the cockroach, for hundreds of millions.

"Man at last might do that. Or he may finish and go elsewhere—as, again, the Sanskrit says, 'Go the way of the Gods.' Or he may split, and one great part of the species specialize at last in a form at last perfectly adapted to this world, perfectly skilled to surmount such waves in the environment as changes of climate and yet perfectly content to ride on forever over the broad tide of time. Then there could be another type which would choose to go on, perhaps not *en bloc* but continually effervescing and volatizing out from the great solid or liquid mass. My geophysicists tell me that the environment, they think, should stay put indefinitely; perhaps, some calculate, it is perfectly balanced on a superthermostatic system and we have only to balance ourselves. Well, I have given happiness to the masses and the opportunity to understand for those who prefer understanding to happiness!"

He stopped, heaved himself up in his chair, half turned, and then chuckled, "My double, how well we have gotten to know each other! You see, we haven't had to get over our differences. Those were smoothed out before we met; and we are also like two identical twins who find themselves washed up on the same lonely island—for we *are* quite alone. I must say I'm more glad of your company than ever I imagined I would be! For, of course, I'm as alone as any man on an island, more so in some ways. It is not good for man to be alone—an ancient quotation, the sense of which

113

I always understood as far as others are concerned but which now I see I must apply to myself. I must not drift away and get stranded and become too exceptional, a kind of stranded whale in the ocean of understanding. My gift, my power, was always to be able to understand the ordinary ranks of men, not one but the whole three, because I had so much of all three in myself. But you are going to fill not only the physical gap and so give me some time off to myself; you are going, I believe, to fill the psychological hollow and give me the company I needed. Didn't I say I always am let invent far more than I know I am inventing and so always, not kill two birds with one stone but get two birds out of one egg? I see how you stimulate my mind and help it to cross-breed on itself.

"When I was going through Napoleon to discover why the second, the political, revolution failed, I found one of the most interesting responses of that small opportunist mind when put up to a proposition—the ordering of Western man—too big for its little activity-fevered grain. He used every now and then to have fireside talks with a number of his body servants, the people right close to him and too intimately small to be thinking of supplanting him. He called it the times when he would 'Ossianize'—take on the romantic phase of the starveling Scot, the pseudo-keltic poet-bard who wrote under the name of Ossian. Then he would try to live up to the intellectual possibilities of the huge opportunity that had been dropped into the lap of a Corsican snob. But always, just when he began to see things on some scale, perspective, and focus that might have defined, out of huge cloudy symbols of a high romance, into a real contemporary picture for Western man, the door was knocked on, we are told, and it was either the tailor come to show him new uniforms or the latest chorus from the opera sent to amuse the animal that dominated that quite large but localized brain."

The listener first smiled to himself. It was clear, all that the queer monster needed was an echo; but as he reflected the humor faded in his mind. There was something coming into the captor's tones that made the captive guest begin to stir uneasily, as when in an easy composition of major chords suddenly is heard a series of minors and even un-resolved discords. He had been carried away with the sheer success story, as Alpha had stormed along. The only thing was to keep on the hat of one's common sense in this blus-tering, boisterous, sunny gale of victory. And then this sud-den turning onto the self with even a suspicion of self-pity —the man who seemed up to that moment to be looking on like a Lucretian god who had suddenly awakened to the fact that, "By gum, the little beggars down there are rather fun and one can make them do all sorts of amusing things." This godlike creature was asking, wasn't he, for sympathy? He remembered a slogan of their old underground training —the man at the top must give but he must never receive, still less ask. But perhaps to that he would be told that it was all pre-psychological, pre-anthropological? But he was puzzled and a little uneasy. In all these days he had now and then felt animal fear and misgiving, but never a hint of the uncanny. Now it stole across to him like an invisi-ble gas through this warm, cheerful room.

He felt he must say something, for the silence seemed to have gone on long and he also had the strange suspicion that Alpha was waiting for him to take up the matter. He tried with a small laugh to make the thing sound light and careless.

"I should have thought," he said with almost a hint of banter in his voice, "that you would have found the oppo-site to be the rather heavy truth, that you would have been overwhelmed with adulation. Nothing succeeds like success, and men and women will worship anyone who has succeeded: when, the moment the magic is gone, they will stamp on him or her just because they are sick with them-selves for having been taken in by themselves."

He paused; that would be enough to try out with. He waited.

Alpha seemed to be thinking over what he said, and his reply was in a quiet, questioning tone.

"There's a double problem there, don't you see? I've done all I could—" and his voice got back some of its old tone of assurance—"in the schools to get language properly taught and to get what used to be called semantics, the reaction between things and words, made clear. But it's slow work, and they who started up that hope put more on it than it seems to bear out. But back to our issue. Yes, you can get, I am sure I have got, remanufactured, that very useful invisible armor, the divinity that hedges a king, and I shall go on, as you'll see, in making that shield more effective. It really would do the world no good at all if I were killed now. Algol—well, of course, would anyone in his senses kill me to make Algol king?" He laughed, a short cough of a laugh. "But one of the underground might succeed in doing the killing and yet assure only such a ridiculous succession. Fancy both of us, the brave little numskull with the quick trigger finger and me the hard-working hub, both being thrown out of the wheel that it might grind along on that police-minded pivot that hasn't a ball bearing or any lubrication in its whole make-up!"

He laughed almost freely for a moment, but then his voice lapsed again: "Yes, I'm getting more sacred at every appearance. I tell you, you'll know, you'll know. It's just like a great white snowball now, growing of itself, every time it turns over on itself. It's all inevitable now—that side of it. I have the graphs of that—the longer even a dictator of the old sort lasted, the safer he was from assassination, provided, of course, that his prestige wasn't punctured; then, as we know, his life wasn't worth a moment's purchase. But the more sacred, the more respected you are, the less you are really appreciated, understood, let be what you are and not lost, like the scrap that the oyster imprisons in the center of its pearl and round which it builds that iridescent tomb."

That very simile, that had been so often in the guest-prisoner's mind, now coming from his host-captor's mouth, gave another queer sense of uncanny kinship, forced friendship, as though some power beyond them both, close but utterly alien, was determined to fuse these two poor little creatures that so longed to be themselves and yet to have something to be liked for in themselves, into one fused, unreflective lump of satisfied action.

"Yes," went on his host, "reverence is the loftiest form of dislike. I know it, for I am exposed to it in ever higher

116

voltages. And in that way it's also true that nothing fails like success. I am being mummified in my own fame before I am dead as a living man. At this rate, I soon shall become nothing but a huge ritualized figure, a great symbol of a myth carried about as the people's Luck and Totem, and not another idea will come out of me and not another breeze of enjoyment fan or reach me in my immense sarcophagus—the box that eats the flesh, that's what that stately word means—and I know, as a living corpse being consumed by its stately, fragrant preservatives.

"Oh, yes, I shall be safe from destruction because safe from life. I shall be free to do as I please because I shall be paralyzed by the process and incapable of any thought, any wish to do anything else and but to obey the immense momenta I have set in motion—or have I? The same genius that talked about the divinity that hedges kings made his chief character, the prince who was frustrated by seeing too far, go further and speak of that other, darker, vaster divinity that shapes our ends, rough hew them as we will. Perhaps we can never get out of the smooth maelstrom of our own success which sucks us down."

He stopped, his voice having sunk to a monotone. The guest roused himself. Well, anyhow, this was another side, a further aspect. He must at least study it, draw out this strange further extension of this fabulous character.

"But, surely," he quested, "granted that Algol and the trusties are hardly those one would choose for fireside talking—"

He paused, and his odd double gave him the sentence his own inner censorship was hesitating to pass for publication. "And granted," said the voice he now used coming out of the original Alpha throat, "granted that I treat you as something less in the picture of actuality than did the Southern women who used to undress before their Negro slaves because they considered them not human, hardly alive, mere parts of the furniture, that you can be my sounding board and amplifier—?"

Yes, it was his thought, and as Alpha One knew it, why should Alpha Two mind saying it?

"Yes," he said, "I think that is an objective description."

And as the other didn't affirm or deny, he went on, "Surely there must be someone you meet in your life who might be a help and not a rival? Most men have a confidential secretary? Someone who is content to admire, support, and be at hand at off times?"

"Did you suppose I hadn't? Certainly I have my confidential private secretary and certainly it seemed that after a number of changes I should be able to pick the person who could play that pretty standard part. And in a way," he paused, "in a way, as usual, I have succeeded, as I always do, far beyond what could be expected—and, as now seems increasingly probable, it has been the very completeness of the success that has made the situation a failure. A woman must be cast for that part, for only a woman can be as really technically clever and orderly and clear-minded and as intuitive and perfectly supplemental as the part needs; and, though you might, in a certain type of man, get someone who had both those gifts, you could not get the third requirement. That's the power with whole hearted energy to subordinate the self to the person served. A man who could so subordinate is a fool; a man clever enough for the intellectual strain of the job is ambitious and so disloyal at heart. Well, all that's mere formula—it's the kind of thing you'll find written up in any of the preliminary studies in employment-agency work so as to guide tyros in the job of classifying jobs and applicants. And I didn't give enough thought to developing it further."

He sighed, "Always there are unfinished pieces and fringes in one's circle of thought, and, this being so close to me, as I was long-sighted on vast plans, I neglected. I thought I had the person. Such persons can't be extemporized; you have to find the raw material and then cut it into shape." He was so engrossed in his own problem that he didn't notice his listener's wince. "It took me years to train the one that finally seemed the best, and all the time we were right in the muddle of getting into the saddle. It had to be a very unforeseen, piecemeal piece of training. But, as far as I could give time to judge, all was going well. She is a wonderful machine. Of course, she's efficient to an

118

amazing degree—has the kind of subconscious that never creates anything and so, as none of its memories are digested or assimilated, they all come out as fresh, hard, clear as they went in; and, as she takes everything from me, naturally her mind is my subsidiary brain, my memory. But she has also the other mediumistic gift or trick. She is amazingly able to complete, and never to distort with a shadow of creativeness or her own originality, what I am going to say or even am going to think. It is never what she thinks, it is simply the thought I have latent, and I have no more to trouble to get it into words. She's thus not merely my memory but in a way my vocabulary and my imagery. And naturally I gave as little attention to her as one gives to one's digestion or lungs when they are working in complete health and with perfect circulation.

"You see, it is symbiosis again, the principle of all higher efficiency; she is merely an essential extension or annex of my brain, to let me get on to more creative work. I can tell her in a couple of sentences what I want for the speech or a memorandum for a line of research to be opened and, when I come back, there is the whole thing with references and developments, but no departures, and not only in perfect order but perfectly elucidated and expanded and made into whatever number of subsections as may be needed for the various ranks of people who must listen to it or apply it. She is my hand and quite a part of my brain and, I thought naturally, that is enough for anyone." He paused.

"But you see the end of the course. Now she wants to be my heart. I should have known from the studies in animal psychology we have used so much: the apparent lowliness of the one partner at any time of the mating-duel is only strategy; and all the more deliberate if unconscious. She does not know that she wished to dominate, and the poor little scrap of personality, which no doubt is quite happy lost in mine, is quite ignorant of the wile it is performing. But the life in her cannot leave alone its ancient game. I knew *that* when I planned for women to be given even more distraction than men in the new world—children and clothes and shows and lovers: yes, be a great actress and novelist,

119

research a bit, explore, become a saint. It is not that a woman shouldn't be serious. It is that she can never be anything too long. Her current fluctuates even more than man's—as far as either of them are individuals—while her substream and undertow draws steadily, remorselessly, to its distant goal; while, beside that, man is a little ephemera who spins webs that the night will break with the weight of its dew. The mother goddess, Kali, is the destroyer. Durga, her other form, dances on the body of her prostrate mate though he is the terrible Shiva himself."

He stopped again. His guest was now on edge. Alpha's voice, however, when he went on had become matter-of-fact.

"Of course, that kind of thing was out of the question. Leaving everything else aside, do you suppose that a man who works as I work has any time for dalliance? My rest is just another kind of work. That's nature's way; metabolism actually increases in the body for the first three hours of sleep. Sleep is just an alternative way of acting—the indraw for the output. If you work with the brain constantly it draws on all else. That's why I have ruled that the one safe and right and balanced place for sex is among my routineers—the dear, healthy visceroes—who, as you know, like their lust, but their real delight is not bed but dinner; bed is the rightful overplus from dinner. Hence in them sex does not get out of hand.

"Well, I've told you I hadn't had time to get round to proper investigations into sex, more's the pity. I suppose, like most men who are work-sublimated, I didn't think it mattered quite as much as it does and that the viscero dinner-bed balance would hold the base of society healthy and childbearing while the athletic samurai-somatoes would get their sublimation in the athletic askesis of exercise and physical risk. Certainly men like myself know enough of endocrinology to know the whole of the ductless-gland system is linked up and that if you are a pituitary-thyroid coupling then all the lower coupling, suprarenal-interstitial, must be drawn on and made simply a feeder system for the upper linkage.

"Well, that's an important issue. The world is based on those who have the 'tamasic' lethargy-lust level just kept roused into cyclic activity by the 'rajasic' energy-anger drive. This drive comes down from adrenocortin. It pours into the blood-stream and, as it were, seethes and boils with the secretions from the gonads. The world of this simple reacting mass is kept whipped in and moving up by the steady-pressure thyroid with its linked thought-ally, the pituitary hormones, giving point to mere endurance. I wish we'd done more work on that; we must; we must know what the pineal is doing up there. Is it waiting to take over as the pituitary took over? But if that is so, then, as this prophecy of man seems foretold *in petto* (as his past is written in shorthand recapitulation in the foetus growth), then above the type that Sheldon so long ago foresaw and I have fulfilled, there must be still another to come?"

In the interest of his speculation the curious creature had clearly forgotten all his private problem, his mind reaching out to this huge social issue. He recognized it and laughed.

"You see how unsuited I am for the part of the secret romance? Why, right in the middle, I'd be gone another five centuries down the future. Woman is always *here*, because she has in her still so much of the animal instantaneity, which is the eternity of the unthinking creature-life. But what are we to do with women? Will they disappear, as the social insects have made that kind of sex disappear, and become mere worker types? Am I doing wrong in trying to get rid of tumors and cancers, so much more common in females, when they may be Nature's hint that here she is offering a way out for the elimination of a type that has outstayed its usefulness?"

Again his mind was carried away by its stream of speculation. At last he yawned.

"Oh, I'm tired, and you see it is just then that one wants some kind of middle rest—between the skilled repair energy of sleep and the activity of waking. Why can't a woman balance on that moment, on those spaces, and give us rest instead of the fever of demand? Why can't the devouring life in her for a moment forget the future? I said, they live in the present; yes, with their surface minds, but the deep animal mind in them, as still and quiet-looking but tense as a stalking cat, is always looking ahead to its spring and its grip of possession. Well, there it is. There is no companionship for me there. She adores and I have to stand it and keep her busy and try to keep her waiting, but she is a strain, not a rest. And sometimes I think I must have rest." He yawned again.

"Sleeping is no problem, now we understand it. But it is in that wonderful, useful, strange, and dangerous borderland between the two states that could be the growing edge of a new restful creativity where we must go open-minded, unguarded, that reason can be assaulted, caught, starved to death. I have used it well, but it's like a piece of overcropped land. Why can't I have a companion who—as in the fairy story an Egeria who meets me, King Numa, only in the sacred grove—just meets me there and nowhere else —when we are outside the body that craves, yes, and outside the mind that contrives, and are—what? Can it be that we are threefold and there is spirit then that rises like Phosphor, the morning star, brighter than all the stars but only to be seen between night and morning or morning and night? Well, I'm growing poetical, and we must both go to the work of sleep. Good night!"

The guest withdrew. But it was long before he slept, and he wondered if in the other bedroom in the apartment sleep was any better.

V

ALPHA'S ALTAR

THE NEXT DAY, however, all these curiously private speculations were rushed from his mind. He was still at his breakfast when the door behind him opened and he found his trainer-in-carriage standing by him. "You are to have a rehearsal at once," and he was led to the door and into the robing room. There, to his surprise, he found Alpha himself, who motioned the trainer to leave, told him to sit down, and walked up to one of the big wardrobes whose doors paneled the walls of the room. He threw back one of these sliding leaves. Inside was a robe of the silvery white he had worn before when being trained; but it was longer, coming to the feet.

While he took it out, Alpha said over his shoulder, "Slip off your tunic," and then, turning round, he came toward him and put the robe over his head, helped him until he stood with it falling to his instep. The full sleeves came just over the backs of his hands. The stuff felt heavy and cold—an unfamiliar touch, and the question it roused in him Alpha answered as he looked at the hang of it.

"This material is of course not woven for anyone else. It feels queer, for it is spun from a kind of quartz fiber. It is commonplace enough to look at under ordinary light. Now, however, come here."

He pointed to a spot in the floor about six feet away from a kind of apse that broke the otherwise wainscoted wall. This apse had a cornice that edged its semi-dome and at floor level a beading that also followed its same curve. The rest of the semi-circular wall was a series of long mirrors from the cornice-architrave down to the beading at floor

123

level. He saw himself standing in this sort of old-fashioned nightgown and thought the whole thing was certainly rather a poor piece of unimaginative dressing up. Then a switch clicked. For a moment he had a shock of alarm. He thought he must be on fire. The figure that he saw in the mirrors was first glowing and then almost blazing.

Alpha's voice behind him remarked, "The light given out by the strips in the beading and the cornice is not visible to the human eye but it fluoresces tremendously, you see, when it hits this texture." The switch again clicked and he saw his figure sink down to a glow till he was once more simply a man in a white nightgown. "Now you have seen how you can be transfigured, I'll put the crowning touch on you."

Alpha came back into the reflection of the mirrors and the substitute saw that he was carrying in his hand a miter. It was a white, egg-shaped cone ending in a finial of cut facets. He placed this towering object on his substitute's head. The switch clicked again, and now the whole lofty figure blazed with light from crown to hem.

"We have come back, by our research into empathy and ritual symbols," said the voice behind him, "to this basic pattern. That diadem was worn by the first kings of the first kingdom of which we know—the kingdom of that middle Egypt from which came finally the lower Egypt and the upper. That tiara is the original papal crown, for, once again, a priest-king found himself repeating the ancient pattern, the unchanging tradition. For this is the papal crown as it was worn when the papacy was at its height under Innocent the Third, and before the pretensions of the tiara that followed it, with triple crowns and all that moss of pretense, showed that boasting had taken the place of fact. Now, take your staff of office," and into his hand was put a rod about five feet tall with a tip which also fluoresced in the same dazzling way. The switch snapped again and Alpha was helping him off with headdress and robe.

"The whole thing has been already timed over, and tomorrow you have to take part in one of the procedures in which that is the central uniform. Now I will explain to you your duties. The entire office has been worked out with psychological precision, so you can't go wrong. You will be fetched early, so your breakfast will be served you at 5:30. You will be robed here. From the moment that you take that rod, those who surround you will not turn their backs to you. They will accompany you all through the day, and all you have to do is to follow till you are ushered to where you will see your concealed conductor. That is all you need to do. Now you can go to your room. I have work to do."

Alpha disappeared through another door, and his captive went back through the door by which he had been brought in, to his own room. He spent the day playing at some new games of solitaire, the cards for which and a book explaining these new patterns he had found in a drawer of the table on which his cigarettes were placed. Then he would pause and try to put together the two last interviews with Alpha. But always he came back to dealing and reshuffling and plotting out the cards. The impressions in his mind were too alien, not only to his own sense of sense but to each other, to make any pattern. He found the games curiously soothing. After the light had blinked over the hatch and he had lunched—a lunch which he noticed was rather more sumptuous than usual—he lay down for a little and found that he had slept till four. At 4:15 the hatch light again gleamed, and it was tea. He smoked from tea till six, for these cigarettes didn't foul the tongue any more than rasp the throat—indeed, they were more a tonic to larynx and palate. At six the hatch light told him that dinner was to be early. He took it out, ate it with relish, thought again it was a large meal, and, after another couple of cigarettes, went to bed.

He woke before five and got up leisurely, feeling well rested, ate his breakfast—which again was a large meal—with relish, and waited, with a certain simmer of excitement. The door opened, and he looked round expecting to find his Dresser, as he now called this deportment and costume trainer. But instead there was a stranger in the door, a stranger in a white overall.

"I have to see you for just a moment and then your

125

dresser"—yes, he used the very word—"will take over. Please roll up your sleeve. This is merely one of our combinations of relaxants and stimulants which will carry you through the day, considering the heightened amino-acid diet we have had you on the last twelve hours. Indeed, something like this is taken by," he paused, "by the principal figure, nearly always now."

The guest captive put out his arm, rolling up his sleeve. Well, if he was to be taken with music and with solemn pomp of flowers to sacrifice, robed and crowned, he might as well go doped. For mightn't Alpha really be repeating a pattern, the oldest of all the kingly patterns, where the creature that has been fed up and worshiped is then robed and sacrificed as the people's totem? Who knows but that in his queer researches in this fantastic anthropological revolution he had not found out this revival of the ancient Sed festival was most satisfying to his vast people? Would it not be what evidently this queer mind was always aiming at—the bringing up to date the primal thing, the psychological force which had hung on as an archeological curiosity, e.g., the Passion Play, and making it real, contemporary, significant, working? They had been told about such things when he went to the university. He had been put into the anthropological classes when they saw his was the inquiring mind of the cerebrotoes who have to be told part of the truth. He had wondered at the time, when his teacher had expatiated on vicarious suffering, and the group-offering found in one man, that, though it had ended in the usual eulogy of Alpha, then just climbed to power, whether the story couldn't have another end. Then he had read on to the rather sinister end, when it was found that the king, who had to be renewed by death, could, and did, get a substitute who died for him.

These thoughts came with signal force on him now—he felt this must be the end. He was therefore all the more impressed by the strength of the injection when he noticed how this black, dense cloud of misgiving which was well over the horizon of his mind, and surely had evidence enough to give rise to it, was driven to dissolve and left his consciousness clean of anything but a sense of tense adventure.

He still thought that this must pretty certainly be the end. But he was full of interest to see the denouement, even if as it broke he must vanish.

The doctor looked at him closely, rubbed the small injection spot on his arm, and grunted slightly to himself. Then he stood aside, and in the door was the dresser.

The remodeled man felt himself striding along with a growing excitement, which, however, had in it no ebullience. He felt cool as a spectator at a show which interests him as a piece of presentation in which he will see a fine exhibition of new skills. There was no fever of excitement in him anywhere. He let himself be robed and crowned, and took the scepter. The invisible lights flashed, and his figure blazed from head to foot. The switch clicked again and the nimbus began to shrink.

He turned round, and he was surrounded. The figures that must have come up behind him had been shrouded from him by his own light. Six men in long ephods or albs stood in a semicircle round him. And as he faced them once again he found his robes beginning to blaze. They did not raise their eyes to him but kept their gaze on the tip of the rod which he held, its butt on the ground and his hand about six inches under its shining crest. In his ear he heard his dresser's voice say, "Now forward." He stepped ahead and, stepping backward but keeping their formation perfectly, the six attendants went down the room. The circle contracted a little in the passage but still kept its formation, and in the elevator they hived round him in the same bee formation as when the workers are near the queen. So in this way they led him out of the elevator, and there another six closed in behind him. He was now circled and could not help wondering where the final close-in would take place.

A dozen steps, which he took as he moved to keep in the center of the ring and prevent it from closing him in, found him—after what had seemed a lifetime—back again in the open, air, evidently in that court whence he had been carried into this building what eons ago. But though it was daylight he noticed that his garments and, he guessed, his infulae and crown still lustered with this dazzling light, as though he were a mirror in full sunlight. Looking over the slightly bent heads that surrounded him and in the direction that the circle moved, he saw a float—the kind of thing that the huge Passion-tide processionals used to bear through the Spanish cities, It was evidently mounted on a powerful chassis and motor, for it was a series of tiers to a central plinth. The circle, seeing now that he grasped the direction, moved more quickly, but still keeping its inturned-face formation.

So he found himself brought to the front of the float and ushered up its steps to the central plinth. When he reached that, his escort ranged itself round him, seated looking at him and, the moment this formation was taken up, the car began to move. He found there was a socket in which his staff could stand so that, while he held it, it gave him support, and, for his left hand, there was a small pedestal surmounted by a globe on which he could rest his palm. The car by now had gained speed and was moving across the main court of the great central palace.

As they approached the great outer gates that enclosed this super-Kremlin they swung back and he saw down the processional way that led up to the citadel. It was crowded on either side by masses of people, all the faces turned toward the gates and, as these opened, through them came the first roar of applause. The car ran smoothly out. He realized that he was meant to make no sign, but his stillness in no wise seemed to check the crowd's enthusiasm. They were traveling some twenty miles an hour, he guessed. But as soon as they had passed through the central part of the city the pace was increased and a screen of glass rose to protect him from the wind. Now, too, there were no crowds in front—the city's outlying districts were as deserted as the central part had been dense. In the glass, however, he could see that there had formed behind his car a vast volume of people; apparently the people who had greeted his start had fallen in behind in linked series of long cars and were making a train of which he was the head. After a half hour's run—for once clear of the city, which, like all the planned cities of that day, when it stopped, stopped cleanly—they went at high speed and soon they saw the country sloping before them to the sea.

He now vaguely remembered hearing (when he had become deep in the underground and so was seldom on the surface) that Alpha had changed much of the nature of the imperial rallies with which the regime had begun and had gone on to inventions in social rituals beside which the efforts of old Moscow and vanished Nuremberg were child's play. In his rehearsals he had had glimpses of the performances. He guessed that he must be about to be led to the new great site laid out for these methods of group-soldering. And certainly the place had been planned remarkably. He remembered once on a high-school trip he had been taken on flying visit to Monte Alban in southern Mexico to be shown the vast layout there. You emerged on a noble landscape and then, as you gazed, you realized that, as far as the eye could see, the natural features of plain, valley, hill had been shaped into a single group of ritual stations and sacred courts. The small hills had been pyramided, the roll of the slopes terraced, the plains smoothed, shaped, and aligned. The teacher in anthropological archeology had pointed out how this achievement—like Cheops' initial effort in Egypt or those at Carnac in Brittany, Dowth in Ireland, and Avebury and Stonehenge in western England —was, of course, not a mere exhibition of aimless energy in building, but the precipitated pattern round which the loom on which the invisible garment and web of consent was woven by the people. Yes, all the education had been aimed to let Alpha make this attempt today. What fools they had been, not to see that if he captured the educated and set each to illustrate his thesis from their specific study, if he flattered them by making their study to have sense and proof and value in his dream, they would support him! He saw now that the educated, more than anyone, were weary of teaching subjects of which they had to tell their pupils, in the end, that they meant nothing and led nowhere.

Yes, they must be coming into the district which had been laid out for this purpose, and, as they crested a slight rise and saw in the distance the sea, he saw that the whole littoral had been taken over and worked into a scheme beside which even the countryside layout of Monte Alban was midget. The landscape sloped down to where the sea made a long shallow inlet. On each side of this natural canal were two low ranges of slopes that ran down parallel till they ended on the shore. The processional road he was on headed straight for the headwater of the inlet. Between him now and this land end of the estuary he saw rising a white cone-shaped pyramid. As he drew nearer he realized that the hill slopes on either side of the estuary had been terraced their whole length, which must have been several miles. They were turned into the flanks of a stadium, and the estuary itself had been embanked, so that a broad paved border of level ran at the foot of each of the slopes. The whole of this area, many square miles in space, had been cased in some smooth, bright pavement so that the place was an auditorium where certainly millions could be seated on the innumerable tiers. Along the whole top range of these great ramps ran a giant fence or palisade of pillars clustering in groups as every quarter of a mile they rose into great shafts big as the old factory smoke-stacks, and then, in between, sweeping down in a curve to fluted slender columns which were no more than the uprights of a terminal grille. Just before his car drew up at the pyramid that ended the processional way he was near enough to the inland end of this landscape stadium to see that already the whole surface was alive with myriads of people.

His car stopped at the entrance to the pyramid and the lines of linked cars, which had been following with the greater part of the capital's population, swept round in an eddying flow and began to deliver their freight along the banks, rows, and ranks of the tiered hillsides. As soon as his car stopped, his entourage, who had never taken their eyes off his rod, rose, and he, keeping at their center, passed up a ramp which he saw would lead him to the summit of the cone. As the slope increased, the circle round him parted in front, then, from a semi-circle, became a train, and, when he emerged on the crest and brink of the tower, they were ranged on steps below him. He was standing out rather like the Nike of Samothrace, launched

130

on a bracket, eagle-like from an eyrie that overlooked the long, densely populated plain down to the sea.

But immediately, through the narrow footplate on which he stood, he could see down into the hollow of the slender pyramid of which now he was the finial, on which he was placed like a tableau vivant of that Carian king who gave his name to all Mausoleums. In the body of the cone on which he stood he could see down below a man seated at a console. As he was being mounted onto this strange altar, his eyes had been too distracted and he had been too busy with finding his place to listen to much. All his orders had been wonderfully given him by hints of movement. But now, as he came to rest and it was obvious that he had gone as far as he could and must wait his next cue, his ear began to tell him that for some time there had been through the air something besides the hum of this huge population finding its places. There was rising through it with increasing volume, pulsations of sound; yes, profoundly deep chords, right down at the very floor of hearing, moving in the very foundations of audible sound. And now they were rising and beginning, like the shapes of whales seen swimming up toward the surface, to loom and take outline.

His ear listened idly and his eye as idly watched the man in the vault immediately beneath him. And then in a moment eye and ear came together in understanding. The eye saw the man at the console make a sudden movement, and a series of stops, it was clear, swept out on each side of his organ, and at the moment the deep, vague, all-pervasive sounds swelled and roared into overwhelming harmonies. The whole place was asurge with the thunder of a giant fugue. The murmuring waves of sound made by this population settling in were swamped under this flooding tide of music. He looked round to find whence this volume could be pouring. Then he realized that not only were these lines of hills made into a giant stadium, they were also laid out as a monster organ, and those lines of pillars that rose and fell upon the uppermost ridge on each side were the pipes of this instrument, some of which must have been a hundred and fifty feet in height. The fugue marched along

131

to its noble close and by that time—so good was the distribution—the population was ranged. The music swept its final chords and there was a silence.

The figure set on this carved crag realized that perhaps a couple of million eyes were turned on him, waiting. He glanced down and saw that, behind the organist, another figure had appeared—some sort of conductor. He held a rod like the one which the remodeled man now held grounded. The conductor, who had grounded his also, suddenly lifted it and stretched it out. The man aloft realized his cue and raised his. Immediately he could see, by a change in the texture of the landscape down which he looked, that as when wind goes over a wheatfield, the population must have risen and bowed. The conductor's baton began to beat; the white figure in its glittering robes—for he understood now that this podium was surrounded with the activating invisible-light strips—waved his rod, and, as when Moses smote the rock, from these long slopes and artificial cliffs and plains broke out an anthem. The organ roared along its miles of stops louder than the sea, had it been breaking in storm instead of lying under a hazy sun, and the million human voices, sustained and ordered by this volume of sound, rose like a gale above a thunder of waves. When the chorale sank—a simple but splendidly harmonized tune —there was again a giant hush, so that at last you could hear far away the faint murmur of the ocean on the beach.

After the stillness had lasted perhaps a couple of minutes the mounted man heard a whisper. Round the edge of the carved curb of the outthrust ledge on which he stood he had noticed orifices and guessed they must be microphone mouths. But out of one of these now a whisper was coming.

It said, "Repeat after me each word as I speak it."

There was a pause, and the same whisper began, "Once more my voice reaches to every one of you, sounds actually in your individual ear."

He repeated the words aloud in his full but unstrained voice—the voice of Alpha which was now his—and he could hear echoing back to him a thunderous tone that rang from end to end of the stadium.

"As the poet of Liberty—the Liberty he prophesied and

132

we have fulfilled—as Schiller said, 'Oh, millions of mankind, I embrace you.' As he hoped, so it is today. Let us give thanks."

No more words came for a moment. Instead, he heard from below and out to the sea a long cry of "Praise, praise!" When these reactions had been let die down, the speech went on, he repeating as publisher each short sentence. What was said was a simple eulogy of what had been done: the happiness, the fulfillment, the discovery that all mankind could find itself and its place, its peace and its purpose in this, the final birth of understanding, after the travail and birthpangs of the age of revolutions. There was to be a future, but one of evolution, no longer of revolution. The world had found a place for, Life had devised a process for, both those who would enjoy and those who would explore. Then there was a self-reference, to the servant that acts as the humble archetype and, as it were, holds back the curtain of the present in order that they, mankind, might sweep through into the future, the lonely figure which, on its Pisgah pinnacle, having led the people through the desert, now may look over into the Promised Land while they should march on into it.

The crowd roared back to this noble pathos, and in their cry he could detect, he thought, something like tears. Certainly their emotion was being raised skillfully. But not precipitately. For after another pause the organ swelled again, and in four huge strophes these choruses chanted their explication of history. The first sang of the tragic effort of the religious revolution dying down into the pathos of a hope defeated. Then another quarter spoke, and the story of the political revolution was recited, its state of effervescent belief in liberty, its desperate outbreak, its collapse back from its fiery lava flood to the cold hard stone of nationalistic imperialism. A third area broke into a rhythmic chant of the economic hope that should girdle the world with workers who had found plenty, security, and brotherhood, and, once again, as the music swept into minors, the tragedy of fresh conflict, deadlocked struggle, and despair. And then the whole of the stadia took up the epilogue —the triumph of understanding; of man at last understand-

133

ing himself, his fellow, and nature; of the riddle of the dark Sphinx, who is both mother and monster, at last solved; of man understanding his unity in his harmony of differences, his liberty in variety of function and outlet, of the soul, having come back to itself, and, finding itself and its happiness in itself, finding at last its abiding peace.

The music sank down in flights of descants and descending sound. The singers were brought back to earth; their catharsis had been begun. They were to be rested between treatments. The organ poured on with its voluntary.

The mounted man was able for a moment to think once more about himself. He glanced cautiously round, taking care not to move. He began to wonder why it was that in between him and the view—whenever he turned—seemed to be an iridescent milky film, rather like the blanched iris on the tail feather of a white peacock. It extended all round and above. Then he noticed the shape of this capsule of faint light, this aurora that evidently crowned the apex on which he stood. He was at the center of a giant nimbus, and then he understood why. The nimbus, he could now gauge, was a vast extension, a luminous projection-shadow of himself. To test his discovery he moved his wand a little, glancing up to the sky on his right. Sure enough, there the nimbus extension moved out a little. Of course, he should have realized it before—this was the invention used in all the movies now: the extension of the actor-image so that it seemed three-dimensional, a wonderful development of the old "Pepper's Ghost" theatrical-stage illusion of one hundred and fifty years ago. His image was projected on a field round him and, like a luminous Brocken specter, shone as a giant of some hundred feet high, visible to people half a dozen miles away as his voice was audible.

Yes, he thought, the problem of bring the man to the millions has been solved. We may not be able to embrace them and mayn't wish to, but we do wish to impress them directly, personally, and we do: each feels that he has been in direct contact with the master servant, *servus servorum*, and each feels a personal devotion to the one man who had put him free and let him do as he likes. He turned from his satisfied investigation of his own figure and looked

134

through the slightly milky mist down the immense files and aisles of this open-air theater-temple. The people were resting, talking, and relaxing.

Then his sight was turned back to his mentor by a flash of light striking up to him from below. He saw the baton rise and raised his; the voice began to dictate in small tones what he translated into thunder. The people now would take part in their ritual meal of community. He was to extend both arms downward. He did so, and as the rod pointed to the earth, out from each side of the pyramid cone which he crowned there flowed a stream of service belts, and on them in inexhaustible supply the food for these multitudes. He was actually presiding over this banquet of millions and distributing them their daily bread. After the first of these delivery lines had begun to extend about halfway down to the shore, the prompting voice whispered, "And now drink and be satisfied, the rock has indeed given forth water of life." He spoke and he could see in the tiers nearest him fountains of colored beverages begin to pour out into basins by each row. People dipped their cups and drank, raising them first to him as a libation.

After their meal, ranks of them came down onto the broad level runways at each side of the inlet and there were choric dances, races, and athletic contests. There were swimming and diving competitions in the estuary, and the various teams and towns of the empire that had sent their delegates competed. Only during this time did a small stool rise behind him, and he was told that for an hour he might preside sitting, not standing. Then, as the afternoon wore on, he was on his feet once more. The champions and winners were being escorted by their singing supporters up to the ramp from which the tower rose. They knelt at the foot. To his hand, from a small delivery band coming up from the tower's center, came a number of wreaths—silver, gold, emerald, ruby, sapphire. He took those, and they slid down from his hands through culverts to where the victors were bowed. Officials standing at the base put the wreaths on the victors' heads, and, singing, their companions led them back to their places.

The sun was now far in the west. Once more the people

were ranged, and once more he spoke to them. The words were of the most obvious but evidently they had been chosen for their psychological, subconscious effect. Given at that pace, with that rhythm, and, at the end, as a kind of recitative with the organ coming in, in chords, between, and giving a background of profound sound all the while, it was clear that the audience was in a hypnotic condition of attention and unification. He could see that their attention was focused on the bright spot the nucleus of which was himself, or rather, his shining garments and his synthetic voice. The whole of the landscape was a white stipple of dots, and each dot was a human face set on this vast epitome, and generalization, of itself.

The final scene of the day-long ritual-act was come—the final words were to be said. Following his conductor, he began to chant and, antiphonally, the audience in the gathering dusk, while his figure burned ever brighter as a beacon of their concentration, sang back. Finally the chorus swelled to a climax and as suddenly the whole volume of sound rose to the sky and was lost. Obeying his conductor, he had raised his arms. He was blessing the millions and dismissing them. He knew that they had fallen on their knees and he, bewildered, raised his eyes to the first star that was appearing in the blue.

Another star appeared and another. They grew rapidly brighter and larger. He saw that the sky was being filled with artificial stars, giant planets. It was a vast fleet of helicopters gently descending, the whisper of their vanes giving a soothing overtone to the silence in which the crowd was bent. As they came closer, ten thousand searchlights of every hue shot up to meet them and bathe these shining hulls in light while they shot down answering beams. Finally the quiet water of the estuary gleaming under this Danae downpour suddenly became fecund and broke. Fountains began to swell and rise, until domes of flashing water fifty and sixty feet high, lit by submarine lighting, and all the water itself made of various phosphorescent incandescences, that shone ever more brightly the more they were agitated, foamed like a long lake of light and lambency. The giant canal was become a great band of burnished gold in which flashed those bosses of living opal. The sea seemed alive, and the long alabastrine rows of the gigantic stadium also glowed with a mild fluorescent flush of inner light.

As he gazed he saw that this steady downflood of light and uprush of illumination had, like waterspout and cloudburst, blended. The lines of illumination subtended: those ascending with those descending forming a vast triangle whose apex was against the stars. The hovering planes had taken up position so that there was first this immense straight-sided arch spanning the giant stadium. Then, from halfway down each of the inleaning shafts of light, drove out a line of glowing squadrons, met and took up their stations. A luminous "A" that linked earth and heaven had been made. This fabulous symbol of light was reared so that, as he looked down, the stadium had become the floor, and there, reared in flame, was a cathedral under whose vault were the representative millions of all mankind. This sheer peak of light, a hollow mountain whose sides were smooth, precipitous slopes of illumination, must have had its apex ten thousand feet above the earth.

He gazed spellbound. How dark had been their mole-like ways that they had not been told of such a prodigious invention! How could the masses hold up against such a battery barrage of suggestion, every sense bombarded and overwhelmed?

He was still gazing, lightstruck, when his eye was deflected by a green flash in the small porthole at his feet through which he had been able to view the conductor. Yes, he was being summoned. The conductor was looking up at him and had taken his long baton in hand. The man below did not beat time with it. He simply spread wide his feet and then, letting his arms follow the line of his legs and putting his hands out so that they pointed down and out in the same line, he held his long baton so between his open hands, held in position parallel with the ground simply by his thumbs. The remodeled man saw that he was meant to take up this posture. Taking his wand between his thumbs and palms, he stood in this position of an offering celebrant, offering his rod of power and himself in the service of mankind—that must be the meaning of the symbol.

But how in the great tent of light that overtowered him would the people be able to see this tiny creature offered up on the high altar of the highest temple ever reared in the whole history of the world? As he gazed up, however, he began to note that the milky, iridescent cone of light in which he saw himself enveloped, and which he had realized projected his image to a vast size, was now growing. Every moment the luminous Brocken figure, of which he was the tiny microscopic heart, the homunculus-nucleus, grew and towered. Finally he saw that it had reached up to the great cross-beam of the Alpha figure made by the planes and their lights. As the light-shadow of his gigantized head touched this ceiling, the spanning rung was withdrawn. His light-magnified figure, he could now see, towered up halfway to that apex which arched so loftily the giant nave made by the stadium. As he stood, with the rod held athwart his body by his down-slanted arms and hands, he saw he was not so much an offering as an intermediary: he had become the giant Alpha itself.

Standing thus, he heard a strange murmur coming up from underneath—a strange sound such as he never before had heard human beings emit. It was certainly not applause—the time was past for the grateful recognition and acknowledgment that the show had been fine, the production superb, the entertainment royal, the day a lovely success and worthy of the approval of a people who had the highest standard of what a show should be. The sound conveyed (from human beings to another human being standing solitary in this heart of light) directly the knowledge that the human spirit had been mastered, overwhelmed, that show and symbol and critical appreciation of detail, acknowledgment of skill and finish and ensemble, had all gone, beaten flat under a tide of impression. The short-circuit had taken place. They were no longer looking, listening, blending impressions, appreciating. They were stunned; and yet in that cry it was not a concussion that those creatures, smitten into one, were feeling. It was, on the contrary, a release. Surely they were stunned out of any defense of understanding, any power of reply. But they were raised, and that cry was one of desire, of yearning for what they could not know.

Here was the true and terrible catharsis which is ecstasy, which, not for thousands of years, had man felt and known, when, meeting in an agonia, a contest of creative, parturitional pain, the deep forces of the earth, of Pan the father of Panic, meet the divine sky forces of a wonder which is unbearable in the promise it offers because it must be beyond fulfillment—so long as the creature clings to its separateness. These masses had been not only fused, they were being raised above themselves, standing high above themselves, and had left their small separate bodies kneeling on the ground. That cry was a vast expiration in which they offered themselves utterly to something beyond any power of theirs to define.

As he looked and listened, caught in the same uprush of the psychic atmosphere, he heard the small prompting voice beginning to recite. And now without any hesitation, still less criticism, but as a hypnotized patient, he cried with the full volume of the Alpha voice, which a hundred thousand amplifications made a veritable voice of thunder that rolled along the vast arch of light and re-echoed off the floor of waters:

"I am Alpha, no person but a principle, the principle of perpetual beginning, the promise of unknown evolution and development. My head and summit is in heaven, my feet, firm-set, wide-spanning, gauge the earth and sea from east to west: from north to south I compass mankind and all its lands, and radiate down overseership and light. I am the initial and eternal Atlas sustaining earth from heaven, yet, as Prometheus Unbound, linking the height with the depth, apex with level. And, in between, I have made a mighty bridge with the rod of my power to carry in ever increasing volume all the lawful traffics of mankind and every joyful excursion of humanity. I am the stairway to the stars and the link of the earth's ends."

The voice stopped, and he waited, as much a tranced spectator as any one of them. What had spoken through him, what inhuman air had passed by, using him as a small

139

reed in the giant tuba through which it sounded? He felt dazed and waited, hardly caring what came next. But when the voice whispered from below, "Step back one pace," he obeyed, though it might mean that he was to fall headlong. He felt the ground, on which his backward step had put him, quiver. Then he thought, with something more passive than content, This is the end, the final detachment of the instrument or the reed from the word. But, instead of falling, he was raised. He had been made to step on the prow of a helicopter, which, while the Alpha speech roared from him, like a tide through a turbine, had come up behind the plinth, and, the moment he ceased speaking and his light-projection was shrunken, had come in to take him off.

But he was not yet to be released from this intolerable pressure of the focus of a million incomprehensible desires. No, the plane rose until his small shining figure was at the very apex of the giant arch of light. Then the whole giant "A" moved out across the plain, and, as it swept slowly away, the supporting aligned batteries of searchlights from the two long ramps of the stadium followed the vast angle and then died like the glow on a mountain from which the last rays of the sun have been withdrawn. Underneath, the crossbar, linking the two slanting columns, had been re-formed by a moving rank of lit helicopters. The "A" that arched the earth moved on to the capital. So it rode, a compass of light, spanning miles of countryside, its moving image visible from scores of miles away. Finally it covered the whole capital in its bestriding, and he, the apex light, was shining right over the palace itself. There the light-symbol stood for a moment hovering, a star radiating down its beams over the place of natality, the spot whence had been projected this final beginning. For a moment he was so raised aloft, like a kind of offering to the stars themselves, and, looking up from the blaze below, he saw their unaffected distances.

He sighed half with relief, half with an anesthetic exhaustion. And as he sighed his station began to sink, the plane was descending with him like a spent ember from a dying bonfire. A glowing spot, he was brought down until the dark flat surface of the palace lay immediately below. His last glance showed that like a setting moon he had drawn back, into the city out of which he had led its tides of population that morning, its hundreds of thousands. He could see its lights flashing from ten thousand relit homes and the sounds rising as men went back to their variety with a new appetite for the manifold after their uplook into the void where all difference ends in the hypnosis of unity.

He hardly felt the plane ground and stood with almost the stiffness of catalepsy until he was helped out. As the engine behind him stopped, the last dike against the flood of exhaustion seemed to be withdrawn. He felt vaguely that he had been psychically magnified, distended beyond all inner power of re-recollection. He had been filled with the focus pressure of loyalty, so that for a whole day he might preside over the monster meeting of mankind. No doubt he had been carefully primed to stand that pressure, but now his system knew that it had used up every scruple of the dosage. As he was helped from the prow-throne, the light of his garments sank. "A ghost," he muttered to himself, "a ghost when midnight strikes and he must vanish," and let himself be led down to his apartment. He was aware that they unrobed him—perhaps the trusties; he was too dazed to recognize anyone, he who for hours had been turned into a symbol and had seen mankind fuse back into a single species.

He slept, for he found he was lying in bed when the doctor came in to him. Then for a moment he was nearly stirred from his coma of anonymity. He looked at the man at first unregardingly. Then a faint tremor of question stirred somewhere in him. The man, who was, of course, one of the selfless or callous (put it as you wished) instruments of this machine that had got its head—this man was trembling and his eyes were moist. When he took the remodeled man's arm his hands shook. Finally he went down on one knee. He gave the injection badly, letting the liquid leak from the puncture. The patient turned with an involuntary impatience from the clumsy stab. The doctor succeeded better next time and then, as though the effort were a great one, bent down. Yes, he had placed his forehead on the back of the remodeled man's inert hand. So, he thought faintly, as he sank into complete unconsciousness, no one can stand against this nucleonic energy we have released. Even the doctor, who knows that he prepared the lay figure, is overcome by it and worships the form out of which the power has gone, the glory departed.

He did not know how long he slept. He woke still with that feeling, as though his base had been taken from him and earth no longer could hold firmly his feet. But he was well. Physically his tiredness was gone from him. He woke because he had been disturbed by something. Someone was in the small room, sitting on the chair for which there was just room beside the bed. He could not remember why he felt as though he had no base. But he recognized the little room and he felt he had been through some unprecedented ordeal for which he had had no defense; all the skills of control which he had been taught had somehow been undermined and overwhelmed by some monster attack. He turned his head to see who was sitting beside him. He saw himself and then, as double images seen for a moment are brought into the unity of single focus with a sudden click of the eye, he knew it was Alpha, Alpha the First, who was sitting there, and he was as he was because for some hours he had endured taking, as Alpha the Second, the weight of the full Atlas pressure.

He realized, a moment after, what he had been through and that it was no subjective impression when he saw the difference in Alpha's attitude. He was concerned, solicitous. This was, he felt as his memory came back and completed itself, even more strange and yet inevitable than the doctor's inability to check the reverence-reaction in himself when he gave the injection as he fell to sleep.

After a moment Alpha spoke: "You see," he said, "something of the pressure. I never suspected it when I made this generator, any more than primitive man suspected that the upper air had in it killing heat or the lower ocean had obliterating pressure, or those poor fools who broke into the other pole of force—the nucleus of the atom of energy—as we have broken into the nucleus of the atom

142

of consciousness—knew the deadly, life-killing powers they released, power which killed all of them by its unsuspected radiation and so withdrew itself again from their meddling hands. Perhaps that, too, is the penalty for us at this other pole.

"I don't know, but I do know you know, and I say it to you, for you alone have been at the center of that tempest of spaceless energy, that we cannot go back. We have gone into the current of that energy hoping to make it turn our little turbines and spin our little craft and we have been caught in that smooth, remorseless flow. We are at the brink. It may be we shall touch some happy isle of stability and plenty right on the rushing verge, as such islets can crest the roaring edge of giant falls; it may be that the deep will wash us down." He paused.

"But we are together in an absolute pinnacle of loneliness, for better or for worse. About that you can now have no more doubt than I. In all the confusion, the practical personal matter stands out for us at the nucleus. We are bonded together by the very pressure of these unsuspected forces which have been released and have, as it were, crushed in on us, and we are tied like the nucleus of the hydrogen atom, the primal and most strongly knit of all the elements."

He paused, and the remodeled man turned round in bed to regard this, his captor, who was now clearly offering him partnership. He remembered that, when he was taking the history of sociology and the professor was pointing to what was then called the goal of organic democracy, they were reading an old author called, as far as he remembered, Herbert Spencer, and how this writer had said that a captor is really as much enchained to his captive as the captive to him. Well, it was true here.

"I thought," Alpha continued, "when you first turned up in my path that you were a masterly convenience. I told you that I was certain this was the kind of thing that befell me—that my ideas fulfilled themselves and my demands were met as soon as I defined them."

He stopped, and his understudy added, "And you went on to say that you discovered there was always far more in the idea that came to you than you had suspected at the beginning or planned that there should be."

"True enough," Alpha owned, "and I ought to have told you further that as time went on I had noticed that each discovery or invention always led to results increasingly surprising and with unforeseen possibilities. It was when I began to recognize that, that I began to wonder whether I might not be in the hands of some power which made me, for its own purposes, believe, as a post-hypnotically controlled patient believes, that I was acting on my own volition, but I was really behaving under the dictates of this invisible hypnotist.

"I knew that I must find an understudy, to take off from me the stunning pressure of these monster congeal-ments and contractions of loyalty, after every one of which I felt more deformed, more typified, and with all my orig-inality, initiative, and enterprise pressed out of me. Weeks would go by, and always a longer interval after each of these monster rites, before my mind could recover from its daze and begin again to think. You see the experience is so dangerous not because it makes its subject insanely puff-ed up and vain but because it somehow depersonalizes him, smooths out the actual convolutions of his character and thought-pattern, and leaves him only a vast passive mask or mirror, as smooth and featureless as a dark still lake on which a million stars reflect themselves because it itself is utterly motionless, utterly without light.

"Once on my travels I was in Libya in North Africa and in a small shack of a museum built near the excavations I came across a colossal piece of sculpture that had been excavated from the sands near by. It was a face some twelve feet high and had been pieced together from the shattered fragments. I was told it was so interesting because the archeologists had become convinced that this was an accu-rate copy of what the ancient world tells us was considered the greatest work of sculpture the Greeks had ever produced on the highest theme they knew. It was a measured repro-duction of that vanished masterpiece of Pheidieas—the Olym-pian Zeus. But the thing that struck me as I stood alone in that little, baking shed, alone with this vast face that glimmered through the shattered stone, was that, though of course anatomically perfect in its scale and proportions and majestic in a way, it was quite appallingly empty, vacant, void.

"The archeologist came in and asked me what I thought of it. I said I had never seen a piece of perfectly competent facecarving that gave one such an impression of nothing, of utter vacancy. It might be technically great, but as something to render expression it was nothing. He turned on me and said, 'Don't you see, you have seen Pheidieas' secret? Only a consummate genius who was also profoundly religious could have done that!'

"Once, we are told, a great sculptor, but not of the highest range, made a Zeus for a Greek city. But when he showed it to the city fathers they were unhappy. They praised its strength and power and emphatic sense of presence—and then paused, till the youngest who was given the task of passing sentence, said 'But it will not do, for that is not Zeus.'

"The sculptor was in despair. But they were firm. He maintained that it had power and majesty.

" 'Look,' he said, 'at the lines of authority, just enough to show the strength latent and ready to break.'

" 'That is just it,' they replied; 'those lines between the great all-seeing eyes, they hint at some partiality, some reaction, some contraction of the wide vision which sees all things with an equal regard and is both kin and alien to the just and the unjust and the evil and the good.'

"The sculptor bowed before their judgment, but they feared he would break under it, for this was as high as he could go. Let this rendering of the divine be refused by his city and what was there left for him to do? It was his authentic vision, true at its level, though inadequate, indeed only inadequate because the theme set him had been so high.

"So the eldest of the judges spoke; 'This is true,' he said, pointing to the great statue; 'it is not Zeus but it is godlike in a lesser, dark way. But it may be a way to Zeus, and men must know the gods of judgment and of doom before they can contemplate and rise to the Father of gods and men who is beyond favor and disfavor, beyond our earth's justice and our human mercy. We will gladly receive your work and give it a place of honor among our speaking symbols whereby the people are taught more deeply and surely than by words. We will set it up, and its name shall be the lord and judge of the underworld. This, in its majestic lack of resentment but still its sad realization of judgment, cannot yet be Zeus. But it can be, because of these very features, it can be and is Pluto, the great god not of Light and Life but of Death and Doom.'

"Well, at every exposure to what is now the wishful-field of mankind, I am smoothed out, and what was once daimonic in me is being so spread and magnified and made sky-embracing that nothing is left but an overarching presence presiding as patiently as the sky itself."

They were silent till Alpha brought back their talk to their immediate crisis. "You seemed made for the part . . ."

The remodeled man ran his hand over his face. Could he still feel those fine spiderweb lines, those finely closed crevasses down which his former face had been sunken and sealed?

"And I thought, here, is my very expression, my person that the world wants, redoubled, so that the face of the die can endure the amount of stamping which it must do without losing its edge and character. But that is not to be, I now realize. I know, as a man in the crow's-nest can see, the direction to which the ship of mankind with all its sails set is carrying me—to complete stylization, to a vast concave which will focus their myriad sounds and give back in a single note, without adding a tone of its own, what they would have said."

He did not wait for his understudy's comments but, as he reached the door, he said, "If you feel not too tired this evening come along to my rooms."

That invitation marked as much as anything the complete change in their relations. It had suddenly become not one of tentative equality but of an unspokenly recognized interdependent balance: they must go together, each was equally necessary to the other. He used to stroll into the small dining room and, if the door that led to the study was open, go on into that. If it was closed it meant that Alpha was having interviews. It was, he noticed, always left open when Alpha was out. And as the weeks went by and Alpha had only small public appearances to make, which the remodeled man shared about equally with him, as the remodeled man found these only inclined to stun the mind for a day or two, so he noticed Alpha's spirits and interest revived. When they dined together Alpha would tell him of some of these notions and how they were going.

"The one thing," he said, "I always keep to myself is the growing point of ideas. By that I mean that I am most uneasy when I find my interest in new notions, new contrivances, new social and psychological inventions and insights is at all lessened. The success of the final revolution was, I believe, simply because I was always open to new ideas. My skill was to see that practically any discovery or invention about mankind could be used and how it could be worked in to the general pattern of the remodeled society. So, though I have delegated all other work, this I keep and do myself. Anyone who has an idea, once they have put the outline before one of my outer staff dealing with the subject, has to be passed up to me: first I have a memo, then a thesis, and then the actual interview. Often I see more clearly than the man himself what he has lit on, and, of course, as he is nearly always a specialist, I see the application of it.

"It keeps me busy, and now that my spirit has recovered from the deforming pressure of being the public symbol, I find this is my keenest pleasure. No! The Mole or whoever it is, or any of his bravest pioneers will never get close to me as long as I keep on the move, as long as the way to new invention is through this room. Why, the underground is like a feeble sportsman who can't shoot a flying bird but waits till it settles, then patiently aims his gun, and by the time he has his sights on the game it has flown off to another bush!"

And certainly Alpha worked hard at these interviews and evidently found them fruitful.

For a few months, then, the balance seemed remade on this closer intimacy. The remodeled man found his own

147

mind settling back, and he concluded—wondering faintly was it rationalization—that he, too, whatever in the end he might decide to do, should first regain, as Alpha had regained, it appeared, his full balance, once more contract to his right size of spirit and real personality. And week by week, in spite of small setbacks, caused by the smaller public appearances in which he had to take his equal share, he found he was recovering. There would not be a monster show with the monster psychological pressure till the spring festival, and Alpha had not yet decided which of them should be exposed to that.

"It's not any sentimental consideration for a man about whom I really know nothing," he remarked when talking it over with what seemed complete detachment. "It is that we are absolutely necessary to each other; we are, in fact, a symbiote. I am the stronger because I have been exposed longer to this thing. Besides, one always has more immunity to something one has self-generated than to a toxin suddenly introduced from another body. I can't afford to waste you if you are to last as long as I, and the last big show made me wonder whether you would endure. It is a very difficult point when you dare no more waste your assistance than you dare waste your own vital resources."

He stopped and seemed to fall into a kind of depressed reverie. He sighed once or twice, then roused himself, and, seemingly to shake off the mood, began in another tone. "I have made you free of this apartment, so really we are living in a single suite of rooms and I know you come in and out. That's right, but I am glad to notice you have observed one rule . . ."

How did the man know, his hearer wondered.

"My desk and chair are, you see, raised on a slight dais. I am asking you never to sit there. That part of the room is under observation; a field makes it visible from outside the room. It was an old precaution—I think unnecessary now: but Algol, romantic fellow, attaches importance to it, and you see one has in part to be the mirror of one's followers' wishes. So use the whole of this apartment as you wish but respect that little dais, if you please, and if you're wise."

Well, it was no use disregarding such warnings when he was already so far out in uncharted waters. He felt pretty sure that he was necessary to Alpha. He felt equally sure that Alpha was still necessary to the revolution that he was steering into evolution. Of Algol he knew nothing and often speculated a good deal. While his mind ran on these vague surface speculations he became aware that Alpha's brighter mood had again become overcast. He heard him sigh again, and again try to rouse himself.

"You have, as I've said, served more purposes than I even hoped, but then that is because I find in me more needs than I suspected. I need companionship. I recover more quickly from mass-exposure when you are about because there is a real person to talk with."

How real, wondered his listener.

"Perhaps I could take on more public appearances? But at the same time," the man was speaking evidently to himself, "the more one has someone to talk openly with and in a way to trust, the more one needs, the appetite grows with eating, the blood flows more freely if sponged with a warm swab."

To be called a warm swab is not flattering, his listener thought, and reflected, That means he really is, as far as he can, trusting, and trusting because he must!

VI

THE ROLE EXCHANGE

THE DIAGNOSIS proved itself correct in the following weeks. True, Alpha kept his interest in his work of interviewing for fresh ideas, and continually worked at new social devices, but his mind, though as clear as ever, seemed to have less control over his emotions. Another insight into his actual state came to the prisoner-companion not when he was with his owner but when the owner was out.

Alpha was to be late that night: he was presiding at a monster banquet of officials—a task not too exhausting; for these meetings, though they had in them an element of adulation, always were occasions on which a good deal of technical discussion was carried on. The remodeled man sat in the study after his dinner had been served him by the trusty on duty. As the man went out of the room after having arranged the fire, the remodeled man looked after him. Would he, too, sink into being such a creature—the highest kind of trusty, but nevertheless a trusty, chief eunuch but still having ceased to be a man? His eye, as he turned round, slowly rested on the desk. Alpha had certainly been mysteriously explicit about it—a kind of tree of knowledge in this little Garden of Eden, he had made it seem. Well, his requested orders should be kept; but obviously it was, as collectors say, an interesting piece and must be more interesting than it actually looked. The remodeled man had been trained in observation. He was also top of his class as a trainee when they did the room-recollection test and he could put things back in the order they had been; that was the second test and a very useful skill when you had done a kidnapping or a theft. He could do that better than anyone in his class.

Suddenly he remembered a useful thing. He went over

to a small cabinet by the fireplace and took from it a pair of binoculars. They were the latest triumph in lens-making and not available for the public. The police used them for keeping people under observation and Alpha used this super-pair when watching crowds and their behavior from the palace roof. He took them out. Their focus was so good and their use of light so economical that though this room was only brightly lit by artificial light he could, when he put them to his eyes, see every detail of the desk as though he had broken the rule and mounted the dais so as to bend over that innermost sacred altar.

There was a memo with heads of points for his secretary to expand with him. There, in another division, were inquiries and orders for Algol. Here in a third wedge of the semicircular surface were questions to be put to new experts to be seen in the next couple of days. And, in the next division to that, the answers and comments from the last couple of interviews; and, camped outside that, the curve of microphones that linked this desk to the high offices and so made it the focus of world power. Yes, it was interesting but obvious, and there seemed no ground for secrecy there. He knew that few power types are secretive unless it is necessary; a certain surface openness is not only a commonplace but quite an effective disguise. It is also a relaxation to the man who has to keep certain secrets, to speak openly about what doesn't matter if it is repeated.

He put the glasses down on the seat in which he had been sitting. He walked across the room and stood so that he could be as near as possible, though still clear of the dais, which stood out from the back of the desk making a small platform about six inches in height and in breadth about three feet. He was now looking across the desk at the chair, a fine piece of carving or molding, for it was of a purple translucent plastic. The back rose like a miter and on it in cloth of gold was embroidered the large Alpha. The arms came out with a fine sweep terminating in two bulls' heads bent down so that the horns were bowed as though the beasts were charging. He remembered that at the beginning the leader had often been called the bull, but that name had gradually, as the party became the empire, been let lapse into the more universal title of Alpha. The bulls' heads were deeply and realistically carved, the horns in the decorative design becoming the volutes of the head bosses on which the hand of the seated man would naturally rest. He scanned the whole thing carefully. Yes, is was a fine piece of carving but so far from being imaginative that it was difficult to go on scanning it for clues. He ran over each detail to memorize it—studied the bulls' heads with care, the back of the seat and then, feeling just a little baffled, sat down—surely that was permissible provided he did not touch the desk or throne—on the very edge of the dais. The high back of the desk rose behind him still more than a couple of feet away. He looked across the room and felt that if he had been on report duty he would have earned a bad mark in not being able to bring back something of value. He ran over, from long practice, all the points that he had noted, and meanwhile his fingers tapped out the points on the carpet which was thick enough to make a comfortable seat.

So it was his finger tip and not his eye which first noticed. Indeed it had already twice made its sounding before his mind turned from its catalog of past data to the present. Then he looked down. The light was quite good there, from the central chandeliers and the wall lights. Alpha did not like dusk effects. He was now upon his knees on the floor level, first examining the place where he had sat and then rapidly transferring his inspection to where his feet had been resting. He did this twice and then sat still for some time—this time on the main floor. Then he jumped up quickly and, taking the glasses from the fireside chair where he had dropped them, began with a renewed eagerness of interest, indeed with greater interest than he had showed at the first inspections, to run over every part of the throne chair.

Finally a smile began to spread over his face. Then he sighed and remarked in a whisper to himself, "How hard it dies. Once taught to hunt, a dog can't help chasing even a chicken. But it's so long since one did a bit of riddle reading that to have one and to solve it—still gives a kind of lift." Then, in a slower tone, "Either it is a hang-over from the earlier regime or perhaps the new regime hasn't really quite yet arrived? Well, that again permits me to wait. But I'm glad of the knowledge." He put the glasses back in their place, found the book he had been reading to put himself to sleep of nights—a Jane Austen—and settled himself by the fire.

It was not more than an hour after that Alpha came in, dropped into the other chair and remarked, "I'm glad you're up. I don't know whether I won't have to cut out these big banquets, even. Somehow they are exhausting and any information I get I could get better in desk interviews. I wonder whether I haven't (sometimes I think it must be true) so lowered, eroded, and damaged my psychic insulation by exposing myself to those torrents of focused enthusiasm as now to be tapped by any small concourse. Anyhow, I'm more and more depleted, and the more I become empty the more they seem to suck on my vitality. 'Pon my soul, if I still have one, I'd like, I believe, one frank look of hate or suspicion. But to see those men all waiting on me, not frightened and cowed—oh, no!—but just childishly pleased to bask in the presence of power, and, babylike, content to identify what they have so largely generated, with me, it is exhausting, for they have psychically the same power that physiologically the suckling has over its nurse, to drain her dry and give nothing save a demand that must be met. There's no going back once you have been the wet nurse of a million milk-addicts. I used to be called the Bull when we were charging our way through the flimsy barriers of that effete thing that called itself communism. By heavens! I've sunk to be the universal cow of mankind!" He laughed, but the laugh trailed off into a sigh.

Then he looked up. "Look here," he said, "can't you somehow put back this energy into me? Aren't I right?" A kind of questing anxious but hopeful tone came into his voice. "I must be, for I know that feeling; that's the feeling I always have before I hit on something big, something that is coming to me and I have only to see it. . . ."

What, thought his companion, is his queer psychic mind now going for?

"You and I are one creature, a symbiote, with two bodies; you are the reserve body. Hence you can recharge me. Transfusions have to be from people of the same blood group. We are of the same psychic group—and there are only two of us—but that's enough. I know now that if you can lay your hands on me I could draw energy from you. That's it! Massage me! It will somehow put me back and restore my insulation. I'll have you taught.

"I've studied the work, that work in the electrical field of the body. Indeed, it was in that work we found our final weapon. All the drugs—which I believe the Mole uses, if he exists, or the body that calls itself by that purblind name—the barbiturics, all the truth-drug lot, were well enough, but the nucleus of the self was largely untouched and people relapsed or only became trusties. I've told you, one doesn't want everyone a trusty. The electric-field work did the trick. There, again, I saw the real sense in all the senseless knocking out of their senses, by electric shocking, those wretched melancholics. But once you have electrically diagnosed any man's 'field' then all you have to do is just reverse a man's field and for a while he's out, and then you set it going at another rhythm and no one can say why he's different but he is. He doesn't forget and be an obvious case of shock and amnesia—oh, no! nothing so vulgarly suspicion-waking as that! He just loses interest in his old interests and grows new, and has admirably sound reasons for doing so."

As he spoke of this final triumph his buoyancy again inflated him, and he went on almost cheerfully:

"Well, I am sure you can do just what I need. Nothing, of course, as extreme as a real treatment—nothing like that at all. Simply massage, just to give me back my self-centering—just to make me cease to be what all this massive suggestion has made me: the natural prey of the mass appetite for adoration which I have awoken. I just can't go on being drained," and something almost like a whimper came into the hard urgency of the tone.

Well, here was an opening, and, of course, one that had been prepared. Was the Mole as blind as Alpha boasted?

"I've had some little training in massage," he said. "I was taught it to use on myself after some injuries and then

154

I used it to help others. I think I might be able to give you some relief."

That last word seemed to erode further Alpha's restraint. "I must have it, I wouldn't allow to myself how far I'm gone. I am keeping myself going just because there is nowhere to fall."

That night the remodeled man found the second skill which had been given when he changed appearances brought into play. From a light hand with pastry we mount to a light hand with pathological muscles, the phrase ran through his mind. Whether it was the self-suggestive power of Alpha or whether the two *had* become uncannily akin, the massage was an immense success. It became his chief duty and hardly a night went without his being called to give this assistance.

"He says the people are addicts on his voice and face; well, now he is an addict of my hands!"

But, though the rest which Alpha gained from the treatment put him more and more at ease, his emotional tone did not harden. Increasingly every night he would run through further and further sections of his life, and it was increasingly clear that this man, so long walled up, and whose only escape from self was to be exposed to the annihilating stream of public worship, had at last found a rest. Ever more clearly came the cry, the demand for sympathy, for understanding, yes, for companionship.

And increasingly the reiterated refrain became, "Why can't I get out! Haven't I done enough? The Revolution is over; Evolution, the natural process, that hasn't got to be worked, growth, natural growth, can take its place. And Evolution can't, unless we stop this dictating. But how can I get out? I can't get away. I can't escape! I'm walled in! Why, this very body has crystallized into a mummy, a bit of type, a great formalized routine stamping-machine, a huge polished die."

"Do you know," he once remarked with a sigh at the end of a series of such self-pitying complaints, "there's a disease that attacks embryos, so that the life-drive goes out of the wretched little foetus. The life which should be central in it, its own life, somehow becomes transferred to its outer flesh. And so the ghastly little man-to-be is degenerated into a great growing mass of pointless tissue. Day by day, as it should be getting on to be born, it is just turning into a rougher, clumsier, blunter, vaguer, more obliterated outline of a living creature. Yes, so terrible is Nature to those that fail to keep free, that in some cases the wretched little mite turns actually in the end into a kind of stone. It isn't even flesh and blood any longer."

His voice was growing excited: "Do you know what they call that monstrous, misconceived thing which can't even be called a misbirth, which can't even get expelled from the womb, but has to be cut out and thrown away, if the womb that bore it is not to be killed by what it has produced, its own tombstone precipitated within it? They call it," and his voice squeaked in its panic dismally, "they call it a Mole!"

He was silent a few moments, sunken in a speechless dejection. Then he began again to argue with himself.

"And the Mole," he muttered, "he or his group are kept alive only by the contrast, by the fact that I am up here, so they have to be down there. Moles are only mice that have gone blind by suppression, or growths that have failed to be carried on by the current of life and so can't get out. If I, as a Bull, hadn't trampled about, they wouldn't have gone underground and tried to tunnel the ground from under my feet. It was all they could do. My success forced them under. But let the surface pressure off and up they will be turned and their destructive digging will be over. They'll live on the surface, again re-get their sight and be able to see ahead. They'll cease to gnaw at the roots of things, and eat, as rats and mice should, the seeds of which there are plenty, and not kill the seed-producing plants. That's the proper balance of life. On the surface their manure pays for their meals. As it is, they are driven down, not only to gnaw at the roots of everything, but to tunnel, ruin the soil and make harvests impossible. The whole earth at last is in danger of being eroded away."

He paused, again exhausted by the sudden strength of his conviction, his overwhelming conviction that his overwhelming victory had miscarried. He sighed again with a gathering despair.

"But it's no use—too late. I ought to have seen this development long ago. I can't get out now. There's no going back when you have gotten up to the pinnacle. Algol wouldn't let me. The road is blocked solid behind me. I've not an inch that I could give, and I can't go an inch forward. No, none of them, from the very base up to those that have their automatics so ready that I can sometimes feel them in my back, none of them would let me go. If I step back, the guns will pitch me forward. Algol wouldn't let me, the people wouldn't dream of it—they *would*, they *all* would, rather have me dead, rather have me mad. I can't get out, I can't get out!"

After a month of this, the remodeled man began to realize what must now be ahead. But what could he do about it? It was unavoidably clear that Alpha had become parasitic on his hidden twin. True, the concealed partner could still give the figurehead relief. He could still get him ready so that he could take one of the monster reviews and rallies. But two symptoms showed the real depth of the inner change and balance. The first was that the great shows, when he, the remodeled man, had to take them, obviously took less out of him than out of the man he no longer thought of as his master. Of course, they were unbelievably tiring, but while he could and did recuperate, the other was clearly losing ground. It seemed that in the end that kind of exposure would kill anyone; and the man who had been at it longest would break soonest—that was all.

The second observation was even more significant of the change and more clear. After each such strain the old Alpha, as his attendant now called him in his mind, ran back to the safety and recharging of this essential stimulant. He had become an addict to these re-tonic muscular caresses. But though his mood was increasingly dependent, that was not to say it was increasingly intimate, still less affectionate or companionable. On the contrary, he was growing more gloomy, and in the shadows of his gathering depression lurked a darker shadow of suspicion, of oncoming paranoia. Though they had this queer kind of muscular intimacy, the human talk between them languished more and more. The attendant felt creeping over him the uncanny feeling that he was being turned into some kind of tamer that can keep a wild beast from attacking him only so long as he can stroke the animal and turn its savage mood to a kind of self-involved content.

One evening they were sitting together. A gloomy silence had fallen. Then Alpha rose silently and went out of the room by the door near his desk. After a couple of minutes he returned and before sitting down—indeed, as he was crossing the room to the fire—he spoke:

"Yes, I knew I was right. I've now spoken to the chief dresser. He agrees. There was something unconvincing in your last appearance. The old self which we thought we had rubbed out is coming back—just like the bramble on which a rose is grafted may reassert its old useless nature. You're here not to have a nature of your own, but to give your coarse vitality to mine." He was growling now. "Get along. Go along the passage; the doors are open. He's waiting for you. We must cut out that sucker-growth at once."

The remodeled man almost protested. Why the devil should he have to do it now! What madman's nonsense, even if the observation was true—which he doubted. But, of course, it was not the slightest use to protest. Like as not, he'd be killed that night if he did. No, he held quite good cards still, and the time to show one's hand hadn't yet come. He got up without a word and went out as he was directed. But he felt sure Alpha's eyes were on his back as he withdrew.

The whole thing, as he returned, he felt was a piece of neurotic farce. The dresser had kept him about five minutes and then, after having put him through some quite perfunctory movements and hardly seeming to attend to what he did or how he did it, glanced at his watch and remarking, "Yes, that's all right now," began to switch off the lights and nodded him to the door.

As the remodeled man re-entered the study he saw that Alpha had become restless. He was just settling into his chair and the door to his bedroom and bathroom had not been latched; yes, and the door to the dining room—which surely the remodeled man has shut when they had come in from dinner—was ajar. But Alpha showed no sign that his companion had returned. They sat like this for perhaps half an hour. Then Alpha rose and without a word went into his bedroom, closing the door behind him.

The remodeled man waited for some twenty minutes. "He's gone to bed, I suppose," he finally reflected. "Well, I'd better not wait up for Daddy's good night." He went into the dining room, shut the door behind him, and so gained his own room. He slept quite well, however. If the man were going mad, well, what did it matter? When he was quite off his head, that might be the signal. After all, a sane man can usually move more quickly and surely than a madman. Yes, he could wait. The first thing, of course, was to give no sign to the tottering mind that he thought it on the brink, that he saw anything odd in its conduct or suspected any change in their relationship. And certainly, apart from the gathering gloom, Alpha didn't say or do anything that was eccentric. But the descent into a self-centeredness and a suspicious melancholy was steepening—there could be no doubt of that.

One evening—it was perhaps a week after the sudden freakish order for that evening drill—the degeneration that had taken place during the day was so marked that the remodeled man felt the time had come to take a sounding. They were by the fire as usual—for winter or summer there was always a fire of some sort, though when the days were warm it was of a fuel that gave a pretty light and practically no heat. The dinner had been dismal. Alpha had pushed his food about but hardly eaten any. And more than once his companion could not help noticing that the figure opposite him was far more interested in watching him than in the food. The attention was furtive, but there was no doubt about it, and that it was furtive made it all the more disquieting. Could the food be poisoned? No: for though Alpha ate very little he did taste every one of the dishes—he was trying to feed. But finally he had risen impatiently and gone into the study.

His companion followed in five minutes. His host was slumped in his chair looking at the fire. He looked so wretched that it was the obvious thing to say, "Wouldn't some massage help?" As it happened, for one reason or another they hadn't had one during the whole of that week. Alpha hadn't asked and somehow his attendant hadn't felt inclined to press it, if the other didn't request it. But the reaction was immediate and even more violent than it was rapid.

"No!" the other shouted. "No!"

And, as though this negative assertion, this protest and resistance, had broken up some jam inside him, there rushed out a flood of words. They were so confused and scrambled that for a little while the attendant couldn't sort them, still less imagine what reaction ought to meet them. Then a drift became clear—it was the old complaint but in a passionate key, and, as it went on, though the words became clearer, the storm of anger evidently rose.

"No one, not one, not a single person! Alone, alone, but ringed in, ringed, not even a wall to get one's back against. But I won't be caught! I—not caught. I was always master. I haven't been trapped. I can see the toils. Keep away, keep your distance!"

The remodeled man had not risen, of course, and now he sat back with deliberate ease. Certainly there was no danger just for the moment, unless one moved. His companion, though, had wheeled round, half dragging the chair with him. But the distance between them remained the same. As Alpha's eyes watched his companion, his hands kept on running over his cheeks, played with the collar of his tunic and the lapels, and worked at the neck. It was the usual nervous reaction of the fingers when the central controls are going. He had seen that before in men that were breaking down, or being broken down, or broken in too fast. Yes, he was working up to some crisis. And all the while this litany of protest and complaint, with antiphonals of defiance, kept on running from his working lips.

"Yes, they all think they have me trapped. And in a way they have. But I have ways out of traps. Well, I was never caught, and I won't be. Yes, a bull can leap right out of the ring when they think he's cornered. They underrated the force, the resource, the drive that's left when, fools, they

160

corner the strongest will and drive in all the world. I'll cheat them. They never thought I could do that. . . ."

It was clear that he had forgotten, or perhaps didn't see, the figure that sat watching him. Yes, that was it, he didn't see really any longer. For suddenly he addressed the remodeled man with a laugh.

"I've had a dream. But I see my dreams are still full of genius; even asleep I know more than the whole rest of them when they're awake. I thought I had a model served up for me, Heaven knowns from where: just found on the doorsteps, I suppose, like a present from Santa Claus. I dreamed he took quite a lot of work off my hands and shoulders and then he used to massage me and that gave him his grip."

He half rose from his chair and began to crouch. The remodeled man felt the moment must now be here. Alpha would now fly at him, surely. Involuntarily he drew himself together to take the rush. The movement was noticed by his companion.

"You're a phantom, a Doppelgänger, but you don't come near me. I know, I've felt it: if you touch me, then you become real and I fade away. That's what's been happening. You vampire that I've created in my fancy, so as to double my mind, you worse than Frankenstein monster, you've gotten your power because I let you cease to be a mental fancy, a kind of splintered personality, a shadow I could project and then make vanish by drawing you back into myself. I let you become a real body, a somebody, yes, final folly, I let you touch me, because you could give me your strength. Why, you were simply the echo of me! I'd made you, and, you shadow, you want life, of course, and to have your separate existence. And for that you have to draw on me, to suck me, to get not only into my mind but to get your hands on me and suck me dry, as a spider sucks the fly empty, like the boa constrictor just twists and crushes its enveloped victim till he's simply a tube of fodder."

The man was almost screaming now. The remodeled man kept still and ready. No: the madman wasn't going to rush him yet, if he didn't move a finger. The fingers of the other kept on playing over his own neck. While in that position he couldn't make a plunge, and this storm of frenzy couldn't last. The arteries in the neck could be seen standing out, and the veins on the temples. The pressure was felt by the victim himself. He dragged at his collar, worked his fingers to find a little relief. He became almost silent and then quite hushed, save for his rapid breathing. He must be feeling some seizure coming on. His hands were trying feebly to relieve some pressure he felt in the neck, in the arteries, the veins and muscles, all of which were dilated. Yes, he was making some kind of feeble effort to massage himself. He worked his fingers back to get the big supporting muscles of the cervical vertebrae into his touch. There, evidently, he felt he must find some relief.

To the man looking on, into his mind there suddenly flashed the queer little scene of the masseur—the first man he had felt any friendliness with, after his operations—trying to show him how to massage his own neck. Well, evidently the poor creature now in front of him was getting or imagining he was getting something of the same relief. His movements became quieter. Though his fingers were hidden from his watcher, the face, too, it was clear, was settling. He had looked pathetically like someone wrestling with a refractory collar stud he couldn't either see or get a proper hold on. Now he was actually at ease for a moment. The eyes too, which had been seeing nothing, cleared. For one moment the onlooker felt he was recognized.

The lips he was watching said slowly, "Yes, you'd have held me trapped. Me! But I found out, I found you out, I'm out, out!"

The fingers slipped up and forward as though he would put them over his ears. His head went forward like a drowsy man's. With a bound, the onlooker was at his side. He slipped his hand onto the neck artery, now flaccid. Then, glancing down from where he stood above the curled-up man in the chair, his eyes remained a moment fixed. Only for a moment, though. An instant later he was through the dining room, into his own sitting room, into his slip of a bedroom and the small pouch for the shaving things. He snatched it open, glanced, and ran back through the dining room into the great study. The man in the chair had not stirred—of course not, that would hardly be expected. But he himself must stir. There wasn't a moment, and he must make speed for two. Maybe he was a shadow; well, shadows must move and they do move fast when what had thrown them is falling. But he must move neatly as well as quickly.

He bent down, placing his fingers gingerly on the back of the neck. Then, with his other hand, he pulled. It came away quite easily, though. And it had left no mark. A moment after you couldn't say where the puncture had been made. But it had been driven home well; there was no doubt of that.

It was all clear now, and as he made his dispositions, his mind gave him all the steps that had led to where he must now, as he was doing, carry on. He had been told—and indeed had seen some evidence of it when he was being trained and let see a thing or two to toughen him—that when the mind goes, when it breaks under strain, very often one of its splinters will pierce and penetrate the mind that had broken it, or any other whole mind that may be about and somehow strike its tangental interest, so that a man who is going off his head will often tell the doctor who is surveying him what is going on in the doctor's own mind. That certainly had happened with Alpha. Somehow, under the strain, he had had this sudden insight. That was why he had suddenly sent his understudy to take that five-minute lesson. At that moment he knew what the Alpha pin was for and had gone and fetched it from where his understudy had put it when he was told he needn't wear it. He'd just stowed it away with the shaving tackle, feeling that after all he did not know when, if ever, he'd want it.

Once Alpha had found it, he was bound, in that mood of clairvoyant suspicion, to find out how it was made, or mismade, how it was made to work. And then he would simply brood, as he had, till he felt, with all the compulsion psychosis that suicides have, that this was the way, the one way, to save himself from being murdered. Of course he knew about the cervical stab—a man as interested as he in the nervous system of men, a man who for half his

163

fighting life had been killing pretty successfully without leaving traces, couldn't fail to know that, the easiest way to kill, even yourself. Yes, mercy killings, and mercy hospitals with gentle, mental remolding of character, all those gentle things of those who had safely arrived in power, all came later. In the beginning, when the letter "A" really meant the crude first start, well, then killing had to be crude, and to kill what you couldn't hold and remold was the only way. And killing must be traceless. That was it, without a doubt, and that brought him up to this actual moment: the cards in his hands, the ball at his feet.

Everything had now been passed on to him. Alpha had just completely abdicated—no, it was more thorough than that—much. The husk which had held Alpha had just split itself open—that was all; the chrysalis had split and the new vehicle had emerged. Alpha's luck? True enough, it had worked with complete finality of proof. For here it was still playing perfectly, playing for the hands that held it, into these fresh hands, but with the unbroken succession going on. Could he doubt it? He had only had to hold himself in readiness and everything just fell into his hands. The way was cleared by the very wish of that which had only in the end wished to get out of the way. But just as clearly, he, the new hand, must do his part. The one thing which was clearly forbidden was to let the move pass or try to get out from the prepared succession. Now that the invisible service belt of fate had fed him up to the top and carried off the man in front, he must take the place left for him. There was no need to think any more; action was everything and inevitably clear and straight ahead.

He drew a deep breath. He knew himself now as a man in full control, alone responsible for himself and for everything else that was going to happen, going to develop out of the situation to which this power, which his predecessor had called his Luck and seemed to the newcomer more Fate-Universal, had brought him. And Time was making up for its pause with redoubled activity. He need wait no more. He could do something decisive, germinal, in every second. And with the call came the character. This was the old life, on a larger scale maybe, but the same calls were

164

being made and his training had made him a ready person, not afraid of the size of what might suddenly loom up on one. His training patterns were well-cut rails. He ran on them without speculating as to the future. He felt the exhilaration of pure unspeculative action.

He took the daggered pin, just glancing back at the body which looked peacefully dozing. It was in that most ancient attitude of burial and abandonment, rightly called "the attitude of foetal humility"—a phrase Alpha had actually approved. Well, it accepted the *fait accompli* and would wait patiently for his orders. He went into what had been Alpha's bathroom and carefully washed the pin, though no stain appeared on it. Then he fitted it back and, with the half-turn, locked it in its sheath. He went quickly back into his room and deposited it where Alpha had taken it from, in the shaving pouch.

Though he was not thinking, through his mind shot two bright, gaudy pictures. They were pin-ups they had in their bunkhouse. Both were of a barbarous amusement the savages of the past used to enjoy—a bullfight. The first was the final scene. The bull is on his knees, spent, it is true, but, at any moment, in the exhausted, exasperated beast, the life might flare back. He is still a very dangerous creature, perhaps the most dangerous of all wild animals, the beast that is wounded to death but may spend his last gust of energy, Samson-like, in hurling his taunting foe to death, one driving lunge and step, before toppling over into the abyss himself. The matador approaches, the man who must gain the final burst of applause or be gored amid yells of contempt at a clumsy botcher. He gives a flourish with his small, lance-pointed sword, and then drives home. If he knows his job, then *"procumbit humi bos!"* and he stands, amid a torrent of flowers covering him and the carcass. If not . . . ! Yes, it is well called the coup de grace, the happy dispatch; and the little weapon was called in the Middle Ages the misericord—the instrument of compassionate release.

The other picture showed another act in this series of savage duels between man and bull. It showed the matador, his gaudy clothes covered over with a white cloth stiffened with plaster, his face and head white, and mounted on a small stool also painted to look like white stone. The bull has charged, but, seeing itself up against a motionless white block and fearing to shatter its horns on a monolith, it swerves and someone else standing on the side can then stab it. But the man who had the nerve to stand still, and whose life depended on his rigid nerve, is the one who gets the ovation and to whom the bull belongs.

Their trainer used to say that both gifts of nerve are needed, and sometimes added, "If you keep your head and learn how to keep as still and expressionless as a block of stone, even the Bull himself may suddenly balk at you. He'll be brought within range and your nerve will have done it."

That had sounded rather odd then, almost nonsensical when most of the class was young and looking forward to making fine-flourished and spectacular thrusts. But surely as his training had gone these last months—surely, hadn't the second picture been nearer the actual facts? He had been obliterated as though he were a carved-away stone, and so completely successful had been the artifice that the effect had been more remarkable than any of the most daring tricks of the bull ring could ever have won. For the bull, baffled by the mysterious image, had fallen at its feet, goring himself to death.

He was back again in the study. The two bullfighting pictures hung high somewhere in his mind acting as decorative orientation-points on the corners of the map of action across which he was, move by move, charting his behavior, as he took his course about the room. He remembered all the things that must be done if murder is not to look like murder and—even more difficult—if a suicide is not to be taken for what in fact it is. He went to a small panel in the room. Yes, that was the place where Alpha—always himself a fine methodical mind—put his gun when he came in. He still carred one when out; more, as he once said, as a matter of method and to remind those who had to carry such things, or thought they had, not to be careless, if they still thought any particular carefulness was still necessary.

It was one of the last things in automatics. Though, of course, all such firearms were on their last legs—they still might be useful at a pinch, and here certainly was such a pinch—they were useful in the make-up of a dramatic picture. You couldn't miss with these weapons. Once you were pressing the stock rightly, they went off the moment the muzzle was aligned with the central nervous system of a living creature and, best of all, when trained on a man, for the electric field of the human body was strongest. It was simply an improvement of that old-fashioned device called Radar and the radio timing device of shells that exploded when any plane or flying bomb flew near them. Along the top of the barrel was an electric tube device, so sensitive just to that electric wave-length of the central nervous system that, up to fifteen feet, the response fire was perfect.

He put the gun on the ground and turned to the chair. True, not a spot of blood had followed out the puncture. He bent down. Even now, in amid the last fringe of down-hair, he could not be sure which poremark was actually the entrance to the lock through which his skeleton key had gone to release the prisoner. He heaved up the body over his shoulder and with his left arm swung the chair round till it was facing the back of the imperial desk about ten feet away. He propped the body in it as upright as he could manage.

Then, after retrieving the gun, he faced the dead man, himself stepping back till his calves felt the ridge of the dais against them. He raised the gun until it tracked across the target. But it failed to fire. Then he smiled with a slight irritation at himself, thinking— Many men have lost their lives through such a silly oversight. Of course, the dead nervous system couldn't activate the firing mechanism. There was, naturally, a safety device on such instruments. He twisted the knob round, to finger-fire, took his aim in the old-fashioned way, pressed the supplementary trigger and heard the chuckling cough which was all these silenced instruments emitted—so little sound, in fact, that he could in the still room hear through its deathly chuckle the whip of the spinning bullet, the dull bump as it bored its way in a flash through the body, and the tearing bump as it, finally, was held up in the tough plastic of the wall panel behind. The body scarcely shuddered, so sharp and clean was the thrust.

He put the instrument on the edge of the desk behind him to his right and walked over. Yes, he was still a fine shot. It had certainly gone through the heart and the body was fresh enough, thank his stars, for blood to begin to ooze through the tunic. There would be no proof that he had shot a corpse; no sign of his real mercy, or of any of his motives, or indeed, best of all, of who he was or who did what. A perfect involvement. He raised the body carefully, keeping away his hands from the blood, and, as it was his duty, he could afford to let himself feel a certain relief that he did not have to touch that red, over-dramatic fluid. He took the body and laid it face down on the floor some nine feet or so from the desk. That's how a man falls, he thought, when he rushes you and you get a heart hit with a high-speed skewer bullet. He looked over the layout carefully, and then sprawled forward the right arm, leaving the left under the carcass.

"Ah, the ring," he said to himself in a low voice, and, bending lower, slipped it off the finger and onto his own. "That's a bit of not unuseful authentication in a case of somewhat confused identity. But I haven't much time. He's getting cold already and he'll be stiff if I dawdle."

He got up, turned and went quickly round to the desk, mounted the dais firmly, and sat down. "The king is dead, long live the king." He repeated the formula of instantaneous succession, of automatic succession brought about by nothing more or less than death.

"Now for the first commands from the reoccupied throne!"

He put out his left hand and took the microphone three and saw the great ring, like a knuckle-duster on his finger joint. That microphone summoned the trusty-watch.

"Number One," he said, "report and bring with you one large mail-delivery sack."

They were just the thing—those huge waterproof sacks in which the monster palace mail was brought in for sorting. There was no answer. He knew why that was so. The

168

trusties never spoke if it was at all possible to obey, and when they could not they had difficulty in speaking unless they were asked a question directly. He heard the connection open and then close. He, too, put back the microphone, sat back and waited.

One glance showed that all was in the orderly disorder that he had planned. There was no need to put a weapon in the felled assailant's hand. The case was clear and more convincing so. The door at that moment opened. But it was not Trusty One that came in and closed it after him. It was Algol.

He was not disconcerted. It was, of course, a very likely possibility. He ought to have thought that some small routine urgency would make the chief of police run in, that instant. Well, better then than earlier or later. Anyhow, Algol would have had to be told very soon. And Alpha had providentially explained very fully to him the kind of simple, restless mind he was now to deal with. Yes, surely it was the Alpha Luck serving up to him the next incident when, nicking the minute with a happy fact, it was most apt. His mind was moving quite quickly enough for the event and he was more amused than annoyed by the contretemps.

"I sent for Trusty Number One. Turn round. See what's happened."

Algol glanced askew over his shoulder and, like a well-trained man, made no reaction.

"He broke under the strain. You know what it is: though most people haven't an idea. And I didn't think he'd break so soon or so suddenly. He rushed me when I was giving him some instructions for his next appearance."

Algol had turned round to him again and smiled. "You're still pretty quick with a gun." Then, with a slight pause, "Forgive an old chief of police being interested in what is probably irrelevant detail, but I thought you always put away that gun in the locker over there when you came in. You said once that, with us to depend on and your work to be done quietly, you didn't want fireworks on your desk." The voice till then had been questioning.

The remodeled man said sharply, "When is Trusty Number One coming!"

The reply, "He's not coming, I've come instead," was said unmistakably and, with the words, the gesture completed the sentence. The chief of police took out an automatic from his pocket and held it lightly in his hand.

"It is," he remarked like a man reading out measurements, "three feet from where you are sitting to the microphones on your left and three feet to your right to the other automatic in this room, which you have obligingly left so well out of your reach. There's been some queerly interesting little piece of maneuvering in this room, which, as an old hand at reconstruction-puzzles, I'd like to get straight with your help.

"You will talk, of course, and you won't move or our talk will have to be shorter than either you or I would wish. But first, let me tell you that the trusties won't come. Ill-placed hopes spoil a good narrative style. You have nothing to look forward to and so will be able to remember clearly what has passed. I have, for some little time, been expecting developments, and, so, like a good guardian, I saw that the lines which go to the trusty office should come through to mine, to my own private telephone; and I have been a very careful sentinel, whenever you have been here, just waiting for this call which has come as I expected."

The covered man had long learned not to move when in such a position. But he parried with a good show of indignation.

"Algol," he shouted, "wake up! I see what you think. You think that that double you provided has succeeded, and that it's *he* who's talking to you and that that is Alpha dead on the floor." Then, when that burst of well-simulated indignant humor had been shot off, he went on quietly, "Look at my hand, do you see the ring? You know perfectly well that it's the Leader that's speaking to you. Come along. Let's get that poor lump into the incinerator and disposed of. I haven't suffered a scratch."

"No, I think you haven't, and I'm glad you haven't. And I'm as sure as you are, that, behind me, on the floor is lying the double and in front of me is the one and only

Alpha that has survived—that has survived." And he began to smile.

The remodeled man was irritated to find his own heart accelerating its beat. He must keep as quiet inside as out, if he were ever to get out of this.

"Algol," he said in a quietly commanding voice, "don't be a fool."

"That is precisely what I have been saying to myself for a little while, and now I am going to act on that advice, perhaps the last you'll give me, but better than most you have." The chief of police drew himself up, weighed the automatic in his hand, and smiled. "I see you don't understand, and I know how unpleasant it is to go away with one's mind all confused. Besides, it will give an extra pleasure to my pretty little piece of work if I share with another and point out in words, actually what has happened, and how I've managed to employ events.

"First, I would say again—*of course* you're Alpha—though now you're Omega, too! For a long while I knew you were in decline. You were fuller and fuller of wild notions of turning the revolution into evolution and all that nonsense. You were becoming no longer the leader of a charge and having the fun and the dash, but a great dummy mouthing out about people having a good time. Oh, it made me sick! But it also taught me sense.

"Well, of course, to cut a long story short, as I'm about to cut another longer-winded storyteller shorter in a minute, I tried to think of some way of bringing back the good old times, and for the people who won to have the prize and to carry on the fine fighting life. We didn't fight and win, to sit about in floodlit nightgowns with crowds debauched with sentiment. But you seemed somehow to have got the great sugary tide, the great oily mass, to suck us away. The police weren't even unpopular; they were treated as increasingly funny, anachronisms! There seemed no way out: but all the while my detestation of you, you old softy, grew. And then your softness made you do the very thing that put everything open.

"I own I never thought that your having a double would serve my purposes so perfectly. But, sooner or later, now I see, it would have happened. You probably don't know that I primed the little piece of carrion on the carpet to make the dash at you by telling the inflated little fellow that he'd knock you out and then he and I would share the prize."

The realization that Algol was reduced by boasting to such a lie, gave the covered man a new sense of readiness.

"Well," he remarked, "tell me why the present situation so suits your cards."

"Gladly, and may I congratulate you on your coolness. I must say, I thought you'd become too soft to hold together right up to the moment that you are blown out. Well, I knew that the one thing that could make all good and plain would be if one or the other of you did the other in. Of course you killed the door dupe. But that's all the same to me. Didn't you see? The one square you should not, must not move on, was, of course, getting rid of your double, at least by killing him. For then, briefly, I kill you because of course you are the double that killed my master and so I revenge my dear lost leader. Macbeth killing Duncan's guards after killing Duncan was pretty crude. But this," and he smiled with a certain complacency, "is, I think you will allow, pretty neat." Then, putting his head on one side, he asked lightly, "Have you any more questions?"

The man covered in the chair crouched back. "Algol," he said, "this is a big mistake, believe me. You are making a colossal mistake, all the way through. Stop this fooling and let me explain. I can—"

"Oh, stop that kind of rhetoric!"

"But," he broke in again, "give me twenty seconds to tell you one thing. Perhaps in that time—"

"Oh, no, I shan't change my mind! But twenty seconds out of eternity isn't long, and no one is coming to interrupt our interview." Algol swung his left wrist across his right so that he could see his wrist watch as his right hand trained the automatic on the man in the chair. "Twenty seconds to so impress me that I shall know I quite misunderstood the situation," he laughed. "Now, go!"

The covered man repeated, "There's just time. It is a mistake. Put that pistol down." He spoke the commonplace words with intense earnestness and, as he spoke, shrank back into the chair, his nervous hands twisting about and fingering its arms.

The smile on Algol's face widened as the muscles of his right hand began to contract.

The nervous fingers of the man he had cornered were now feebly playing with the bull's-head terminals of the chair-arms, while he said over again, "Stop, it's not too late."

"Fifteen," counted out Algol's voice and, in mounting triumph, "sixteen, seventeen."

Nothing moved in the man opposite him, save those twisting fingers. Now even the fingers were all but still. Only the thumb of his right hand still feebly played with the short left-hand horn of the right bull's head, pushed at it, till it suddenly bent.

Algol's right hand, at that moment, opened widely, made the kind of gesture that a Bali dancer makes in explicating a movement, a fan gesture with all the fingers splayed; and the automatic—just as a flower that has been played with is, then, tossed to the audience—leaped lightly from the flattened palm, bounced onto the desk, collided with a couple of the microphones on the left, and was still. Algol carried through the movement of his arm. He had risen, evidently, on tiptoe; he twirled round; his neck and head spun in the same ballet gesture, and then, as quickly, swooped down behind the desk.

The man in the chair fiddled with the loose bull's horn again. A slight sound of shifting came from behind the desk out of his sight. He played with the small tusk of sham ivory again, listening. But no sound now came from the desk's other side. He took his thumb off the bull's head, raised his hand and then, rather wearily, his body. He was taken with an immense yawn. He turned to the right, skirted round the big desk, and, when he was on the other side of it, looked down. Algol was lying with his hand still in that rather unsuitable dancer's gesture, but his other arm was under him and his face was on the floor. His observer bent down, waiting for a moment, then ran his hand under the body on its left side, nodded and immediately rose.

173

He collected the automatics, the one on the right-hand corner of the desk and the one lying among the microphones. The first he placed by the twisted hand that still seemed reaching out for something. The second he took into the bathroom. He emerged wiping the stock with rubbing alcohol while holding the barrel wrapped in toilet tissue. He put it back in the small locker in which Alpha had kept his insignia pistol which now was serving a more practical purpose. Then he returned to the desk, took the microphone three. The contact opened.

"Trusties One and Two," he directed, "come up with two mail-delivery sacks."

He heard the contact close and waited, watching the door. It opened and the two familiar house figures entered, each carrying a voluminous textile sack.

"My defender saved my life but lost his," he remarked, watching their faces. Perhaps a shadow of commiseration or admiration might have passed across their eyes: certainly not of surprise. And now that cleared and they were evidently only waiting for orders.

"Place the bodies one in each sack." They handled them as though they were clumsy parcels for the post or pillows limply being pushed into their pillowcases. "Now, carry them out with me." These men were chosen for powerful build, and they swung the sacks on their shoulders with one heave. He opened the door for them and led the way to the large elevator. They all got in. He slammed the gate and pressed the lowest knob.

"Dispatching outgoing mail," he found himself repeating in a whisper. "Two loads: one white mail, the other black mail!"

The whirring stopped with a cushioned jerk. He swung back the gate when they had grounded. He knew where they would be. He was down, with his cargoes, at the incinerator level and at this hour they were out of action. He went over to the wall in which, like built-in marble sarcophagi, the electric furnaces of fused quartz gleamed dully in the strip lighting of this vault. He picked the large central one that dealt with hard garbage at high temperature.

"Open that furnace and deposit the sacks in it." They

obeyed adroitly. The pale white cave, like a cool sepulcher, received the two swathed lumps. "Now you can go back to your quarters, and remember to send down the lift to wait for me. Bring me some hot consommé in another half hour."

He heard the elevator door clash behind him. Then he spun the resistance knobs at the side of the furnace door and stood, his eyes at the observation slit, where, through translucent deep-tinted quartz, the interior of the furnace could be viewed.

For perhaps two seconds all was black. Then a red sunrise spread over the scene on which he looked, a flat gray landscape from which rose two low ranges of dark mountains. The landscape flushed quickly as though the sun were rising somewhere behind him, flushed and then glowed, glowed and then glared. And the mountain ranges, as though the place had suddenly become volcanic, burst into flame. The flame enveloped them and the landscape became a solid bank of fire enclosing an atmosphere of fire. The mountain range in this climate rapidly began to shrink. The atmosphere which for a few moments was heavy and dim began to clear to a fierce brightness. The two ranges were rapidly shrinking, melting away, or rather withering away. They shrank and twisted as fine paper in an ordinary fire will twist and shrink until it finally contracts and completely vanishes away into gas.

Finally he could tell that anything had been in that consuming mouth only because, on the quivering heat of the floor, the smooth level surface seemed to be slightly raised along two tracks by a low silt of incandescent dust. He had been told that the heat was so intense that it pulverized bone and tooth and that all that was left was a little pure white, very fine calcium dust. It was evidently true. He switched back the dials to "Off" and heard, as he retraced his steps to the elevator, the gentle tick, tick, coming in slower intervals as the furnace made the very slight contraction adjustments that was all the reaction it showed to this tremendous upsurge and downrush of temperature. He got into the elevator.

In the apartment he gave himself a leisurely shower and

then, as he heard the trusty come in with the soup, he bathed in a tub of radiated water that stung and needled your muscles till it felt, at least to him, better than any massage. Putting on only a robe, he went in to his late supper just as the trusty who had served it withdrew. He felt hungry, tired, and curiously content. Empty, too—finished, in a way.

His mind did not want to speculate, to think of the future, or to reflect, to live over the past. It stood at a dead center and he was well content to let it do so, while he looked after his body. He knew he had left out nothing and that he had taken all the moves offered him. He felt like a piece on the chessboard that has been played with to considerable effect and now waits until the consequences of what its moves have brought about, develop further.

After drinking the soup he sat smoking while he listened to one of the modern symphonies on his radio and wondered detachedly about music's strange history: how man, the patternmaking animal, had gone on developing this most lovely and deepest of all the abstract patterns—gone on developing it, regardless of the plenty or poverty, the tragedy or happiness of the successive ages. That lovely medieval music rising like still columns of thin blue smoke serenely in the evening sky, out of a landscape black, at ground level, with auto-da-fé fires. Buxtehude and Bach weaving and unwinding that inexhaustible cloth-of-gold, of fuge and concerto, while their Germany was struggling exhausted out of ruin and even the cannibalism of the Thirty Years' War. Yes, even in the spirit of man, even in the spirit of man the technician, was something that went on with its serene evolution and explication, be the earth never so unquiet, and the bodies of men and the passions of those bodies never so cruel or terrified. He turned in to bed with his mind as serene, detached, and vague as a cloud which passes above the sunset and melts in its passage away into the darkening blue.

The next morning he woke fresh, immediately recollecting his position, which, indeed, he had taken care to make clear by moving into the master's bed. And his mind now saw clearly its inevitable next move. As soon as he had dressed

176

and had eaten he went to what already was his desk. Taking microphone one, he gave an instruction and sat back. Within two minutes it was answered, and he was already so sure of himself that in those two minutes the only thought that ran through his mind was a query. He was asking whether his predecessor might not have been actually right in his pet fancy: If you put yourself into the position to have certain progressive, significant ideas they would come to you, hit you. A pole, put high enough on a dark night, will suddenly appear shining white in the high dark, because it is intercepting the beam of a searchlight passing over, but otherwise unseen, in the clear dark air. Certainly he gave not a thought to what he was going to do. It was all obvious, and simply flowed from what had been forced on him.

The door opened and closed. Waiting for him to speak were the two subordinates of Algol—the two who, those other lives ago, as it happened, were the couple that had picked him up and been the first flight of pouncing falcons which were to carry him up to this present eyrie. Well, certainly, they, no more than he, knew what they had done. He smiled at the thought and they, seeing that the world-master was in good mood, smiled back a little sheepishly and placatorily.

"I wish," he began, and they were all deferential attention, "to give you instructions which are important and will be for you, I know, profoundly satisfactory."

He paused and looked again at them. These men, he knew, would commit any act of toughness, if it were their orders; and yet here they were not shamming the part of deferential and even gentle loyalty. As long as he was leader he could draw that side from them—or, for the matter of that, the other—by a single gesture. They were just domesticated wild animals, dogs absolutely faithful to their master and brutes to all else if he set them on the wretched stranger. He remembered how much the old Alpha had learnt and used animal psychology in handling his new giant agglutinations of mankind. How he would point out that his whole success was because he had seen the way between the horns of Hobbes and Machiavelli on the one hand and Rousseau and Owen on the other.

"Man is not a brute," Alpha used to remark, "in the old romantic sense of that word, but in the new natural-history sense. Nor is he a charming, sane individual making social contracts and contacts and loving to be amiable with all, just because he likes those he knows. Bear cubs love their mother, true enough. But skin her and they will nestle affectionately in her pelt and eat ravenously off her carcass lying beside the pelt. I, without my mask and robe, would naturally be eaten. Someone else who really could wear the giant's robe, would get the worship due from cub to she-bear."

Well, the poor old fellow had been right. He had prophesied truly. The successor found his mind so clear and detached that he could think these amusing things while giving these cubs their shaping licks and pats. Again he saw that ex-Alpha had been right: a little position might make a man vain, but when your position went beyond rival or equal, then you yourself became self-debunked and quite detached. But could he keep it? Had Alpha, who had gone? Well, he would keep it if he could keep going, and it was clear what he must do and was doing with these tough kids with their child minds. He let the phrases of vague promise run until, as it were, their psychic saliva was flowing. Then he gave them their first lumps of actual food—real news and what it would mean for them.

"I have to tell you that your chief, my faithful servant, has now made an act of incomparable nobility. As you know—and may often have felt with some heaviness—his life had been overclouded in this new dawn, by what he, quite wrongly, but convincedly, believed was a personal blot on his record and scutcheon.

"The revolution had already entered into evolution"—he paused, and they bowed with eager anticipation—"but he felt that he had failed to present me with the thing that was therefore overdue. We have peace and progress. But in his own province those great facts were overcast because he had failed to root out, expose, and bring before me this figure which he calls the Mole. I begged him to leave aside such things, showing him that we had victory, so why trouble about missing some of the steps! But, like all great technicians, his joy was in his work, and he assured me that never could he think that my reign was safe, as long as, however far underground, there lived one who could question it.

"My advice could not avail with him and so finally, with regret, and seeing that without it, he would never have rest, I permitted it; I sent him to what alone could be, to such a man, his rest. He told me that he was sure that, though he valued your services as highly as I do, this work could only be done alone, by one man singlehanded. He must go down alone, for, as he said, and you and I know, the mass attack had failed to penetrate. It had driven back, but only driven deeper the nucleus. To get down to that and behind it, a single probe and lance must serve, alone could serve. And for that supreme task he offered himself and I, for his peace of mind—for of my security in your hands I felt no doubt—I reluctantly permitted. Nor did his sacrifice end there. He would wish that I should make this farewell for him, and I will, with a fitting eulogy. He may be a-way long, he may be away for good and—here attend to me—when he returns (though that I know would be sufficient for such fidelity) he could only be known to me."

He saw with pleasure their puzzled but entertained interest.

"Think what this man has done, how completely, in order that he may succeed in his task, he has obliterated himself—for he was always of that nobly extreme type, almost unsuited to survive in a world where the right has the right of way and open passage. He knew that the only way whereby he could hope to penetrate down to the depths he was determined to plumb, would be for him to do nothing less than to disappear, disappear utterly. He must have his outward self completely destroyed and leave no trace of it and go on alone, an obliterated man with nothing again to recognize, to reward, to re-establish, lost to his one consuming purpose."

They were still at a loss, but their interest certainly not less keyed.

He watched them almost wince as he remarked quietly, "Therefore he has chosen to have his whole body transformed, facial surgery must cut away the face the world knew, and bodily surgery must change that fine body, of which, as a master athlete, he was so proud." He paused, "He has gone, already he lies somewhere utterly changed, never to be restored, but set on his traceless journey to the unknown. Yes," he said in deepened tones, "only I, only I can gauge what that sacrifice must mean. But I am glad that you, too, can share my understanding."

He saw their sentiment, in their moist eyes, swilling over for a moment, their self-interest and excitement—self-interest, that a chief they no doubt liked as little as Algol had liked him, was out of the way, and excitement as to what further rise must be coming to them. He switched over to the proclamation manner.

"I am giving you the first orders for a new advance, soon to rally in a new drive of progress the greater part of mankind. The age of struggle and hidden wrestling closes with this wonderful secret act. Now we all come out openly in spectacular leadership. The age of secrecy closes at this moment. You stand on a new divide, and I name you two as deputy leaders of the two great orders of marshals of humanity.

"You," he said, turning to the one who looked least muscular and most spectacular, the dramatic type rather than the man of action, "you will be Grand Master of that division in to which I am going to divide all the police, and your division will be called the Guides. It is for you to give mankind the lead and the initiative in every manner of communal invention and advance, in all the ritual of their living, in the full and manifest pattern of social beings which must be continually enlarged and enriched. It is for you to see that in your deployment, the forces of humanity shall not develop energy without an adequate expression-pattern. It is not for us to repress but to expand, to find expression for all the yearnings, aspirations, and inspirations of mankind. Repressed, they become revolts and conspiracies. Let have their outlet in the chosen and designed and changing patterns of living and they become a power of cohesion binding man ever more strongly as he grows in magnitude."

He turned to the other—a tough, if ever there was one, and as simple and action-hungry, as risk-requiring, as a boy of twelve.

"You," he said, "will head the other order. While this, your companion, your fellow consul, will take out and expand the uniformed police into new advisers, friends, and inspirers of the common man, your task is to take out and explicate the destiny of the secret police, the plain-clothes men. I name you, therefore, the head of the order of Oblates. You have had to live too long as delates—men who had to live on the informer, on delation. That day closes this moment. The red dawn may end in a clear sunrise. It is for you to use the readiness, the power of taking risk, the carelessness of reward, the power to dare and to hold on in secrecy, for a new high. You will use your honored forces—you will set the pattern for them—in a life of continual frontier expansion. At every limit-line of mankind, there you will be marshaled to lead mankind on, to lead it out into new territories. Wherever there is the risk of radical exploration, of the breakthrough into an unknown world, with unknown prizes and unknown dangers, there you must and will be the pioneers."

He paused, and he saw in the eyes of both of them that simple swimming glance. Yes, they were impressed. The language was commonplace, the tasks obvious, and yet, somehow, said by him and with the trappings and initiative it would give each of these psychological adolescents, the whole thing became a vision all the more powerful and compelling because so vague. He faced them with an intense stare and saw their eyes, which had been fixed on him, waver and sink. He rose.

"I hereby," he said, "appoint you to these offices and, incidentally, each of you will carry the rank and the salary of our late vanished friend."

They smiled up at him, as he stood on the ramp which was higher on his side than on theirs, like boys receiving their first prize. He raised his hands and, as though he had ordered it, they sank on their knees. Their heads were bent, bowed over the edge of the desk, as over an altar rail bend neophytes about to receive a sacrament. He put out his hands and laid them on these bowed scalps. He felt the skin move—and remembered the queer old word Horripilation—that gooseflesh-raising of the hair as the nervous system feels the oncoming and presence of a power which frightens and yet excites. So, the ancients said, so is found the man who in the sacred grove or in the inner holy of holies has suddenly been found by the god, looked on, and left happily dead. The heads trembled for a moment under his fingers.

Then he withdrew his hands and said curtly, "Go; the patents of your rank will be prepared immediately. Be prepared to undertake your offices, division of the force, et cetera, at once. Announce that Algol has gone on a mission of the utmost and highest importance and is therefore seconded on an indefinite leave."

He turned back to his seat and as he sat down he saw the two, become curiously boylike now in his eyes, back out, bowing, through the door.

VII

ROMANTIC REACTION

HE SAT STILL for some time after they were gone. Like a
refrain through his mind ran the phrase, "It's as easy as
that, as that. You just go ahead and say what should be
done and it's done." He knew, without a tremor of doubt,
that the orders he'd given, would, though so simple, break
out like seed in the long downward slope of subordinates.
All he had to do at the high and steep elevation at which
he had been dumped, was to set a small trickle going in
the direction he intended, and then, inevitably, he could
foretell that in a few weeks there would be a great rushing
torrent of purposes and skills, orders and arrangements pouring down and out onto the plains of what the world called
action and actuality. And in a few months there would be
cut out a great bed, and what had been a torrent, strong
enough to carve its way with some noise and thrust and
some resistance overcome, would have become a great calm
river, "with pomp of waters unwithstood," that flowed on
so resistlessly that people took it as being part of the very
order of nature.

As he thought, he twisted something on his finger and
looking down he saw that it was his central insignia, the
signet ring—what old Alpha had called, with his curious
gift for using old terms and making them slightly different so as to serve new evolved purposes, the Future-Man's
Ring. He had never been able to look closely at it before,
for although when he was sent out deputizing he had to
wear a reproduction, he had noticed that Alpha there had
shown one of his curious reticences—perhaps when he
had talked of the inevitability of his inspirations he had really meant just this—a superstitious sense of his own luck
and that, like most men *au fond* superstitious, he had identified his luck with this object.

The reproduction he had worn had had the bezel uncarved. This was elaborately carved. It was a large luminous stone of a crystal of electrum tint, and the whole table of the stone—quite an inch in length and perhaps three-quarters in breadth—was taken up with a full and deeply carved design. It was evidently one of those abraxid rings of Gnostic influence. He took a magnifying glass from a drawer in the desk and examined it. It was certainly a striking and suggestive design, and maybe this was the source from which Alpha had gotten his basic idea so that he felt his luck was somehow held in it. It showed, from top to bottom, a giant figure of a man in the stance of the Rhodian colossus, uniting the lands of the east and west with his huge straddled stride: he was also clearly an Atlas, for his head was bent forward a little so that he not only regarded the whole earth stretched out before him but held the full clouded heavens on his bent nape, both a diadem and a burden from which he saved the earth. His arms ran down each side of his body and were open outward in an attitude of achievement and bestowal.

Yes, it was clear from where old Alpha had taken that ritual act with which the vast symbolic service and ritual of mankind culminated. From the loins of this superman—this Adam-Kadmon, archetypal hominid—there swooped down an eagle, on the landscape between his feet ramped a winged bull, while, flying out from the inner facet of each kneecap the winged man and the winged lion seraphs met, making the crossbar of the giant "A." Yes, certainly something in the creative paraconscious of that curious medium-creator that had called itself Alpha, had seen in these ancient Minoan symbols something archetypal and still been able once more to find a contemporary expression and give the stamp of their mold to one more of the social-heredity patterns of mankind.

And as he gazed at this curiously complex but congruent pattern, he found his own mind beginning to see further extensions and applications of this mythic design. Surely, to use formal language, here was an actual instrument of government. Alpha had been right here and he had been right also when he was still looking ahead to further evolutionary development, further unfolding of the latent idea.

The time, his successor began to see, as he pored over this minutely carved elaborate symbol, the time *had* come for the next stage, and while he gazed at the primal Alpha, the new notion took form in his mind. Surely, Alpha's work must be carried on. He had, like all the priest-kings, when his power began to wane and the Shekinah to leave him, he had to be set free by his successor, who then would further fulfill the idea which had done all it could through that last vehicle. For him, then, for him, Alpha II—the one so closely identified with the office that the join between I and II would never be known by the world—for him the task was, with the renewed life which he brought to serve and to incarnate this idea, to take it a step further in explication. He must and would with this sacred signet make a series of proclamations for and as the voice of mankind. He saw it now: he could speak directly to the people and issue on their behalf, and with their worldwide acclaim— and he smiled at the aptness, the inevitable aptness of the phrase—Bulls, hominal bulls, bulls of humanity, charters of mankind. So the last priest-king had from Rome issued his papal bulls to the city and the world; but it was a vain and shrinking boast—or, rather, a prophetic hint as to what the real ruler of the world, when he came, should, could, and indeed must do.

Now, the hour had come and the self-assassination had been merely a purely internal and strictly private move, a small internal digestive act, while the great development processes of the growth, of a solidarified, physically integrated mankind, went on. His mind had become clear. All he would need now was to work the actual wordage out with that curiously mediumistically-minded, psychic parasite, the secretary whom, with all the other gear of command, he had inherited.

He turned to her microphone and waited, with his mind filling with a mounting certainty and definition as a cistern fills steadily from base-inflows. The small panel that was in the wall between the fireplace and the door to his dining room slid back silently and she entered. He had never had a full look at her, always having to be out of the door as she entered, but the impression he had garnered and sheaved had been right. Quite likely she might not know that he had seen her, that he existed—for certainly Alpha I saw the advantages of other people being in the dark, as well as anyone. But she had formed quite a strong impression in his mind. She entered now obviously only knowing that she was once again in the center of life, once again in the presence of the man who had made meaning of the world, for everyone, supremely for her who stood closest to the actual sun of being. How could she distinguish, in the heart of that universal blaze that lit the whole of mankind, any peculiarity or particularity! Again, he knew he was so much his office that not a chink in its smooth shining surface would let through a hint of whatever he might have been or had been. He was secure and now need never fear, a heart grown cold, a head grown gray in vain. The curious aptly inept lines from Shelley's eulogy of the young dead Keats flitted along the word arrangements of his mind. Well, it just showed how everything converged—the priest-king from the undocumented past, the poet from the wordy but ineffective romantic movement.

She stood waiting, quite content, and in a way quite unself-conscious as long as she was in his presence and was waiting his command. He told her to sit down and he would talk out his next process. She took one of the chairs from the fireplace and arranged herself in a relaxed attitude.

"You see," he said, "we have reached the place when a new expression will be given to all that has been latent. The flower matures a long while in the bud form and then in a moment it breaks into full bloom. The moment has come for me to proclaim mankind to itself, to call it to waken and to expand to its full world compass. For some time it has been clear that the Dominium of Alpha, this society of freely integrated mankind, has been mankind proper, and outside of it there has been only a fringe of peoples hanging onto outworn patterns and archaic procedures; just as when the age of revolution began and Western man found mere physical power he found a fringe of peoples who were left behind, the pagan and untechnical societies which he called savage. But Western man was one-sidedly cocksure. His rapid advance in physics made him blind. He did not understand his disbalance, and over against him he had Asia the misconceived, the underrated, Asia whose psychological knowledge had to match and complement his dangerous power of crude physical expansion by giving him power of psychological cohesion. The Revolutions are over.

"There," he said, "that is the prologue. There will be a big ritual act and this will be my inaugural. Then I shall go on to tell them what is now due. For the last twenty years what have we seen? Why, history repeating one of its automatic solutions! When the Roman Empire had made its first striking successes and come out as the leader of all the whole Mediterranean lands, then, as nothing succeeds like success, it was called in from every side:—Here, as when the Attalids bequeathed to the people of Rome their kingdom; there, where nations who could not solve their international contacts and trade intercourses, had to have an arbiter and overlord to give the international peace their economy demanded but which their power was incapable of enforcing and their agreement inadequate to supply. So today we see by the inevitability of success, the flow of outer peoples toward our order and into the field of our higher efficiency and superior integration and extended range of the balance of happiness—of order and freedom. The time, then, has come, to proclaim this, make it explicit and, as it were, to make actual what is latent—in short, to incorporate mankind."

She stirred in her chair with an easy movement of content but made no other reaction. He knew both from immediate feeling and from what Alpha had told him, that she had grasped it all, not with a critical, constructive sense but with the power of the great actress to express it in detail and its full amplification. She would actually know how many subrenderings for the different stages of representation of the central idea would be wanted. So he ran on and gave her in such dotted outline the scheme for the great inaugural ceremony also. How he would, with his signet, and in a meeting of mankind, with television showing it to the whole world and bringing them every word, make actual the unification of mankind.

They worked in this way for perhaps a couple of hours and, so easily had now the flow come, that he was able, with part of his mind, to observe her, not as an instrument which he found it perfectly easy to play with full volume and mastery, but as a person in herself, even in a way a mystery. Clearly, she was good looking in that standard classic Greek way which was the facial fashion of the time for those who wished to be professional women. And she had been sufficiently sure of herself to let the pattern not be quite completely the polished and finished style of the pure mode. She had retained one or two slight dysplasias and asymmetries—it was not a fine font of print, it was an extremely good freehand calligraphy in which she had rendered her appearance, and made her impression. He went back to his outlining.

"Tell them," he said, "that I join them, I, the supreme bridge-builder, the *pontifex maximus* of the final bridge which spans the great river of Ocean, uniting, at last, mankind. The common man can just stride the ditches of personal differences and so sustain family life. The dikes of different social heredities divide them. Only heroes can leap such, and super-heroes swim the sundering rivers of nationhood, bringing mankind into empires. But only avatars, the spiritual amphibians, can pass over the oceans and so found world communions. So I am the ultimate avatar, the Pharos of mankind, the concluding Abraham in whom all the nations of the world shall be blessed.

"I have made those synthetic extensions of consent whereby the natural fibers of the human heart, strong but short, may be woven out in the vast loom of communal experience and ritual apprehension into the great seamless robe and garment of mankind. The word *cosmos* is at base the word for a robe, a wrap, an enveloper, and in the great pattern of mankind, in the great golden net of interwoven and shining orders and ranks, loyalties and interrelated creativities, I have threaded all the pearls and jewels of mankind in a shining diadem."

All she said when he stopped was, "That will go into

eight graded sections—two of preliminary proclamations, two classes of special ranking orders, one code of instructions, two divisions of protocols, and the inaugural speeches. The re-rendering into the textbooks, and the school recitation passages, and the recasting into the choric ritual odes will go to the college of choric production by next fortnight. Yes," she mused, "the distributions and subeditings should be through in six weeks," and she rose.

His mind, as she made these rapid distribution gradings, had gone back—for it was finished with its part of the task—to thinking of her and watching her obliquely. This, of course, was the uniqueness of the woman: a mind which, on the surface completely lacking in anything but the power of accurate echo, could, nevertheless, take the simple initial sound and, as will a large vacant dome, quietly and quickly distribute it into its harmonics and octaval parts. Indeed, this mind of hers, he began to see, had a power and beauty of those large vacant-faced goddesses such as the Aphrodite of Melos. This is, he reflected, a beauty so lacking in any accent of expression that it is the complement of that great sky-vacant void Zeus of which Alpha spoke. Such an accepting, unchallenging mind, is as it were, a womb, a vast, quiet, patient egg in which the small struggling seed, the feverish sperm, finds its rest, its development, but also its consumption.

It was then, when his mind with its new surety had reached this firm conclusion, that, on the clear sky of his assurance, the first mist-cloud of doubt began to form. Alpha had spoken of her hunger, her demand, held in cheek but with a gnawing vigilance always trying to break through the rider-rod on the balance bar of their relationship and upset it. But he had to own that though he could sense a loyalty that was indeed symbiotic, he could as yet not sense the intrusive yearning for identity that would destroy balance. He was too trained in observation to spoil this first fine impression with distorting overlay of conclusions drawn or imposed.

No, he felt, there are two possible explanations, it is true, but I must not as yet draw either. What I know, and all I know, is that there must be some change, for old Alpha

189

was a good reporter. His power was in judging men and women. That's the *sine qua non* of all super-leadership. Anyhow, in either case I must note and move carefully, for of the two possible explanations one must be that the difference is due to her sensing, at some deep depth, that I am different, that the Alpha of today is other than the Alpha of yesterday, that she is stepping today into another stream. Do I, I wonder, smell different? He smiled to himself: The woman's flair subconsciously realizing that she's lost the scent? Or, and this other conclusion is as serious, she must have found some assuagement, some deflection of the full pressure of her dependence.

After a few moments it seemed she had made the rapid allotments of the grades of presentation his message would require.

She rose, evidently sensing that he had finished, and said, "There is only one interview that has passed through the preliminary sortings and would be worth your attention. A new psychoanthropologist has passed the tests of thesis-originality in his application to see you, and as the basic ideas can't be found to have been presented to you before, and his correlates, though original, seem sound deductions from physiological and psychological reaction patterns, it has been thought you might find value from drawing him out. His notions, though no doubt in themselves worthless when actually applied, might prove a trigger stimulation to the latent ideas which you have further to give to the world."

She spoke this rigmarole quite quietly, and he knew what it was meant to convey: it was a formula to say that a psychological inventor would repay his attention so that he might take his thoughts and weave them into his further constructions.

"When have you given him?" he asked.

"In the middle of tomorrow afternoon. His mental processes have been timed and it seems he should take some forty minutes to discharge. I am, therefore, ready to confirm with him that 3:30 would be an hour at which he could be seen."

He nodded. "Be here, then, at 2:45 to give me a précis

of the present interlocked field of psychophysical experiments and large-scale tests. I shall want to know how far the schools and the colleges and the adult education are using the new psychophysical methods and the grading out of the various types."

She gave the gesture which her rank gave, the right hand held down near the body but turned out at right angles with the flat palm presented to the floor. When he looked up again she was gone. The timing in himself told him that he had done his work for the day. There were no appearances—and all the lieutenants were charged so that the developing processes would keep them engaged. The wave he had sent out would be gorging the upper turbines for the next forty-eight hours.

His mind also obeyed his sense of position and he found himself able to spend the remainder of the day neither exhausted nor restless. He read, listened to music, saw in the television that evening's vast opera—an enormous mythic rendering of the voyage of the soul. The basis of this, though as immensely enlarged as the Greek drama enlarged the simple folk tales out of which it grew, was the Tantric Mahayanan Bardo Thodol.

It was, of course, superbly done, with every aid of the modern stage craft. The great circles of lessening light, of rainbow belts of glory, and smoky mists and fumes of miniatory gloom, were shown with perfect representation, and through it could be seen the small sparklike soul traveling its way, dreeing its weird, until the great climax. After the pleading recitative voice of the attendant lama had tried to restrain it, the rising wind of fear-desire, that bore it away from the first lightning burst of the Clear Light of the Void, carries it onto the lee shores of the underworlds, when, last seen through the refraction of these dark belts of murky light, the forms of the peaceful deities rise with ineffective pleadings, the goddesses and gods of compassion, the redeemers and the grace-bearers, their hands held out in last appeal. But the gale rises higher, and down on the gathering blast sweep the awful marshaled bands of the wrathful deities, and the soul before this typhoon can

191

only scud for safety to the close harborage of a womb and one more birth.

The vast mythos was rendered with a volume of rhythmic sound equal to the light-controls, and the modern composers, with their enlarged orchestration, with their new instruments of siren sweep, with notes and super- and subsonics that shook the central nervous system, were able to charge the whole audience with cathartic ecstasy, to which mankind had been alien since the Greek play ceased to be the actual rendering of the deepest needs of humanity.

The choreographers of this day had also now found, in these great transcendental themes, at last a way out of the futilities of the romantic movement and the boy-meets-girl ineffectiveness. Here were designs worthy of their art, and techniques. These designs at last carried on that cosmic interest and concern of mankind which had been stifled since, when the Greek play was silenced, the miracle play of medievalism had tried to substitute, only itself to peter out with Punch and Judy!

Audience and actors, as of old, were one, and in the tremendous choruses, though they were led by the special singers, the whole of those present partook, while, as the great movements took place on the central stage, the attendance was also conducted so that it too moved in sympathic rhythm, though on simpler pattern, with the tragedy that was explicating itself on the vast altar-stage round which they, the attendance, were ranged. As the great process of dramatic ritual closed, with the small central figure falling down in the great cosmic swirl of desire, down, down to where opened to receive it the billowing ocean trough of the Sansara, the heaving, traveling sea-womb of reincarnation and of time, the music swept broadly forward to a climax in which acceptance and agony were in strophe and antistrophe, until the lights sank one by one, the general vision faded, and the vast view of the single cosmic process shrank back into the manifold and the discriminate. The audience found itself once more in the phenomenal world —its revels ended, the vast altar-stage empty and the world once more around them to be lived in what could be remembered of the outline of meaning which had been shown as in a glass, darkly.

As the show closed and his ground-glass screen, through which he had viewed it, clouded to its quiet opaque gray, the new master of the world sat back. Hadn't they climbed somewhere beyond where men had gone before and carried a step further the possibilities of vision and understanding for mankind? It was true the Fourth Revolution had come and had completed the three preliminary efforts. For they, the new masters, had given the answer to the blind demand of the First Revolution, the Religious Revolution, the need for man to have religious freedom—the right to have his views of the beyond, where the state could not get them or go with them, where every man must go alone. Alpha had seen that the people had a right to have their views rendered for them in the most splendid way that modern means could present the archetypal ideas and hopes and intuitions of ultimate justice and mercy. So, too, the demands of the Second Revolution had been met and man had been given all those political freedoms, that right to liberty and order which had been the blind demand of the Political Revolution—which had till now only ended in military dictatorship and giant armies and the revolt of all peoples outside that small district from which, first, had come the idea of liberty and, next, the armed force which exploited that generous hope. And likewise with the Third, the Economic, Revolution, the demand for the right to plenty, to liberty from breaking toil, the right to find that work in which one's inborn creativeness could find its expression and the man be satisfied and his community benefited in constant and generous reciprocation—that, too, had been blindly and ignorantly demanded. And today, at last, that rightful part of the demand had been found solved in the final solution. The chord of the three demands had found its sudden resolution in the final bass note of the fundamental understanding of man, of the psyche, the true center, while all these others were but epicenters, of those great shocks of readjustment which the rapidly condensing psyche had made.

Now, at last, the true center had been found and it was

henceforward possible to keep pace, or, rather, to balance up one side of the demands of man for expansion with his equally vital but till then overlooked demands for an equilibrium of corresponding cohesion. If man expanded his physical powers by deliberate invention, so he must, by the same use of deliberate invention, forge a new tensile strength in his consciousness, in his psychic capacity, to hold together and remain integrated. The traditional assumptions, loyalties, rituals, and beliefs—even had they held fast and not dragged their own moorings, fixed as they had become in too small a cosmos-picture—were capable only of balancing a traditional set of crafts and skills and technical "mysteries." With productive science working at one end, productive science must work at the other. The old-fashioned gun barrel of simple steel could hold safely a charge of black powder. The high explosive needed a new metal in which steel was increasingly reinforced till it became only a partner in a new scientific metal which nature had never forged but man invented.

The more he thought, the more he felt the inevitability of the whole vast process. How could the Mole fight it? Wasn't the Mole perhaps merely that rather futile opposition which only serves to bring out the full inventiveness in the side on which has fallen the decree of success? Wasn't he no more than the recessive characteristic, which is masked by the dominant, so that, perhaps, by that effort of masking—as in a healthy body a toxin produces more antitoxin than the body requires and so the body gains a still higher and more general health—the rightful orthogenetic pattern of living which is dominant may become even more inventive with its victory than he would have been had it won by a walkover? "To him who hath shall be given." The old gnomic saying capped his thought.

He went to bed with his mind at a new balance, with avenues of fruitful choice opening out before him. One thing he knew: he would not hurry, he must not hurry. He had succeeded to, he was crowning so much of, the imperial efforts of the past that in him, too, the great imperial motto could again flourish, the motto of evolution itself, "Festina Lente."

He got up the next morning noticing that no shock met him, even of surprise to find on returning to consciousness what his position had become. Even that strange remodeled face—that, too, with its extra fifteen years falsely written on it—was not that a gain, also, to look forty-five with all the maturity of success and yet, in point of expectation of staying power, to be thirty—one of those master secrets he could keep as part of his inner regalia?

The morning passed quietly. There were a few documents to be signed, a few orders to be confirmed, the notices of some series of honors to be issued. The various secretaries of these chancelleries called, waited, and humbly and gratefully withdrew, clearly having had a lift just to have been in his presence and received his smile. They would report to their families all the little detail they could gather from the routine interview, and the quietly accumulating pressure of loyalty would grow of itself like the strands of a climbing vine wrapping round in a steadily strengthening coil. He lunched early and then sat reading some interesting reports till he had annotated them to his liking. How well everything was presented so that the actual decision was easy and clear, only requiring a top man of undoubted authority and fair general understanding to make it. Could one doubt! This was effective government.

But after he had digested, a small old-fashioned want made itself felt. He would like to take a long, fine, solitary walk in the country—to swing along and let his mind wander, being led from one vague, pleasant line of feeling more than thought, as his body swung its steady soothing measure. Of course, that was out of the question. The captain must stay on the bridge, and he could get enough outings in the great processions. Still, just to be out, not to have to choose between this cooped privacy or that tremendous pressure of exposure—a vacuum or a supercongestion. . . . Well, it had to be. But while the thought-feeling swayed him his body rose and he began to pace the room.

He made several turns and then, as he came to the upper end farthest away from the desk, he glanced and saw how neatly the bullet tear had been mended in that chair. He bent over it and then looked behind to the wall and saw that where the bullet had lodged had also been carefully covered over. You could just see where the punch had been made but really only if you knew.

He was in that position of inspection when he heard the panel by which his secretary entered slide smoothly and he pulled himself straight, altered the position of the chair as a kind of covering movement—though what could she know about it?—and then turned slowly round. He turned to his left. She would have taken her seat to the right of his desk, so, to avoid passing near her, for he still was not comfortable in the field of her emotional pressure, he would go to his desk by its left side, toward the door that led to the elevator landing. He had taken a couple of steps, then, before he noticed that his way was barred. He looked up and his irritated surprise at the failure of his maneuver went up another gear into a shock, as he saw the figure that stood in his path to the desk was not a woman's at all; a strongly built young man confronted him.

"What are you doing here?" was met with the curt command, "Go back and sit in that chair and perhaps I'll tell you."

As the command was enforced with the wave of a hand that held an automatic, Alpha II retreated and sat down. Time must be gained, and no doubt this latest piece of madness would explain itself. It looked pretty obvious as to how it was meant to end, but if one could understand how it was brought about that might give one a chance of seeing one's way out.

He began quietly, "Why may I not go to my desk?"

"Because then you'd be armed."

"But, then, why don't you ask me to put up my hands?"

It was always wisest to keep people who covered you with guns talking as long as you could; that was old underground advice. And the answer, though still more disconcerting, was interesting.

"Because I know about you. You don't carry arms when at home. You depend on another defense—clever enough unless you're caught off your perch."

The young man backed a little, keeping his victim covered, and then, when he was near the desk, glanced quickly over his shoulder, remarking, "The switch is off," and with that sat down on the step of the broad dais that ran round the desk.

"Yes, it is a neat little trap, isn't it?" he said, stroking the pile of the carpet with his left hand. "Of course, if the pile just on this dais is a bit stiffer than the silky nylon that makes up the beautiful checked pattern of the rest of the carpet, well, it has to stand more people standing on it, doesn't it? A quite natural precaution in good housekeeping. But, of course," and he patted the strong nap, "these bristles are pretty stiff, aren't they? Naturally you could have had those silver squares made of a glass fiber as fine and silky as the super-nylon on which you tread, and the gold bronze squares made of a super-conducting copper-aluminum alloy just as floss-soft. But then would either of them have stood without fusing or shorting the quite big currents that you wanted to be able to shoot through them at a moment's notice should your visitor make a sudden suspicious movement?"

Frankness would now serve best, he judged.

"Now, tell me," he said in a perfectly quiet but interested tone, "how do you know so much about this room and its occupant?"

He looked at the young fellow narrowly. Whom did he remind him of? The face was curiously familiar. Then suddenly he had to smile to himself. How slow he'd been! For, from the first, in spite of the intervention of other interests and questions, he had been puzzled by the look of the lad. Of course he'd seen someone like that before. Never in the flesh, as far as he remembered, but in photos. The fellow was a pretty good rough likeness of what Alpha had been some twenty years ago. The early pictures had not been popular with the later regime but you could yet find them, and naturally the underground had a series.

As the fellow paused, and it was essential for the covered man to keep the conversation going to postpone action when his part was so patently passive, he added, "Of course, I can see part of your passport. It's written on your face." Then suddenly a great laugh took him as the solution flashed.

197

The laugh evidently shook the lad, who looked positively offended at the levity.

He called out, therefore, through his chuckles, "Sorry, but I was laughing at myself for being so slow. Of course you could only have come through one pass; of course I saw the sign that some traffic might be on that pass, when I viewed that sentry yesterday."

"What do you mean?" It was the turn of the intruder to be disconcerted.

"You're like what Alpha was when still boyish," he explained rapidly. "Alpha's secretary naturally adores being near the world's success but would like to possess the idol of the people's heart. All that is no secret. It is merely the inevitable formula. You want to kill Alpha, again a quite common wish among males, as common as the wish among females to marry him. So you get to know Alpha's secretary. You satisfy part of her desire. She has her husband in two pieces as it were, or served in two courses—but at last the second course decides to swallow the first. Hence, you, somehow, having gained her confidence, put her temporarily out of the way and, having learnt that the old devil is unarmed, again from our Delilah, you pop up and pop him off and no doubt then both of you will, you hope, live happily ever after."

The effect of this bright piece of deduction was surprising but quite hopeful—as the end was to gain time.

The young man burst into indignant protest. "No!" he shouted and in his excitement actually uncovered his victim. "No, she's not to blame. She never betrayed you. She couldn't. It isn't in her absolutely loyal nature. But you pushed her too far. If there has been any betrayal it is I who with a conflicting loyalty have sacrificed her."

He paused and was evidently so taken up with his own romantic dream and sorrow as for a moment to disregard his prey. He had to justify himself.

"I'll tell you. I'll not have even you go out with a wrong impression of that woman, absolutely loyal even to such an object as you, and to me, just because she felt that in me she could see what you must have been, and, who knows,

198

may, before you went to pieces, have been. Yes, you shall know."

"Well," his selected victim reflected, "we must be thankful for assassins' sense of the dramatic! Probably they would never take the considerable risks and ardors of their trade were they not always dramatizing themselves as statuesque tyrannicides. I suppose I felt like that once. How much position changes conviction! And, of course, when they have to carry out their crowning act as it were in private, naturally they may never be able to run through the scene again, even by themselves. Hence we have the epilogue before the last act."

He was right, the young man was going to unburden himself and show the full height of his rectitude.

"You starved and exploited that woman. She was your chief victim. Out of a vast population she was on the summit of your holocausts." As he spoke his words moved him more than they interested his listener. His voice began to tremble. "I don't know what I've done. I didn't know what I was doing. Here's the story, and you can go to your tomb with perhaps the first piece of straight truth you've heard for years. I was young and hotheaded, and, like the best of my class, I hated you with your debauching of the people with pleasure. We wanted a fine, hard generation, one that lived and grew tensile on contest, struggle, and war. And you were turning them into slops and drabs. Oh, yes, all prettily turned out like a beauty chorus in a low show. Well, when I'd been like that for some time, I heard that there were some people who hadn't gone over and who worked humbly, strongly, unremittingly."

"You mean the Mole and Company?"

"Oh, I suppose you know what your chief of police tells you. But you can't know the spirit of the catacombs that burns deep down there, a true volcanic flame under all this ash and garbage. It will yet clean up all this dump!"

The boy's rhetorical prologue was giving him back his spirit. But a moment after he began again to waver.

"Well, I hadn't been long in, before we were electrified to hear that our chief—yes, the Mole—had at last made a perfect plan, so that he could insert, like a hypodermic needle under the hide of this great bull beast, one single germ and the monster would collapse. We were told that somehow he had been able to pick one of us and train him somehow so that he would be able to get through all the defenses and then, at the center, knock out the center pin. Then the whole wheel of oppression would fall in pieces and we could give back to mankind a clean, open, athletic, strong life.

"We were told that the training had been successful; we were told that the torpedo had been launched, that it was approaching undetected the giant hulk, that it had actually pierced its way through the torpedo nets, that the charge was now in contact with the central magazine. We waited with an expectancy that grew with the days—and then nothing happened.

"I was one of the first to dare ask, 'Is success still expected?' Indeed, the first to make the question an open challenge. I was court-martialed. It was insubordination, of course, even to talk about the plans. We were told, not in order that we should comment, but could be ready to co-operate should we be needed at a moment's notice: to show us what sacrifice we could have to meet and could meet, and to keep up the morale in that dark where there is never any clear news, only rumors . . ."

How well his hearer knew! The boy sighed, and then squared his shoulders.

"I owned that I had done wrong and could be literally fired but said they had better make a last use of me. I said, I'm like what the brute Bull used to look like. I told them that everyone knew of his secretary's state of heart. Why couldn't they send me to my death that way? Why not let me try the oldest of all ways into a citadel, older than the Trojan horse, the way through the harlot's house that is upon the wall, the way through a hungry woman's bedroom? That's the real sop to Cerberus—"

He paused, tired of his literary showing off, and added, "I thought it led to death, but noble death. But perhaps it only leads to hell after all. Well, they condemned me to death for insubordination on active duty and when I was waiting in my cell I received the reprieve: that I was to try for six weeks if I could make that entry, after which I would be picked up and disposed of. Yes, I succeeded—" the thought of his success did not raise his tone—"I succeeded. I was well trained and a good learner. First, I found out some of her friends. I should just have time for that necessary circuity. I was able to interest one of them greatly in me—for she, too, was one of your superfans and the likeness was what she wanted.

"Of course, as soon as we were really intimate, she had to boast of and commiserate about and so patronize her more successful friend. She told me at great length all about your secretary's hopeless passion. We sympathized together and she got so much enjoyment out of this absent patronizing of her powerful friend that, sure enough, in less than three weeks she actually thought she had suggested that I should see the great lady. We met, and again I saw that I held the card I hoped. She was hungry, right enough, poor kid, and she needed me. Then I had to play a part as difficult and dangerous as all the rest."

He leaned against the back of the desk almost relaxed as he lived over again the old nervous tension; the ancient intimacy springing up in that odd corner, the age-old confidence of one man telling another of the time he has had when the woman he has made fall in love with him has still to be kept in ignorant attachment, while he goes on to make a further attachment to the woman who is his prize but perhaps also his captress.

"Well, the hand played itself out. Yes, my face was, if not my fortune, my fate. She had fallen, right enough, after the first interview. I kept the double game going and before the six weeks were over I was able to report back, 'Can claim further reprieve of six weeks. Have now access.' Yes, I became her lover and shortly she was allowing me to be in her apartment here. I was dressed as one of the palace attendants. She found me a post, in one of the kitchens, as it happened. I used to bring her up her food and spend the evening with her. So I could say to the hyphen woman-friend that I was being kept by my work. But though she no doubt loved me because I was what her sane body knew you ought to be and had once possibly been, I—" he paused—"I began to love her for herself."

Then he shook himself. "Oh, don't flatter yourself I'm getting soft. Maybe I shan't kill you for the old reason but I'll kill you for a better, because, as long as you live, she won't love me completely. That's the real male reaction and you'll get it, never fear. But I hated deceiving her and, heaven knows how she'll take what I am determined to do.

"She trusted me at the end completely. It was only a couple of nights ago when she was in my arms and she sighed with complete content. 'This is perfect,' she told me, 'for now I feel safe and I also know He is safe.' I had always spoken to her as if I, too, were a doting fan. 'You must,' she added, 'often have the same fears for Him that I have. He is so brave and I know that though all kinds of people come in to see him he will never have his automatic on his desk. He calls it a piece of unworn insignia that he hopes soon to discard even abroad. But,' and she put her face closer and whispered in my ear, 'a few days ago he left me alone in his room. I couldn't resist. The throne was still warm where his arm had rested. I crept from my chair, went on my knees on the dais, and just laid my head for a moment where he had been sitting and, while I caressed the arm of the chair his hand had been on, I found that one of the small ivory horns of the symbolic bulls' heads was really a switch. I turned it and nothing happened. I left it on and stood up, looking round the room. I know it was wrong, but what woman is not curious about the secrets of the man she adores? As I gazed about, a large moth with purple-dusted wings suddenly sailed out from the great bouquet of flowers on the mantelpiece. It floated down through the air and lit on a corner of the outside of the dais which I could just see. There was a small flash and it was gone—utterly gone. I spun round, turned off the switch, and was back in my seat in a moment. But my heart was high in spite of the shock. I knew he had his defense and, thank heaven, he was wise enough to keep it from everyone.'

"Well, after that I knew the way was open. I just couldn't miss and mustn't wait. I'd have got you anyhow, had you been at your desk. But you see how fate rules and insists? At the moment I enter you choose to take a stroll and be ready to sit for your death mask in that convenient chair where you will be neatly executed."

Sitting back in that chair, Alpha II imagined that he could feel with his back the exact place where the hole had been repaired through which he had sent the bullet that confirmed Alpha I's dispatch. The lad, too, had evidently almost finished his tale, when of course, he would have nothing to do but shoot.

"Well, I had to drug her, drugged her tea as I brought it to her and sat with her, saw her sink away into stupor, and her last word was 'Alpha wants . . .' Well, *you* shall want nothing more, I promise her that, and when she wakes the way will be open to a sane, rational, heroic love."

He wound himself up with the winding up of his story, heaved himself onto his feet, and his fingers closed round the butt of the automatic.

"You are sure that you *are* killing Alpha?" his victim remarked quietly.

"Why, where's the doubt *there!*" the lad replied half in contempt but with almost as much question in his voice.

"Come here," Alpha II commanded. "You know I am unarmed, and I will put my hands in any position you like provided that you will put your face close enough to mine for you to see precisely."

"What are you up to?" the other asked, obviously nonplused.

"Well, it would be a pity if, after all your skill, sacrifice of feelings, and considerable courage, you killed the wrong man. If you went back to the Mole with the wrong extraction he would not thank you and might spoil your oncoming marriage. If Alpha has really got away you'd be the fool if you only killed the dummy put up to distract your fire!"

"But of course you're Alpha. *She* knows it. Nothing would deceive her!"

"Well, to some extent, you have."

"That's different, quite different."

"But did you, considering the way you went about to

get in, considering the type of disguise, your looks, that got you in, did you never wonder what method was used to get in your predecessor on this deadly but hopeful route?"

The boy was evidently now mainly won over, and, to the second command, "Come over here," he did obey. He held his automatic ready and his hand was more than half tensed round its stock. It was a tonic feeling to watch those muscles and wonder how far that thumb-tendon would have to rise before the neat little piece of mechanism his palm contained would cough out its deadly phlegm right into Alpha II's lungs. But the young fellow reached within two feet of the elderly looking man seated in the chair and the gun had not hiccuped.

The young face, which was the rough model of the face it scanned, looked up and down the lined and worn features. Sure enough, that must be Alpha; it was only a wish to gain time. And this was what time did, this was what he would be some day. It was high time to throw off that old husk, to finish his job, for now he'd never be safe with that old powerful parody alive. He must get through the formality of firing and get back to the poor drugged girl downstairs. He must be with her when she woke and all this must be in the fixed past. But the man who was, for all intents, dead and with his arms, as he'd been told, locked behind his head, did not seem blanched with fear or even shaking with any nervousness and he was speaking quietly:

"Now that you are close enough, look over my face, or *this* face, and see those fine lines, like very fine cobweb marks, fine, white, straight, very keen, cuts—for that is what they are; they are white because they are sharp, deep surgical scars. Now, for you can take any liberties with it you like, raise the upper lip." Gingerly, the lad obeyed and hardly prevented a slight shudder.

"Yes, you see, the jaws have been cut in the same way and the teeth extracted. Go on, look well all round the inside of the mouth, and you can trace cuts and slashes and long incisions right down to the windpipe. The whole mouth cavity

and throat are as scarred and mutilated as the outer sur-
faces of the face."

As the boy kept the teeth exposed, the voice mouthed
its words in disgusting accord with the exposed build-up.
The boy let the lip fall from the grinning dental sets and the
great, bulging, pink plastic mounts in which they were set.
The mantle of lip fell over the sham frontage. He drew
back; his fingers nervously wiped themselves as though he
had had to handle a badly reconstructed, ill-preserved
corpse that, as he touched it, might collapse upon him.

Filled with this uncanny sense of strangeness, he couldn't
resist asking, "Who are you?"

"Your predecessor."

"But . . ."

"Yes, I got through and I have done my mission. Had
you killed me you wouldn't have killed Alpha, you see.
He's gone already. They never told you how they prepared
the first double. You think you have taken risks and paid.
Look at me. What would you have said if, with your looks,
that fate had faced you! And I was better looking than
you. I can say it, because that 'I' was flayed off my bones
in the depth of a prison long ago. Yes, I was made into a
living clay and not only obliterated, but, out of my flesh,
with me still imprisoned in it, I was made into the very
image of the man I most detested. Whether I succeeded or
failed, I was always to be like what I loathed and, incidentally, as you have proved, always be in danger of being
killed by any young spark that thought he was getting rid of
the Alpha spirit. Spirits, I now know, are not killed so easily; they simply pass like a flame from the candle from
which they have been blown onto another prepared to carry them, and be consumed by them."

The boy had retreated. He was sitting on the floor, his
weapon dropped beside him, looking up at the face that
looked across over his head. A very old quotation from the
prophetic passage that described forever the type of the
supreme suffering servant came into the mind behind that
face, "A face more marred than all the sons of men."

"Haven't I," he asked, "received the mark of the beast?

Isn't this to have the stigmata of damnation etched and spliced and grafted into one's flesh and bone?"

Yes, the younger man had been brought to a standstill. There was a silence while the elder man thought, Haven't we both come to the end? Wouldn't it have been better, after all, not to have won this round, too? And then the sense of destiny took him again. Was it possible that so much had been taken from him that now he couldn't fail, that he had become like a kind of wandering Jew that could always travel and never reach his journey's end, a Tithonus who could age and shrivel but never die? They sat like that for some time.

Then the boy said, "Do you think I might go to her? I think she may be coming to by now, and it would be less of a shock to her; indeed, I might be able to explain it all away if I could be with her when she wakes."

"Yes, go," said the elder man. "You will be able, I think, now to put things right with her. Just tell her that the drugging might have been one of the Mole's devices and she received what might have been meant for me. She will be happy, and you and she can enjoy that happiness. You had better stay together till I call for you. It would be safer for her, I think."

The boy said, "Thank you," simply, and was gone.

VIII

SKYSCRAPER'S VIEW

ALPHA II RAISED his eyes when the panel had slipped into place and they were caught by a small disk near his desk which began to glow. He remembered, as on it appeared: "Certified interviewee No. 1 for"—and then followed the date and hour, 3:30, 352, 1996. Yes, it was time. He would have to do without his secretary but the process was going on. Time and Tide wait for no man, or no mask. And it was well: The tides can wash away everything in the end, even Lady Macbeth's hand, even a remodeled face. He might, in the end, forget that he was ever a private person, a particular man, and be washed by the flow of process into the vast shape of the mask into which he had been cut and thrust, a great depersonalized object, a smooth-worn hub or pivot of the turbine through which raced the waters of the endless flux that drove mankind. He gained his desk and pressed the switch of assent.

Within two minutes the door on his left opened and his visitor mounted the dais, facing him over the desk. At first sight he seemed the inventor sort that he should be—the cerebrotonic type in almost excess. There was the long, high-arched skull well seen as it rose above the small, flat-pressed ears, for though not bald the scalp was covered only with a fine down, almost like a cap of silk. The forehead was high so that its narrowness was compensated by its upward sweep. The eyes so deep and in such caves that, though there were no brow ridges, yet the upper part of the face gave no doubt as to strength, and, though the whole face was narrow and long, the eyes were set so much on the outer part of the skull that they were wide apart, giving a wide-angled look and nothing narrow or peering in the stare. In their cave of fawn brown they shone like acqua-marines, pale blue in a fawn setting. The whole skin was fawn and, though unwrinkled, it gave the sense of considerable though perfectly healthy age. The nose was finely shaped but of that one-size-too-big proportion that marks with distinction but mars for beauty the hyperpituitary type. The mouth was wide but the lips so finely and slightly curved that there was neither looseness nor tightness about them; there was the hint of a smile, a smile of constant interest and understanding. The chin, again, was a trifle too long for the proportions to be beautiful but gave a final accent of focused, intelligent resolution to the whole appearance. It was a face you might pass by, but once you looked, you looked again until you had mastered the whole, for it had much to tell and yet was quite obviously uninterested in impressing or in being in any way emphatic. He was dressed in one of the long mantles worn by the elderly who in this age were not afraid to be known as old. The only slightly unusual thing about it was its color—a fawn ocher, not a common tint in this day of bright tones. But it matched his skin very well.

Alpha II had time to give himself this careful inventory, as his visitor made no haste to break the silence that followed his silent bow. The face was worth perusal and, as one read over its smoothly written record, it was pleasant to contemplate. From it there seemed to come to the onlooker that kind of quiet completed sense of pattern that is given by a well-carved steatite head of a Boddhisattva. There was, of course, a personality made manifest, but a personality that fitted with perfect ease the calm, symmetrical conventions of a hieratic artform. And the voice, when he spoke, was as much an expression of that pattern as was the face.

"I am glad that you have been able to see me. For the expressive ritual forms of the state now seem to have reached a level when further knowledge of research in psychophysical interreactions may help. We also need to know more about quantity-quality correlations in regard to the sociological problem of large-scale education through group movement and affirmational action."

"What are the facts with which you can provide me?"

208

was met by a series of closely argued propositions, formulae of behavior patterns and tables—all given without a note—of correlations of learning-rates, metabolism quotients, emotional reactions, subconscious resistance rhythms, and assimilation curves. As he listened Alpha II began to reflect how in spite of success, how hit and miss, how amateurish had been the efforts of the Party, the victorious Psychological Party, in their shepherding of mankind.

"Please provide me personally with all these tables and graph records," he said as the exposition came to an end. "I understand that with these you are certain that experimental methods and tests-out would show a very great improvement in solidarity and reduction of the wastage rate that requires will-treatment and mental reduction?"

"Undoubtedly," the other replied.

Alpha considered his next remark, and then, "I suppose you are aware that the span of your work, its width of correlation, its insight into the whole new problem of government by assent and anthropological comprehension, goes far beyond what is contributed by the usual social inventor or researcher?"

The "Why, *of course*" of his visitor made him react with the same words, "*Why* of course?" with an accent of real question put on them. "Why come to me if you know so much? Did it not occur to you that the head of the state, the chief correlator, might not welcome one who not only could give him information—" he hesitated a moment, and then said, "Alpha must always be open to that—but could see the whole interlocked relationships in a wider angle of vision than the state had yet shown signs of perceiving? Knowing as much as you do, you must have known that about humanity?"

He put his question partly as a challenge to try out the man in front of him and partly from clear curiosity. In those few minutes of demonstration the figure and the mind behind the figure came together in a sincle focus and he knew he was in the presence of a species of intelligence, or rather of high character, that he had never met before. To ask the man who he was, was a temptation he must resist as long as possible. Meanwhile he must find out indirectly all he could. But his curiosity was the more roused the more he realized that here was a creature who had the power to reveal as much of himself as he chose and who had shown only a small aspect of the type of mind, of which the clearly expressed radical knowledge just given was merely the specimen he at that moment required in order to gain Alpha's attention. His visitor was, it was clear—and one would be all the more at his mercy the less one faced up to the knowledge—one who was not only aware of whom he was talking to, of what would interest and hold at that moment in that place, but also as clearly of what impression he himself was making. Alpha II felt as though he and the fawn being in front of him were two pawns put in confrontation and that an intelligence which radiated from above the fawn figure was directing them both. The initiative lay wholly on that outer side of the desk, because it was the stranger who knew precisely where he was and what could develop, what reactions would be made to each of his measured disclosures of information.

The answer to his challenge did not come at once, and then was indirect.

"Do you think you will be able to use the information that I have been able to put at your disposal?"

Alpha's quiet retort, "Of course," was to have been followed by a demand to know more of the informer.

But this time he was cut short by, "Then we can get on to matters of more concern. The management of this huge business of mankind incorporated, the company of humanity unlimited, unlimited liability, is, of course, a task which needs endless additions to managerial knowledge. But, once it is running, once it is understood, as it is now understood, as an anthropological problem, the frame of right reference has been discovered. And, though there may be errors in application, there are no longer those cardinal and crass errors of fundamental misapprehension, such as, in the efforts of intelligent and devotion men. As one hundred and fifty years ago in surgery we passed out of the prepasteurian, pre-disinfectant stage and then understood why till then all major operations, in spite of the highest surgical skill, had to fail and fall in sepsis and septicemia—" his listener stroked his face as he listened—"so today we know the place and power of antiseptic force, of non-shock, non-violent manipulation—that handling (for that is all that surgery means) whereby the necessary molding of mankind can be done without heaping up a counterreaction that drags all back into disorder."

"Then you approve of the Government!"

"I am, sir, making an objective diagnosis. Of human bondage and human liberation, even of human happiness and sorrow, of the choice between the charms of plenty and peril, of ease and excitement, I have not spoken."

Then Alpha II felt his excitement justify a certain rashness of direct attack: "Who are you?"

But it was met with a return back to himself: "You are aware that the first flashes of your further development in the pattern of mankind have been released and have awakened great pleasure."

He nodded. He had not seen the actual announcements but he knew, by the timing his secretary had given him, that, though it had seemed a speedy piece of work, the preliminary headline hints would be wide over the world by now. "The controls of mankind were to be increasingly thorough, finding out what people wanted and giving the right to have it." Yes, that was both true and popular. Well, he must try to find out about his visitor by building him up from piecemeal reactions.

"You approve, then?"

"I am here because—having, I believe, convinced you that what you are about to do is in the line of the inevitable development, of which you are the prow, and can also be implemented most swiftly by the means I have indicated (and what I have given you is merely a specimen)—I believe we can now come to the matter which is increasingly central."

To his question, the answer was almost curtly, "Yourself."

Now he would call the man's bluff. "Nothing of me," he said with a grim smile, "till something of you. Who are you?"

"An elevator man."

An answer which irritated him to react with, "Joking is a grave matter when on secret matters of state. After all, you need never leave these buildings again, if I choose, and even if I let you go, it can be managed so that when you do, you will have left all that you had and were, in our hands."

"Boasting is even more serious." The answer was given with such detachment that it was a diagnosis rather than a retort; and, before he could re-attack, the voice went on, "A description literally true, can, and indeed always does, seem funny to one who has not the general information to see its relevance. I am an elevator man for two reasons. The first explains why I am here: I have been sent down to give you this information which you require—the more important part of which I have yet to impart. The second reason explains whence I have come: I have come from the Elevated, or, if you prefer a title which may seem to you less traffic-worn and high-brow, let's say the Over-Heads. It really doesn't matter. People who have learned the importance of anonymity haven't really any names, only temporary numbers to indicate temporary functions. Labels are libels."

Alpha II tried to break in on this play of words, but for the first time the other raised his hand; it was a hand quite startlingly long and thin, so that as he raised it, it looked less like a hand than a small-shafted rod, imposing silence.

"You know that in all the metropoli of the traffic epoch, when the surface population-pressure rose above a certain density per square mile, there were three traffic reactions. First, there were subways, trenches which carried the fastest traffic in trains just under the streets; that was the first underground. Next, when the ground permitted it, there had to be a still lower and freer run-level found by driving tubes totally below the earth, quite unlit by any daylight and fed by special fans for their air. And, as we know, as the density still mounted, there had to be added an elevated system, first in old New York, then abandoned but finally resumed—until you started redistribution—at the high zoning level of the standard skyscraper—the 700-foot elevation, so that the cable ways guided the air gondola-trains above the city in the highest speed-circuits. Well, this pattern of population circulation, this necessary three-layer traffic to keep the masses from congealing and seizing in a super-jam, was also followed by the necessary flow of the forces of movement, of government, of opposition, and of overseership, as they worked upon the otherwise steady stagnation and breakdown of the forces of blind increase. The task was to find for an increasing population, increasingly supplied with economic necessities, those psychological stimuli which would prevent them from degenerating."

"What do you mean by classing the opposition with the Government!"

"I am speaking as an observer. No government till now, not yours even till today, has, as a matter of fact, been able to command the active loyalty of mankind unless there was a threat and enemy against which to marshal the forces which otherwise corrode of themselves the whole structure. And as there are no longer those physiologically and economically ruinous, but psychologically stimulating, tension-balances produced by the odd structure of nationalism, the stimuli now have to be generated by the struggle of the state's subway forces with the opposition forces driven into what we may call the tube system, the catacombs of ultimate resistance, where men, who have sacrificed themselves to become moles, try to countermine and sub-sap those somatotonic types which you draft off, with their otherwise dangerous energies, to man the trenches of the subway system."

"But what's all this got to do with Elevators?" he spoke almost irritably. Only the queer force of the man himself had kept him listening to such queer illustrative byplay.

"The Elevated is the third level, the level of overseership and as needed as the others."

"That's modest of you! Why don't you claim that your little bunch, whoever they are, could govern with their left hand, while, of course, being too good to let their either hand know what the other's doing, keep going with their right the necessary stimuli of the treason which you are pleased to call opposition?"

The man questioned smiled, "I think I can answer to

213

your satisfaction and without delaying you longer. You have reached the point when those who do survey, but do not intrude, or indeed intervene, save to put information at your disposal, feel that the tube system of the Mole has served its purpose. Henceforward the real balance might be an open, and not a blind polar, relationship between those, the government, yourself, who must be chiefly interested in application, correlation, and maintenance. And so, as I have said, I will conclude. I will and can.

"You are the key figure: And it matters as little to me who you may be as a physiological figure, as it really matters to you who, in that respect, I am. We both belong to various blood groups, no doubt, but that does not affect the meeting and blending of our minds. You need me, and, because I exist for the purpose of giving that kind of help, I need you just as much. You see, there is a world picture, a picture in which I have shown your position in general and your particular next step. And as you in particular have to take that step, you are the foot, the upraised foot of mankind, I have to help that foot to be balanced and strong that it may land firmly. The step is right, the ground is ready. The foot remains for us to view. You know," he suddenly became emphatic, "you *know* that you cannot safely any longer expose yourself to the psychological pressures which have already been generated round the focus, which you have become. And yet we know your intention —inevitable, essential—is that these pressures shall now henceforward, and with a sudden critical step-up of pressure, be immensely increased. They must be. I have, then, two services to do you. The first, we will take when I have received your consent to the second. I can, with the first, relieve you of a pressure which now has served its purpose. But the second, of that, with my help, you must relieve yourself. You see, you must break?"

The part which the man in the chair had been playing, almost under the pressure of his position and because that position seemed to impose a false sense of initiative on him, suddenly seemed to shrivel away. Where was he going? Was he really simply going to slip into the pit, the huge crater left by the burning out of Alpha I, and so lie

214

there embedded and finally fossilized, part of an ever more slowly turning tide of settling mud of custom, settling into a crust of custom, or being broken by some unsuspected revival of success from the deeper level of what his visitor called the mole-tube opposition?

Could he go back to the Mole? No. Before this call he knew that was over—those tubes went just as much in a circle as the subways that ran above them, and shot down into them, shot down into them fresh energy just to go on revolting, revolving, revoluting. And if the Mole came to the top, what would he, of Life's necessity, become? Simply a rather more lively, rather less vigorous, rather more widely seeing rat? The sewers or the ultimate sinks, the street culverts or the final cloacas—those were the choices. Unless there was, as this man (who ought to be mad but for his skilled mass of technical knowledge) suggested, a third process of overseership, the Elevated? Besides, wasn't it true that Alpha I, who certainly was not less tough than he, had broken under that pressure of popular famation which was psychic deformation, and he himself, even at the lower pressures, which now he was going to step up, had felt himself utterly enervated? *Of course*, it was out of the question to go on. He was simply blinding himself in order not to think and to go on to the brink because there seemed no place to stop. Now, however? He must gain time. He must keep this man and somehow test him. He might be a raft or only a bundle of waterlogged straw. An idea flashed in his mind: he could keep him longer and test him without his knowing he was being tested.

"We can consider that all a little later," he said, stroking the lines on his face. "There is, as it happens, a small problem which is at this moment affecting office efficiency and, if you are the expert you would say, you could help in it."

The visitor seemed quite unsurprised at this procedure and stood quietly while Alpha II switched open the secretarial circuit. There was a small check at the other end and then his secretary's voice, with obvious strain, answered. The voice became even more constricted when it assented to to his order, "Come at once and bring with you your visitor."

She entered and not only was it clear that the effects of the drug that she had been given had not yet wholly cleared but also that the nervous shock she had undergone had reduced her self-control to the thinnest of films. The conflicts going on in her loomed through so that she seemed more to be two persons than one. She stood ever so slightly swaying, between the boy who was just behind her and Alpha. Revulsion and devotion not only were keeping her mind in a crisis of confusion: it was clear that she could not say from which of these two poles she felt these conflicting tides to be arising. Her mind was not merely looking at something about which she could not decide whether to fly or to submit; she had a kind of double vision, for she could not decide where stood the object of her real devotion.

She did not notice the visitor, but he was engaged with her, and before Alpha could enter on an explanation—while he was framing words—the saffron figure said to her, "Come and sit here." He put her in that chair which had already borne two crises.

To the lad he said, "Sit in this other." To his clumsy, protesting courtesy, "Where are you going to sit?" he replied, "When operating it is easier to stand."

Then, turning to Alpha at his desk, "This situation is known to the world, in its outline, and one glance at the third party gives the conclusion. The detail does not matter and might easily confuse the issue in its clarity. I am not concerned about what accident of apparent intrusion brought this physiological counterpart of you here. In the deepest sense it is a convergence—it could not be avoided—and in relation to what I have just said to you it can be used with effect to help liberate you all."

He paused, looked at the secretary for a moment searchingly, and as he looked she collapsed. The boy made an effort to rise. He was waved back to his seat. The visitor went over to her and put his thin fawn hand on her shoulder.

"I am going to use a very ancient language to you, so

216

old that it is dateless. 'Woman, why weepest thou? Whom seekest thou?' You are a woman and you have sought a man on which to rest. And you thought that a superman must be a man of men. You would have the supreme man. No. Woman must not seek to mix a dream, a political dream, with a racial fact. No man who serves mankind can serve a woman. You have loved, in your dangerous wish to have a genie lover, not a man but a huge projected shadow of mankind. The rainbow is real enough provided we never try to touch it. It exists in its great span of beauty because it is always at that distance from us. That which sits at that desk is a simulacrum. Why, you cannot know that is even the same physique which sat there seven days past: the whole of the wave-lengths of energy that make it up *have* passed away, and been replaced by others which have been made to take on the same form. You have already made your choice." He took her by the hand and placed her on her feet.

"You are simply trying, with a false consistency to your own belief in your dignity, against your deep sane sense of your happiness, to fight your rightful fate." He took her and turned her to the boy. "Man, here is your woman; woman, here is your man. Go; the way is clean open to you. You were nearly trapped: but now the road is wide open; don't be your own jailer."

She struggled for a moment. "But will *he* be safe?"

"This is the surest way of making him safe. He has no danger but in your balked husband."

"But all those awful people of the underground who hate him?"

"That, too, will pass away as quickly as this closer peril will pass. The man who is to be your husband will help us at that last solution."

At that there was a hesitation, and wavering, she put out her hand onto the boy's shoulder.

"You're not going to put him in any risk?"

"You see, already he is yours! But he'll remain yours all the more, if you do not with him, what you did with his great shadow over there. You must let him be what he is, that he may be to you what you need. And now I'm going

217

to explain to you quite briefly where you are and who you are, in order that you two may go ahead with that private sane happiness which is your main contribution to the happiness of the whole.

"The reason for my *visit*," he stressed the word slightly and looked across at Alpha's seat, "is that your society has reached a crisis—not a crisis that leads to a crash but one that might lead to great confusion. You know, you men of action, how easy it is to take action. You must already have suspected how hard it is to stop action, to get back to the freedom of being able to wait and take your time and let things develop. That is the effect of too much violence; it is first intentional and then goes on merely by its own inner momentum. I want to persuade you just to carry on, to let things develop and to cease pushing them to and fro. For I know that if you will do that, then the rest is easy."

"But you own that it is hard, damned hard?" Alpha II interjected.

"Not too hard if once one sees why it should be done."

"Can you show us why?"

"Yes, it's inevitable, and if you, if we, don't do it, it will be done with a good deal of trouble, but done it will be."

"How?"

"Well, it's already practically hatched: all you have to do is not to prevent its coming out."

"Explain."

"Surely you see what you have been the tools in shaping? At the beginning of social history there are three great realistic Utopists, Manu, Vyasa, and Valmiki. You might do worse than put up monuments to them and name their feast days as the Founding Fathers of Mankind. For they *were*, though they have had to wait for some time before humanity was prepared to study itself and so understand their insight. They saw that four types of men as a matter of fact are viable, do get born, and insist on living their special kinds of life.

"We have seen violent efforts, revolutionary explosions which tried to make mankind fuse into one level—atomistic democracy; then as violent re-revolutions—called mistakenly reactions—when men tried to correct this false simplification and get on with two: masters and men, officers and privates, labor and management. But this balance was too simple and therefore unstable. The Alpha experiment—" he did not look at the present occupant of the seat—"was important, was inevitable, because it marked the end of the third revolutionary phase, the recognition of three types: The masses left to enjoy themselves, in fecund plenty; the hard-working technicians and officials,; and the directive of men of ideas, pure research, theory, and oversight. This is the system which this revolution, the psychological or anthropological revolution, took over from Sheldonism, and that is why the poor old dual system of applied Marxism went down before it, or rather vanished like an outworn idea, as spent as was the idea of the Holy Roman Empire.

"But Marx was right in one thing. His vision was narrow, but what he saw was there. He saw that his revolution was bound to take place, was bound to demote the old political revolution based on democracy and on all men being equal to all the possible pressures a complete society generates. Marx was wrong because he thought his Economic Revolution was the final one, instead of the penultimate phase."

"But Sheldon is final, isn't he?" broke in Alpha II.

"Final, yes, if you mean that, with his revolutionary insight into the nature of man or the natures of men, the whole revolutionary epoch is over, for it then reaches its fourth phase, ceases to be revolutionary, and becomes again, in accord with Life, evolutionary. It ceases from convulsions and goes back to growth. It ends the age of crises and cataclysm and enters on the epoch of development and understood advances."

"You're not going to take all the adventure out of life?" the boy broke in.

The man in saffron smiled and, looking at the secretary, who had been turning from one to the other in a distressed way, remarked, "That remark, daughter, is meant for you, really. Do you see, he's telling you about himself and his rightful needs. That is why, just as much for your happiness, for his, and for this job we are on together, I have a piece of work ready for him as an engagement present.

"No," he went on, "no, we won't take the adventure out of life; rather, we are going to take the blinkers off mankind's eyes so they will see for the first time—at least those who want to—the immense size of the adventure on which they are all launched. Sheldon was nearly right; and so, beside the statue of Manu I would like you," he turned again to Alpha II, "to put one to that remarkable thinker. Manu spoke the first word, Sheldon spoke the second. But Manu was misunderstood and hence caste resulted. And Sheldon is in danger of being misapprehended, too; and if that is so, then we are left with the present state of affairs: true, it is a more workable, because more detailed and worked-out, system than Manu's. Instead of rigid hereditary castes, Sheldonism, as we know, permits men to be picked, somatotyped, and graded. They can be shown the body-mind type to which they belong and then by vocational guidance and leading put to that position in which—" he paused, and then said with emphasis—"in which, if they don't grow and there is no basic development through life, they should stay. But if life is a hatching, then there is growth. If we are embryos in this life, psychic embryos, then we should grow."

" 'It is not growing like a tree, in bulk, that makes man better be.' " It was the secretary humming the famous Ben Jonson glee song. He nodded and smiled at her.

"Sheldonism has been, we know," he glanced across at Alpha's seat, "expanded by further glandular knowledge. His three types are somewhat rigid outlines (though, of course, he himself devised a system of elaborate intermixture definitions) of glandular states. Now, today we know that those glandular states are not rigid endowments, settlements for life, but rather delicate balances which we are free to shift and bring forward in a rising series of efficiencies."

"What do you mean?" broke in Alpha II, at last taken out of his self-interest as this scheme began to unfold. "Aren't Sheldon's three types full and final? If everyone is seen as a compound of these three elements, haven't we a system suited to mankind and one in which, as you say, and," he paused, "I have become convinced, the revolutionary epoch ends? And, surely, then, mankind rests?"

"Rests, yes, as a recovered patient rests from fever but is also up and about; rests in the recovered energy for creative and steady work. Now there's the point, and it points to your future. Sheldon's three types are balances and balances which we can now direct. The first type, which we all now know by his title, the viscerotonic, what has it shown itself to be? That basic type, that child type, that finds its drive in life from the polar balance of the interstitial glands of secretion balanced against the suprarenal glands."

"Then," broke in Alpha II, suddenly recalling the last time Alpha I had been prophetic, "then you *would* have a type of person whose energy cycle was circulating chiefly through the pelvic balance center and whose easy acceptance of life was kept from becoming sloth by being shot across with the secretions for the glands of combat, while these adrenalin secretions would be kept from making the man a constant fighter by being soothed by the easy lustiness of the interstitial. Yes, you've made your point there, right enough."

"And I can give you two further confirmations," the man in the saffron cloak went on. "This basic type is mainly what the Sanskrit physiological sociologists called the Tamasic type crossed with the Rajasic, an easy-going acceptance of what comes, balanced up against constant injections and dashes of the noble rage that protests. And secondly, this is the basic type whose demands made the First Revolution. But to that in a moment. For, just to finish with the two other types: The somatotonic," and he nodded at the boy, "if he is to be the balance that really works (Sheldon knew that a pure type would not be able to survive but would die of its own excess), he in turn is a polar glandular balance—this time between the suprarenals, the glands of conflict, and the thyroid, the gland of sustained effort. That is clear, without a doubt. A tiger has huge suprarenals and a small thyroid; man small suprarenals and a big thyroid. The somatotonic type is central is society and is made of a central balance of the central glandular couple."

221

Alpha II turned his ring on his finger. All this was indeed confirming his predecessor's last attempt to see ahead and grasp the Life trend.

To be certain, he asked, "Then mankind is an immense extension of the actual body of a man, and our social progress, is it marked, is it ruled by the advancing, ascending progress of accent and emphasis in the couple-linkages of the inner glands?"

"I believe you are right," the other replied. "The notion of Adam-Kadmon, the primordial man, which I detect in that somewhat abraxid signet on your hand, is, I believe, one of those true insights. It's the same as the Hermetic, 'As above, so below,' and the whole fertile conception of the Macrocosm and the Microcosm. Anyhow, what I have to tell you is that this evolution can be continued by anyone who wishes to pay the cost of the psychophysical training. There is no need why they should. They can rest where they will at any of the stages, any of the 'mansions' up that great ascent of Mount Carmel, the trackway of the Spine. As long as they come to a settlement with one of the balance-couplings, they are viable; and indeed they have their social place, use, value, and enjoyment."

"But what of the further levels?" Strange to say, it was the secretary who was asking, but it did not seem to surprise the speaker.

"There," he said, "we reach the present highest stage, the level to which, as the revolutionary age closes, mankind has been reared. For here, of course, we have the next coupling, the thyroid-pituitary balance, and that gives us the cerebrotonic type, the present master administrator, the man whose steady drive of persistent energy (which comes from the thyroid dominance, and which by itself becomes simply the unimaginative hard worker, the indefatigable official and civil servant) is pointed, aligned, and lit by the gland which the glandularists of the West have a little prematurely called the master gland. For above this third linkage-balance is a fourth: the pituitary now in turn becomes the assistant partner, the backer-up. And the initiative passes to the final gland system, that of the pineal."

"Yes," thought Alpha II, "yes, here we reach my predecessor's thought-frontier."

"Of course, the West is still wondering what it can be for, for they have found no use for it, for they have not given it the uses on which it could deploy its supreme energies. It is the gland of vision—for there, the Sanskrit thinkers saw, was the inner eye, 'the aperture of Brahman,' the final look-out point of man and mankind. Hence we obtain integral thought and, when this opens, then the man has climbed the long internal tower which it has taken him about a million years to mount. He emerges out into the sunlight, sees the whole of his past pilgrimage lying below him and the whole of the kingdoms of the earth, and is ready for his flight out into an element which only those who have seen and touched it can know."

He paused, and was already, they saw, looking out from his top of the tower over skyscapes they could not see.

Alpha called him back, "Does history sustain your vision, or is it mere prophecy?"

"No, it is fact. First as regards individuals: we have in our records a valuable old picture book. It is a collection of portraits put together some seventy years ago. But the portraits themselves range over some sixteen hundred years. It is a typological series of a very particular type. The book is called *The True Likeness of the Saint*. A great number of these pictures are contemporary portraits and not a few photographs of the person when alive, or lying dead, or the death-mask. Their interest is great for somatotyping. For it is startling how many of these men and women of outstanding energy and ability are obviously at the very limit of glandular balance. Some are, like the popeyed, gaping-mouthed, swollen-throated Saints Ambrose of Milan, Teresa of Avila, and Joseph of Copertino, obviously excessive thyroidics: others, like sickle-nosed Saint Carlo Borromeo and Saint Pius the Fifth are, as clearly, excessive pituitarists. Yes, I have long had no doubt, these are the first natural mutations of that oncoming emergent type which we today are already becoming able to release scientifically and which your new order needs more than anything else as its new faculty for entering on and developing this its new world.

"But to leave the sporadic individual and turn to history in the mass. History is the clinching proof of this progression that I have been outlining. It is that second proof I promised you when I began this sketched-out demonstration. For look at the four revolutionary phases of this epoch of the last five hundred years which now closes its great revolutionary epoch.

"The first was the Religious Revolution, and the force driving that from below was the viscerotonic type. They wanted a profound emotional experience. The old convention, tradition, religion, had ceased to be able to give it. It had become dried up in its later scholastic disputations. The popular cultus in consequence became morbid: first of all the dreadful Dooms, and soon after the grotesquely dreadful dances of death and then devotions based on blood, five wounds, and bleeding hearts.

The second revolution, of course, has long been recognized as political, the turning from devotion to direct action. But we have only lately recognized who made it, what type. The puritan is the somatotonic protestant fighter, and he turns from religion to politics, from Cromwell down to Carnot. This is the age of action *per se* because men of that type must do; and, soon, doing takes the place of all thinking. Nationalism and imperialism are the two poles, one of contraction and nuclear resistance and the other of expansion and explosion, whereby the maximum of contest and struggle is achieved; the atmosphere in which the ungeared, uncomprehending middle type, the somatotonic division, finds its expression—but society's destruction. Mercifully, it cannot last, for it is energized by only one-third of natural mankind.

"And the turn comes for the third—concerned with planning, with supply, with production, with increase; in short, with economy. After a scatterer comes a gatherer; yes, nature can always use the pessimistic proverbs of mankind to as much as fro. But, of course, in this, neither, is there finality. The Economic Revolution made by the thyroid-pituitary type has to pass. When old Stalin brought back the ballot and then the Church, people said, 'And now we are back at democracy, nationalism, and orthodoxy.' But there is no going back. He was simply handing back the cards to the force we call Nature, that THAT might deal them for the fourth hand. Hence we are come to the fourth revolutionary phase which closes the revolutionary cycle."

"Then you mean," said Alpha, "that you bow yourself onto the stage as the final fulfiller of the law of being?"

"But not to eliminate, only to complete and help the other levels to understand their place and pleasure in life."

IX

THE UP-TURNING OF THE MOLE

ALPHA II SAT still a while and the others watched him. Finally he said, "It's a proof, but is it a process? Can it actually be lived? What would you do here and now, *here and now*," and his voice became almost harshly definite, "with this young couple? With the Mole?? With me???"

"You've put the series of questions rightly," the other remarked with a smile, "but before I can answer them I must begin even before the young. I have to say something about myself—why I venture to answer these your questions. I described myself accurately as an Elevator man. I've already said that there are three levels on which the present process is working; the lowest is a protest, then the middle is a pretext, and, at the limit of what I can see, is a prospect.

"I see," he smiled again at their bewilderment, "that my effort at definition hasn't cleared things much for you. All I want to say is that the three levels, though they may seem antagonistic, are really three points in a circuit. But two poles are better then three. I have been sent, as I said, on a double message. One is to you: to open up your circuit, if you will, in the direction toward which you are feeling your way. But you can't find that upper objective until the lower is closed. So I have come, also, to close that lower."

"What do you mean?" was said first by the man in the chair but was echoed by the other two.

"Well, perhaps I have said too much before doing enough. That is why, I believe, I am sent on these missions, because I still like talking, and at the same time they can see that I get mixed up in a good deal of action—I have to prove my words. All I wanted to make you see at this point was that the Elevated isn't something that looks down detached from the earthbound traffics. You can see the design of life either laterally or vertically, perpendicularly. Seen that latter way, the three levels are really three piers of one bridge. 'This world is a bridge, pass over it but build no house upon it.' Man must be increasingly a mobile organism, not sessile. So, you see," he said, looking hard at the boy "everyone who rises to office is simply an officer; his name, whether it be Osiris, Indra, or Alpha, is simply the title and description of a place on the bridge, on the wheel."

The boy looked bewildered, so he added, "Your lesson from that is twofold. First, nothing is gained by killing the man who holds a post. As long as you can't destroy the post, something, somebody, must fill it. As long as there are pockets on a billiard table and the balls are running about, balls will be filling the pockets however often you empty them. The second thing is even more welcome to you. Don't you see, the higher you get up the less you are a person, the more you become simply a packet or quantum of energy moving from one engine of expression on into another. Freedom to be one's self, to be a person, to have one's own life and likings and love—that belongs to those who still, and at their level, rightly wish for such things.

"There, that's enough. This story starts with a mass of moral and then turns into a romance or fairy-tale—a sound reversal." He turned to Alpha. "This young couple are going to marry, of course. That we approve of it is merely that we consent heartily to the Process of Things. So will you be so kind as to do it with a good grace for me? Please set them up in life. Of course, you will remember that though they are still going to enjoy themselves greatly as individuals, they are already beginning to hatch into something else. If reincarnation is true, this is the last time that they will have the boy-and-girl experience—and so probably," he smiled at them, "it will be at its best, for they are pretty certainly more experienced in it than they can remember.

"You two," he was again addressing them, "you also, won't forget that, will you? You," he was looking at the girl, "you mustn't keep him from those other activities, those rightful risks which he must take in this life, for they are the bud-activities, the foetal organs being developed for the life he will live after this. If he is nothing but a lover he will be a creature that has outstayed Life's welcome. Now, before I tell him the first thing that I have for him, the first fine bit of adventure, you, Alpha, tell him if you have a place for him in which he can live this saliently balanced life."

"Why, of course," Alpha II smiled. "I remember hearing it said that when you have to steer the ship of state ideas come to you that are going to be far more useful than even you imagine. I have just instituted the order of the Guides. As a wedding present I name you as a lieutenant general of one of the junior corps."

"Yes, that will do," the Elevator man remarked, as the boy saluted. "And now, without delay, he can win his spurs. I spoke of my second job. For that I shall need both of you. I came to see Alpha and have enjoyed my visit and will have a good report to make on it. Now, with you two men, I am going to call on the Mole."

There was a silence in the room; attention which had become general with the increasing feeling that happiness lay ahead, suddenly congealed.

Alpha broke it. "You know, of course, that no one knows him, that some people doubt if there is one man." Then, glancing across at the boy who was already eyeing him, "Some people have wondered whether there may not be different groups all of which are confused as Mole-workings."

"Well," the other blandly replied, "you told me that after I had settled with the young couple I should say where the Mole came in—I say here, and I will prove it."

"How!"

"You can't get at him—none of us—" The boy paused and flushed.

"You think that I'm just suggesting we walk out, ask a Public Relations and Information Please man where the Mole digs and call him up out of his burrow! No, I have my plan as to how to summon him. And you are my Open Sesames. It's quite simple. Of course you don't know him.

Do I know the person who sent me on this mission? Does anyone really know," and he nodded in the direction of the desk without looking at it, "who actually sits there? As those powerful realists the mathematicians long ago discovered, functions are enough, without bothering about entities." He stopped. Then, speaking carefully to the boy, "You will need today to send through this message." He repeated slowly, " 'Have made contact: work completed: can bring forerunner and prize with me: send instructions.' You know you can send that."

The boy hesitated, actually blushed again, and finally said, "Yes . . . yes, but—"

"You mean," the other cut in, "that if there is a highest-up, or, if you like, a lowest-down, he won't see you, no, not you two. Well, trust me for that: he will. If you say you both are bringing the prize with you, and if he is lying as deep down as the sounding would seem to indicate, then he certainly will not let that interview take place through anyone else or with anyone else present."

"Are you sure?" It was Alpha's voice, with almost a tone of anxiety in it.

"Yes," was the reply, "the more lonely you are the simpler you become. If there is a single man who has sunk himself at such a depth from human contacts, and the complexities of reactions that such things awake and activate in ordinary men, he will be becoming even more simple, more predictable. There's not a doubt of it. That message assures that we three—two of us, and maybe the third, being the two or three men he would rather see, and study, alone, than any three men in the whole world—will be granted an unwitnessed interview. Yes," he added quietly as they still hesitated, "believe me, it will prove as simple as that. I feel sure I know my man." His voice was grave but not solemn, and a moment later it brightened.

"Now, boy, get about your work." And to the girl, "You see we are giving him an adventure good enough to keep him quiet and contented for quite a long honeymoon!"

The boy saluted and this time included in the sweep of his hand not only the man at the desk but the small saffron figure which already had sat down with ease and complete lack of ceremony on the floor.

"He is to report back here in twenty-four hours?" Alpha asked.

"You can do it in that?"

"Yes," said the boy to the man on the floor, "if I get through at all."

"Oh, never doubt that," said the floor-sitter. "Moles and we flittermice of the sky have this in common: our reactions are fundamentally the same, we see in the dark, and I know we are going to be seen!"

The boy was well disciplined. Without a look at the girl, he was through the panel, and they could just hear in the silence the muffled purr of the private lift descending.

"That's good," the saffron man said as the purr faded, "good, that he was able to go even without saying goodby to you. He will stick to you if he has that sort of self-control."

The girl found hers at his tone of voice. There was certainly a certainty about it that was reassuring. She obeyed then as promptly when told in the same assured way, "Now go, and go to bed. Your life these last few days has made you short of sleep—being drugged is no substitute—and you needn't go into your marriage like a tragedy queen."

She even smiled at his quip as she followed where the boy had gone. Left alone, Alpha heard his name called.

"Now *we* will go to sleep—and I trust you have learned to sleep when you can and when you wish."

"There's a small apartment next to this," Alpha offered.

"I don't need a bed," the other replied, "but I will sit in any room where I will disturb the routine of your place least."

When Alpha left him to go to his own bedroom, the saffron figure was seated on the floor looking more calmly settled down than most people when tucked up in their beds. The next morning Alpha worked all the forenoon and his visitor had not called on him. At lunch time he looked into what had been his apartment during those breaking-in days.

230

The saffron figure which was still seated on the floor looked up at him with a smile. Alpha's invitation to a meal was accepted and his guest ate some fruit and drank one of the warm beverages with evident pleasure. He seemed to be fully alive in every way. They were sitting for a few moments in the study after the meal when the notice panel flashed that the visitor who had left yesterday with certification of return was waiting.

The boy was before them in two minutes. He could hardly wait to be questioned.

"You're right," he said, looking at the saffron figure, "it went through—well, I've never known a message go and come back so quickly—and what's more, we are to report at six-thirty this evening."

He was almost a little daunted by the advice, "Then we'll all have another rest—and you a real sleep. No: you will stay here, please. You can have the bed I don't use. I shall act as your warder and see that you sleep well. And we two will also take our siestas in our own fashion. We may be up all night. People who haven't really talked for a long time are apt to be loquacious when at last they can."

He was as good as his word; he led off the boy, made him lie down, and in two minutes made him go to sleep. He then visited Alpha and left him in the same condition as quickly. Finally he went back to his chosen place on the carpet in the small sitting room and settled down into his posture. Gradually a smile spread over his face, a smile that did not break but seemed to smooth all the features into an ever deeping rest. Yet, though he never stirred till the clock's hands on the wall behind him were at five-thirty, as the minute hand hung straight down, he rose without any sign of stiffness, went in and roused the boy, told him to wash, and went himself to call Alpha.

"You will ask," he said, "that your secretary see that we are passed out through her entrance where there will be a car for us. Also, please provide for me a hooded cloak such as you two will wear."

The order was given, and five minutes later the three of them slid down in the small lift to the basement level where the cars coming into the palace parked. A car was ready, the boy gave the driver an address and in silence they rode for perhaps half an hour or forty minutes. The saffron-cloaked man was now wrapped in a dark green mantle and had drawn the hood completely over his head.

The car stopped and was dismissed. They crossed a small garden. They might be in the suburbs. The house to which the garden belonged was one of those of that zone, a house for a family of five. These houses were detached. The children needed the fairly large garden. This house, however, was quiet even at this hour and no lights showed. The boy led the way. As they gathered in the porch the door swung open. The boy entered and they followed, hearing the door latch itself behind them.

In the dark within, which was now absolute, a whisper, which had no character of tone about it, said, "The spot of light ahead of you—" they saw a spot begin to glimmer—"is an elevator door. Enter it."

They groped forward. Alpha was first to get his fingers on the panel and to slide it aside. He felt, he had to own to himself, a small shudder, as he stepped on the trembling, unsteady floor, and could not help a feeling of slight relief as he heard the others step in quietly behind him. He put the panel back in place and almost at once the floor gave under their feet. The descent was certainly swift and long. Certainly, if this was the way to the Mole, he did live according to his lights—very far down. At last, with a slight joggle, the slipping motion stopped.

Alpha heard the door slip back and the boy begin to say, "We should be there," but his voice was cut short by the same whisper they had heard above, "Straight ahead."

They stepped along, able to keep their eyes aligned by a single glimmer of a spot light that glowed ahead. Their feet had been on some hard surface, but at a certain point when they were apparently nearer the glow-spot, the floor surface seemed softer.

"Now, stop," said the whisper, and they heard a door close quietly behind them.

"Well, one of you has been away far longer than is wise,"

began the whisper again. "The other has to make a considerably fuller report than he has made; and the third is someone who it is to be hoped is going to stay—but, of course, all three will be staying, and the third, even if it is a case of mistaken identity, will stay . . ." the whisper paused, not, it seemed, out of uncertainty, but rather to be sure of giving emphasis, ". . . for good."

Alpha II felt utterly at a loss, the boy was silent.

After a moment then, the whisper went on, "Well, that is all right. Identity is hard to establish in the dark when no assistant can be used. A little light must be thrown on the issue."

Alpha suddenly realized that this continuation of the whisper must be coming from another spot. There was a longer pause, and then gradually, like a rather sickly dawn, a faint, suffused light began to spread in front of them. A greenish glow was cast up in their faces. He saw the boy's profile to his left and between them the cloaked and hooded figure they had brought with them. And now, across the stand, on which the long shade of the light rested—which he now saw was a desk—he could detect faintly a man's figure.

"Yes," it was still a whisper but now surely it was coming from the hood, "you will need more light to be sure of the identity."

And in answer to this the light did glow more strongly. Indeed, it grew so strong that it was possible now to see the whole room, a small room, a dark carpet, a desk, and someone at it. But before he could make out more by deliberate checking over, there was a small movement at his left, and, from the other side of the desk, a quicker one, accompanied by something that was surely a gasp. The saffron man had thrown back his hood; indeed, the cloak had slipped to the floor. He was standing clearly shown in the light; but, more, he was leaning right over it, looking steadily at the figure that was still only dimly seen at the other side of the desk.

And almost at once he began to speak, not loudly but with the greatest emphasis, "Now put on the full lighting."

The whole room came into full illumination glowing from

233

the walls. It told the onlookers nothing more about this small dugout. But they would not have attended if it had. What held their eyes was what was going on over the desk. The saffron man was leaning forward and had caught the attention—and caught was the exact word—of the figure that sat on the other side of it. For the saffron figure was poised over the desk, like a falcon when it has made its strike and holds its prey. And drawn back in his chair sat a man who should have been the formidable master of the situation.

Certainly he would in any other situation have been most noticeable, indeed dominating. For the head was immense —a great bubble of a cranium, so that it looked as though the brain had blown out gadroons and apses to give it larger working quarters. The eyes, naturally, under such top hamper, were built over by the overhanging bulge of the forehead. And the nose, and the lateral lines that shaped the mouth running down to the chin, and the chin itself, were merely delicately drawn support to the hypertrophied brain case. They ran up and out like lean, fluted, shafted buttresses to support that dome.

But the oddest thing in this odd image was not in itself. That lay in the contrast and complement. There could be no doubt about it: the saffron, hawklike figure that bent over the desk and the dark form that was drawn back, though the one was a marvelous balance of extremes and the other as definitely overbalanced, an obvious hypertrophy, yet, in some odd emphatic way, they were complement and supplement—balanced doubles.

The only other thing that appeared of the man were the hands on the desk. They had come forward, evidently to give him some grasp under severe shock, and they were utterly different from the fawn hands lightly poised, like an alighting bird's, just short of them. They were, instead of being clean-sinewed, crabbed. They were very strong and knotted and the fingers were long. But nevertheless they were coarse, twisted, with blunt, powerful nails and like a hogged main there ran down each finger a crest of black hairs that finally met in a small mat of such bristlings that covered the hands' backs. Everything was still, save these hands. Nor did they move much. Rather, under their white coarse skin you saw an inner wrestling going on. The mount of bristles was rising and falling as the sinew tensions flickered underneath.

Suddenly the play was switched to action. The right hand slid with the speed with which a spider, till then brooding, will suddenly move. It darted so quickly that it was already into a shallow drawer to its right before it was told to stop.

The saffron man had said, again quietly but if possible with more manifest emphasis, "No, you can't move your hand."

For a moment the two figures remained. Perhaps three feet divided them, but both the onlookers felt and knew that they were as closely locked as though they had each other gripped into one solid mass of impacted muscles. In the silence it seemed that one must hear the vibration of that immense torsion. But not a sound or movement gave outer evidence of the wrestling match.

At last the two onlookers could see a minute change. The man seated at the desk was managing, it seemed, to exert some freedom from the hold that had him pinned. His head was drawing back and his eyes were being raised. A tremor even went along his outstretched right arm. The eyes' color couldn't be told but it was possible to see the pupils. They had been small when they first became visible. They shrank as though focusing to a still finer point as though, with their concentration, to break through the pressure that was against them. Then in a moment they dilated. The hand made one more scrabble in the drawer and slid out of it, helplessly hanging down by the chair in which the figure now lolled.

The saffron figure raised itself up. "Brother, I am sorry to have had to use such force. It is my fault as much as yours, I had to take the risk of coming here without knowing whether I could succeed, knowing only that the time had come. For one thing I did know, I must remedy our joint mistake. And the world—macrocosm interlocked with microcosm—needs that you should finish with this your aphelion and return to perihelion. The path you have taken no doubt, you had to take. But now it leads up again; you have touched bottom—come home."

The man sunken in the chair stirred a little uneasily.

"You are wondering how you failed," went on his confronter. "You failed, primarily, because you had finished what you were doing and so lacked power to keep on. And that led to your immediate failure; you shifted your forces in the struggle and that lost it to you. Till you put out your hand, I did know that you could not shift me but I did not know I could make you give. Then, when you reached for a gun, then it was clear that your forces were divided. Your faith in the methods we know had flawed. Your doubts about the power of mind robbed you of the power to use it even in self-defense.

"I knew that this must sooner or later happen. It had to follow on your general increasing misgiving and the corresponding growth of your black faith that physical violence alone can count. The fencer who takes his eyes from his opponent's eyes, because he wants the better to direct his own sword, is, of course, done. You turned from apt force, pure will against pure will, from the direct action, to the indirect attempt to solve things of the mind and spirit by hitting the body of your opponent. Then, of course, you had to collapse. You became distracted, you turned to physical force, you felt fear. Hence we are now open with each other again."

He turned to the other two: "Please go out into the passage and wait for me. I will call you when we are ready to go."

They went out and he shut the door. They sat on the ground in the dark and they could just hear two voices in steady exchange. At last, after what might have been a couple of hours, the door opened. The man in saffron seemed just the same. The other had risen. They were of the same height and build. Both now were wearing dark cloaks. All that the man in saffron said was, "We can leave now." The man who had been behind the desk led them to the elevator after switching off the light in the room. As it went out, Alpha II, used to noticing if anything had been changed in a room, could only see that on the desk, which

236

before had been empty, now lay a sealed envelope. As far as he could see, on it was written a code number. The dark-cloaked man pressed the knobs in the elevator and it rushed up like a bubble to the surface of the water from the floor of a pond.

X

THE NEW CIRCUIT

HE SHOWED them through the house, let the door latch behind them, and then the three fell in behind the man in saffron who wore his cloak loosely because the night was warm. The streets were full of people not hurrying—for hustle had been discouraged now as poor taste and ill health. The crowds walked about at their ease, and whether they were going to some appointment or simply out for the air they clearly had enough time to enjoy their walk and look at things as they passed. And things were worth looking at. The street had been laid out nobly: houses and groves of flowering trees, avenues and groups of buildings, had been arranged with an eye to design as well as to convenience. Water was used with fine effect in every vista and now that it was night the fountains, falls, and culverts were all lit with fluorescent fluids while the buildings that rose above them were floodlit. There was no attempt to compete with day—but night was given enough illumination so as to be seen in its contrasting beauty.

The lighting, of course, was so good that everyone could recognize one another as well as by day. This suddenly awoke alarm in the boy's mind as he came with his companions into the more crowded boulevards. He turned to the form of Alpha who was walking a pace or two ahead of him. Catching him up, he glanced across at the face better known than any one's in the whole world. It had gone. The figure that walked now beside him was quite unrecognizable. He saw a man whose worn face hung in folds and puckers; the whole lapsed mask hung from a disproportionated pendant nose and was caught in at a shrunken chin. Of course: with a quick sleight of hand, a pass or two, as deft and curious as a conjuror's, he could make his appearance vanish—he could disassemble, or should one say dissemble, his personality. He was, when assembled, mankind's figurehead. Take that mask to pieces and what was left? Disassemble an engine, where is the engine? Yes, he was safe. The few ill-looking people that were about were always treated with a courteous lack of attention. It was taken for granted that they were undergoing facial treatment for some accident or disease or that they were gallant incurables. The crowds eddied by with gentle disregard of the queer little group. "If they really knew who we four actually are," the boy couldn't help feeling, "even their long training in good manners would break down!"

When the four reached the place where the great palace boulevard met them, the saffron man, who had been walking a little ahead with his new companion, waited for them to come up.

"I am to suggest that you two go back to your headquarters. I and my friend here will be crossing the street now."

Then, speaking to Alpha II, "With your leave, I will call on you once more—tomorrow afternoon if it suits you."

Alpha II said nothing, but bowed, and the saffron man and his companion were gone.

"We'd better enter by the secretary's entrance, don't you think?" the boy suggested when in silence they had almost reached the palace. "I'm known at that door and I can now send in a call that I and a companion be let through."

He took one of the small pocket telephone sets out of his tunic, fitted it to his head, tuned it, and in a few seconds was talking. On and off in the street—as smokers pause to light a pipe or cigar—you saw someone pause and go through this same procedure of making a small-beam radio call. The boy put the set again in his pocket and nodded that it was all clear.

They went on together, passed into the small entrance, and gained the private elevator. The boy got out at the secretary's floor. Alpha II went on. In a few seconds he was back in what already seemed his room. He went to his bathroom and, turning to the wall, moved his loaded hands about his mouth and face. Then he turned to the mirror.

It was true, as the likeness that had been built up on him and for him, was remounted, he felt the strange subtle change from doubt to assurance, from bewilderment to inevitability, the ability of inevitability. He went to his bedroom, undressed, and lay down. He noticed with a certain grimly intimate amusement that he now preferred to sleep as he was remodeled and not lapse back even when alone into shapelessness, even in slumber. It was something deeper than appearance. It was a matter of fundamental feeling, kinesthetic sense of being actually in gear, in mesh and physically integrated. He felt the need for the tonic comfort of these inner supports on the great nerve trunks of the face and neck, as the foot feels the need for a firm and level stance. He needed the support of this armature even when relaxed, perhaps even more so, as a dozing body needs the embracing support of an easy chair.

He slept well. Waking, he shaved, dressed, put on the ring, looked at the self that faced him in the pier glass, considerately. Yes, he was once more the part and no one else was it and now no one, even in the lowest depths, was left to challenge it. He was once more the part and for good, and the part was he; he had no part in life but that part, it made him a whole. Besides, where else would he go? Who was he? Who remained? He had been a spearhead of an upthrust of final revolt, which spearhead, in order to pierce the defenses of oppression, had to be keyshaped. And now, broken off in the lock, he had become part of the lock while losing touch with the haft that had driven him. This was the path of non-returning. But whither did it lead?

To shake off that question he went to his desk. Again he noticed that subtle but compelling force of place, point of view, perspective. He remembered that when they were being trained in psychophysical controls and inhibitions and were being taught some hatha-yoga techniques, he had read in one of the original texts that the actual spot where a man day by day sat to realize what he really was, and what he intended to become manifestly, his asana, his seat, became so charged that anyone taking that place must either be hurled from it, or, being able to sustain its trans-

240

forming power, must become like the master whose throne he was fit to succeed to. Well, hadn't that happened to him? Could he doubt it?

His eye lit on the memoranda for actions that had been fed through the various ducts onto the desk divisions which dealt with them. He ran his eye as along a review of the convergent reins of power. In every case he saw with a certain sense of unhurried interest the answer that should be given, that anyone in his central coign could and must give —and yet without that correlative position might be at a loss to provide. He began making these answers. He told his new General of the Guides, in passing, about the boys's promotion, as along the small television line he and this new acquaintance—who thought he was his old chief—discussed commanding personnel for the new cadres.

So the morning went. After his lunch he rested, but with real ease and hardly dozed, so that he was ready when by his bedside flashed the extension from his desk telling that the man of the inventor class had called for his authorized extension of interview. Alpha II had just settled himself back at his desk when the saffron figure came through the door and stood in front of him. But said nothing. Nor did Alpha. They stood looking at each other and there was a sense of completion in the confrontation. They looked at each other as sculpture reflects sculptor and sculptor regards sculpture.

At last the man on the throne remarked to the man who stood waiting before him, "And now . . . ?"

"Surely you understand?"

"I do, when I'm working, when I'm seated here, but directly I get up and try to understand, as a private person, try to think actually where am I, then I don't."

"Why try?"

"Can I go on without knowing more than that?"

There was a pause: "Well, if you know more, then you must know considerably more."

"Explain."

"Well, you yourself, you know now, though you may be fighting it, that you are not a person; you are now, you have been turned into—as in the old true tales of magic—

into something which is both you, in a way, and not you."

"Yes, I have faced up to the fact that there is no going back."

"Good, you see you have been spliced and grafted into something else. Your way, then, is to go on. You must and can grow still further into something further than either the Mole or Alpha made, unintentionally, of you. Dharma—the Living Fate—drove you into growing beyond their expectations. They thought they were making a tool, but on the contrary the tool turned them into hafts and molds."

"But I can't just go on playing a part. . . ."

"What are we all but playing parts, creating parts?"

"That's what I mean, I can't go on repeating a role my predecessor had found had come to an end."

"That is why I said, if you would know more, you must know considerably more. You must know not merely what your part could develop into. To know that you must know something of the play, the plot, and those who are acting with you. That's why I've come back, for the last time."

"But can this part I'm playing lead to anything?"

"Assuredly. But remember, the whole of this life is a knife-edged bridge. To cross a bridge not knowing your orientation, your true direction, is to find it not a bridge but a precipice."

"But I do want to get on."

"Very well. Then learn the next thing: that on a one-way bridge traffic must go in sequence and at a certain pace. There must be no doubling and passing."

"Explain."

"You have two cars ahead. One is the vehicle you see in front of you at this moment and the other was your chief and is still your forerunner."

"You mean . . . ?"

"Yes, you had better understand that. Life works by doubles and by pairing, by coupling and by symbiosis. You were sent to double with Alpha. That boy was sent to double with you. We each have a partner, sometimes an understudy, sometimes an overstudy, but always a study: part of our process of emergence by education. And I, too, have my blood brother. In the world to which I belong, the next range of social life that integrates with this of yours, we, too, as in all the great orders has been the rule of life, have our companion, our spiritual twin, with whom it is our task to grow in reciprocation—the marriage of true minds. Well, years ago, I was given as the man who was to grow up with me—and who would then be able to take my place that I might move on to my next upper step—I was given one who was picked by the higher understanding as my supplement. He was selected for me, as later on, when I had lost him and he had lost his way, in a mistaken and blind way, he picked you.

"He knew the formula of this mysterious, inevitable succession. But he had forgotten its real significance. And so, thinking to destroy Alpha, he actually supplied Alpha's successor. It was inevitable. The process can't miscarry. But the way it actually befell was my fault largely—though no fault is any man's wholly. We were very like, and I had for him a great devotion. The devotion that is awakened by the man who is to do things you yourself cannot do—what a real fulfillment of parenthood that is for us: you prepare that he may create. But it holds its particular parental dangers. Yes, I felt his powers so appreciatively, I was so sure he would go beyond me, that I forgot to gauge enough his lack of vision. He could not stand knowing and yet waiting.

"We see, we have to see, from our position so much, that he must indeed be strong in deeper vision, that vision that sees far beyond what is actually happening, to be able to endure such information of actuality, of the immediate crisis and agony. Time and again he strove with me: 'We must not,' he urged with increasing passion, 'be cold escapists seeing all the tragedy with chilled superior gaze, content simply to understand and to wait, to wait for others to wish sufficiently also to understand. We had, we have, powers equal to our vision? Then we must use them!'

"He was told that that showed he must spend more time in contemplation, until, on his time-lengthened focus, the vast meaning-making background would emerge and he would see of the travail of the soul and be satisfied. But he reacted all the more strongly. 'That was simply callous spectatorism, the cold cosmic artists' escape.'

"One day he was gone, and soon we heard that revolt at last had behind it a mind so that it was not a blind reflex any longer. But we knew that it had still no vision really. I begged that I might pay for my lack of care and of insight by being let go after him, to check him; to throw him—yes, I was willing to do even that—off the life course—if only I might save him and the world more quickly. But those who are as above me as," he said it without any personal accent, "I'm above you, ruled that I must not. I must pay for my error in the only way, the slow way, in which all error is discharged. The process must run its cycle and then I might fruitfully take my call, take my risk and, the process ripe, pluck the fruit."

"Then the Mole was one of you—you elevates?"

"He wished to be and he will be."

"And you let him do all that violence when you could have stopped it!"

"Once I had failed to lead him to where he would see, where he could accept the full sum of suffering and know that it has meaning and that it runs its course till the individual wishes it to cease, then his higher powers had to be spent in what he called 'service,' and 'the sacrifice of the cleanliness of his private soul.' "

"But in the end he was a ruthless monster."

"In the end he was what his partial vision, and his powers in excess of that vision, had to make him, no more, no less."

"But what of the people whom—" the man seated at the desk touched his own face and neck—"whom he—he mutilated. Do you have any idea of the number he broke and marred? What of all these—not even his enemies, his slaves!"

"Surely I need not tell you that they need not have come within his deforming grasp had they not wished in their hearts to do as he had found himself forced to do, and to become as that doing had made him?"

"But what of the people, the masses torn between these two hidden wars, this undeclared but quarterless civil war? Have you no pity for them?"

The man in saffron bowed. "I have great pity, pity that still has in it such heartbreak that it is often in danger of becoming useless. For I have not yet risen to the station where I can understand all the fates of mankind and so see with actual direct vision that each man suffers what he himself has earned, what indeed he still stubbornly wishes, and that his deliverance comes and can only come when he sees that and knows that he has chosen what befalls him."

He actually sighed and then, with a regathered composure, added, "But I have those who do so see, immediately above me. As they pointed out, had I had that vision, then my younger brother would never have slipped back to the false short cut of violence."

"But that doesn't really answer things. Granted that settles the personal destiny of that miscarried man we called the Mole, won't the Mole's machine go on, grinding out ever more blunderingly, pain and mutilation and death? And for no end!"

"That is why I was sent now, at this particular time. Before this, had I intervened, that might have been the result. But not now. You see, he had finished, he was finished. The process was clean worked through. When he," he paused, "forged you, he knew that if you failed, he'd failed. It was his last despearate throw, when he had tried all else. And I know him and so know he knew he might well fail. He was desperate. The boy, even, you know how cornered he had become. There was none of that at the start."

Alpha II knew the truth of that.

"The Mole alone held the movement, was the movement. All undergrounds have to become one-man shows or come up and become simply obvious. The Mole had not only centralized everything in his own brain (and that's why we, of course, could get directly to him), but only he any longer really believed in his own cause. That note which he left on his desk dissolved the underground and it will dissolve it. Because every other element in it was ready to get loose, had no longer any stake in it save the Mole's power of will to pin them down. They knew that the surface had won. Al-

245

ready, like released bubbles, they have flown up with relief, and broken free on the surface into the general air."

"I see," said the other slowly; and then, "but then what about Alpha and the successful conspiracy that's now left in the saddle? What about that?"

"It, too, is only the other side of the medal. I told you, that the time had come for the Mole to be released from his steadily deepening purgatory because (as we must always wait to happen) his own deliverance could take place —and could only then take place—because the process in which he had taken the wrong action had to work through, and at last had worked through till it had yielded its strange good."

"What do you mean?"

"I told you he was due to go, because the old order you have now been put into (and from which his complement Alpha had already been abstracted) was now over. The balance was no longer needed on that lower cycle. The time had come when the upper cycle could be switched on and into."

"Then are you going to take over, be the stimulant to the state which once came from underground revolt, a sniping from the top of skyscrapers to keep us on our toes?" Alpha II smiled but was uneasy.

"No: we shall not intervene. The intrusion that I have had to make, is, you should see, very rare, very irregular, if you will. It is, I hope I made plain, in order that I might remedy a mistake of mine that led to so much suffering."

"Then you are going to retire again into your invisibility?"

"But not out of vision."

"But what's the use of that?"

"Surely you see! This is the middle world. You are on the middle pier—or, if you like a homelier simile, all our forms, because all our consciousness, are simply like the iridescent trail which a snail leaves on a stone as it oozes its way along. The gleaming smear fades out as the new opalescent smudge is laid down. I think—at least for this epoch—the Mole level is closed, and you are now basic."

"Then why did you intrude at all? Wasn't the whole process of elimination going to work itself out anyhow, the gra-

246

dualness of inevitability—as the old socialists used to say?"

"That's just it. You must go at your pace. I did have to intervene to recover the rhythm of natural process that had been lost. It is what musicians, of all artists the masters of insight into time, call 'rubato.' "

"And now you owe it to us to carry on."

"Oh, no," and the other smiled, "now I owe it to you to clear out. Don't you see that what those who see can do and must do, is that? When they have to put things back that have gone wrong, *they must put them back*. This is the middle world, because it is the world of free choice. And what those who are above it and who, as they see it ever more widely, see it with more and more interest and less and less anxiety, what they do, is just that—they put back, they give back to men the power of freedom, the gift of choice, which they had lost, for which they were made and for which this world was made, to give the possibility of that creative exercise."

Alpha II sat silent. Perhaps it was true, certainly it was a getaway which if his visitor chose to take no one could stop him. Obviously it was as useless to attempt that, as for a mammal to try and keep a bird on the ground. Alpha II's mind had no recourse but to go back to his own problem.

"And I? Am I to be left arrested here, thinking up fresh shows to keep people happy?"

The man behind his desk smiled, "I think I hear 'Ajuna the Bull of the Bharatas' slumped in his chariot complaining to his charioteer, and as Krishna I must answer, 'Go a-head, and after the battle which will only last a day or two, then repeat your demand for release and it will be granted.' "

"Oh, we read that, of course, for the yogic training part. It was one of our preliminary texts for study when we were enrolled as Undergroundists. But does it really make sense, really answer my problem? After all, you've said it and, Heaven knows, don't I know it—this pressure in which I am to live even at its present level would break any person."

"True enough. But then, surely, the answer to your question is quite obviously another question: Why be a person?"

"Oh, please don't fool! Can't you see my sanity, and maybe the social future, rests on finding just this answer? If the prow can't stand the pressure at which the ship drives it through the seas then it buckles and the ship of state founders. The head must always be something of a madman, always increasingly insane! Hasn't that always happened to autocrats?"

"That's precisely why you must cease to be a person. No, no; don't interrupt me. I'm not fooling. I told you, at our first interview, I was sent to yield you two services. I have given you already pledge of my word. The first service is now discharged. I have turned up the Mole and mutated him and closed the underground. The second service, I told you, you must yield yourself, though I would help you to do so. There are two reasons why you must cease to want to be a person: the first is personal, the second public. By so ceasing you will then be serving not only mankind and able to endure the actively-passive mobilization and service to which you are called, you will be serving yourself also. For only by ceasing to be a person can you be relieved from your own personal deed. I believe that is the real meaning of the Gita. Look at your own case: Had you had real power you would not have had to kill, no not even in self-defense. Because you have killed—you see I don't blame you: I state a fact of causality—you must discharge that deed. You cannot get free and rise to where real power lies until, by willingly ceasing to wish any longer to be anyone, you will have repaid that debt you contracted when you were forced by your helpless lack of any real power to force a blind creature who wanted to live by killing you, to be himself killed.

"And now for the second reason, the public and future reason why you should and must cease to be a person. First tell me, who are you?"

"To tell the truth, a pretty muddled person."

"Only so if you will try to cram what you are into the queer little success picture which when you were an adolescent you tried to make of yourself and your future."

"Well, who am I?"

"Look at that ring on your hand. There you see half the chart. There are the great legs firm on the earth bearing up the rest—the great viscerotonic mass of mankind. Next there is the huge torso, heart, chest, lungs, and arms, the up-drive of energy. Above that the head, mouth, eyes, and brain. And that is the visible Apex. But seen with more insight it is really the junction, the focus. For what has there come to a climax, is really a junction. From there what has been convergent again becomes expansion. One day that ring will have to be changed. The arms of the Adam Kadmon will be raised and Atlas will not be keeping heaven and earth apart, he will be the ladder, the great X, the Saint Andrew's Cross, that unites them. But that higher part must be invisible to those below who see only to the visible Apex. You, however, have reached that junction and focus and you now may look on."

"But does that really answer the question, Who am I, even if it does say where I am?"

"If you really know the one you know the other. You are what you see and are as great as you can see far." Then with a sudden intimacy, "Listen: you have come to the point when only the hang-over of a wish to be a person, someone who in privacy hugs himself thinking, 'Here is little me and I have climbed up till, though the world doesn't know it, it is little me in the vast megaphonic mouth of the world statue who speaks to them. What fun, this is indeed 'fame!' That is the nonsense, the childish nonsense, that has undone nearly all those who have been carried to the station where now you stand.

"You are equal to the height of your office if you will do two simple truthful things. First, you must cease to want this secret gloating, of trying to live privately in the past looking up to what you are in the present. Be what you are. Live now. And the second part of that is, live so that every moment you pass into that next moment completely. Be at each moment what that moment makes you. Don't cling to this moment when it is past any more than you cling to what is now past. And don't see the moment as something you are viewing from outside to bottle its bouquet. If you try and straddle like that it will pull you in

249

two. But if you go, give, yield, you and it will be one. It then can't hurt you, for you yourself have become the wave that you feared would engulf you. Move along. This is a bridge and you are at the peak of it. You must move that the others may move up. The circulation of life depends now more on your continued mobility, on your not settling down, on your further vision and viewpoint still leading you on. Mankind depends on that one fact now more than on any other."

"But where can I move?"

"As I've said, you can move by continually becoming."

"That's just gnomic nonsense to me."

"No, it isn't. Something in you knows it isn't."

"Something in me knows quite plainly one thing and it doesn't like it. You *are* leaving us alone, aren't you? And won't we relapse?"

"But don't you see that is freedom—there cannot be certainty, no, nor security, and liberty." Then, even more quietly, "Can't you understand? That is the nature and power of that supreme mystery, Liberty. It is the power not to know what will happen. No tyranny, no autocrat, has been strong enough to be able to endure that creative ignorance. Freedom is the supreme achievement of, because it is the supreme answer to, Faith."

"Look here, I'm not being difficult. I now do want to co-operate. But honestly, I don't understand."

"Don't struggle so hard with your mind. That's not the way, and perhaps I'm not the right teacher. I always talked too much. No one can fully understand as long as they are in Time. As long as they act they do know in a way, but only by doing and as long as they are doing. If they stop halfway to ask what it means they are utterly confused. But when at last the doer has acted long enough—as you have nearly done—so that he no longer asks for any return for himself—no, not even to see the results he thought he saw would come—then at last he can begin to see things as they are, then at last he can understand what Freedom, Faith, and Anonymity are—three words for the three-fold nature of the One!"

"Well, you told me I can't understand and certainly you have proved that!"

"But I have told you that you can implicitly, indeed actually, understand by doing?"

"But still, how?"

"Because your doing is your way of becoming."

"Then we, Humanity Incorporated, are achieving something, not simply involved in an endless round-dance of which I am the petrified Maypole?"

"Assuredly: and as you can ask that question and are its President, its Conductor, I can tell you faintly and in symbol what you are doing. This human life is a hatching process. It should be good in itself but not good enough in itself. It is a prelude, a prologue, an embryo state. An embryo must live fully and well if the post-natal life is to be properly and fully achieved. The first wise man of the West gave us our sailing orders when he ruled, 'Here we are as in an egg.' And you are the very nucleus of the germ. Now you may, therefore, cease to be actual and become wholly potential, no longer a man but a seed, no longer a personality but an idea. Now you *must* see it?"

Alpha II smiled very slowly with his large alien mouth and nodded.

"You see, it is as simple as that, as inevitable as that, as inevitable as the fact that unless the grain fall into the earth and die it cannot give rise to the next harvest. Now that you are throwing off, discarding all your husk of personality, you can go on. This is the true Sed Festival in which the priest-king is renewed. You are dying to rise again. So I hail you, because you die, as immortal. What is your title? Alpha—yes, and that's what you are—the first letter to the whole Alphabet. But once you are said, then the others have to follow in their sequence. Look at that letter in its old significance: in archaic, ideographic Hebrew its sign is Aleph, the camel, the broad-stanced beast of burden, the archetype totem of the desert-ship, the wilderness crosser from oasis to oasis, the pilgrim beast who carries his own water and food in himself.

"You, Alpha, are the successor, the culmination of those other three priest-kingly offices and titles, Attis, Adonis,

Osiris. These were once men but they became ranks and because they were ranks, don't you see, what till then had been a blind alley, became an open way, a bridge. You pass through these stations to attain a still higher position. You are Alpha, the manifest and salient, and if you will really rise to that and leave all the petty nonsense of personality behind, you may at last pass out, leaving another Alpha to take your place as imperceptibly as you have taken the first Alpha's seat. And you can then be completed because you can become Omega. The most ancient pattern shows it—what we call the egg and dart—the salient pointed angle which is the structure of the Alph or Alp and the circle of complete rest, the Omega—the dart of the sperm and the globe of the ovum—penetration blended with comprehension. There that is all. You have nothing more to do but to go on—develop, and the future will and must open."

He stopped. His voice became almost personal. "I won't say I hope we may meet again. It is impossible to step twice into the same stream. I shall not meet again that section of the process which I am speaking to now but of which the real you is the whole. I shall, of course, meet that river again; indeed, our waters may well be running in the same channel long before we both enter the ultimate estuary."

He raised his hand and had turned out of the door before he lowered it.

Alpha II rose from his seat uncertainly. His mind was mixed; he wanted to go after the saffron figure. He wanted to get back to his old student self that was going to live its own life, of course generously, adventurously, but its own, with its own intimacies, its own units of affection, its privacies, its personal possessions, its particular character. Then he smiled slowly and felt those great foreign lips move and slide over those artificial jaws—no, that was cut short, literally cut off.

His eyes, without seeing, had been scanning his desk. Yes, there were the outlines of the next vast symbolic rally and titanic myth-performance. They were going to show the rise of the Psychological Revolution, the emergence of Alphism. They were going back further than ever before—

making the story cover a far wider span of history. Till now they had been content with showing how all the modern age, the age of revolutions, the last five hundred years, had led inevitably to this the Psychological Revolution and explication. Now, it was suggested in the memorandum which he was to enlarge, that medieval and ancient history might be brought in at least as a prologue—the vast swaying conflict-balance of the Papacy and the Imperial power and back of that the Imperator and the Pontifex Maximus blended in one office by the Roman Principate.

His eye had begun to read with increasing interest. Back of all this there must be something more primal. There must be shown the strange figure slowly circling that primal tree of life that grew by the shores of that lake of Avernus, that pool where ancient man felt that the unseen world and the seen, life and death, met and mingled. The old lines began to run in his head from the old ballad: "The Priest who slew the Slayer and shall himself be slain"—the Priest of Nemi guarding the sacred tree on which grew the Golden Bough that lit the dim isthmus linking the living and the dead. "Light amid the vanished ages: star that gildest yet this phantom shore." He began to see how this huge historical mythos could be handled.

He put out his hand to open the circuit that called his secretary. He heard her answer cheerfully. He sat down, his mind ordering itself for work. The words ran through his mind, Attis, Adonis, Osiris, Alpha, and Omega. Yes, that was the circuit. As she entered he did not look up, only sensed her happiness and rapport and began to dictate.

Here's a quick checklist of recent releases of

ACE SCIENCE-FICTION BOOKS

F-titles 40¢   M-titles 45¢

If you are missing any of these, they can be obtained
directly from the publisher by sending the indicated sum,
plus 5¢ handling fee, to Ace Books, Inc. (Dept. MM),
1120 Avenue of the Americas, New York, N.Y. 10036

CLASSICS OF GREAT SCIENCE-FICTION
from ACE BOOKS